Words of Christ in Red

Robbie Dorman

Words of Christ in Red by Robbie Dorman

www.robbiedorman.com

ISBN-13: 978-1-958768-22-8

Cover design by Robbie Dorman

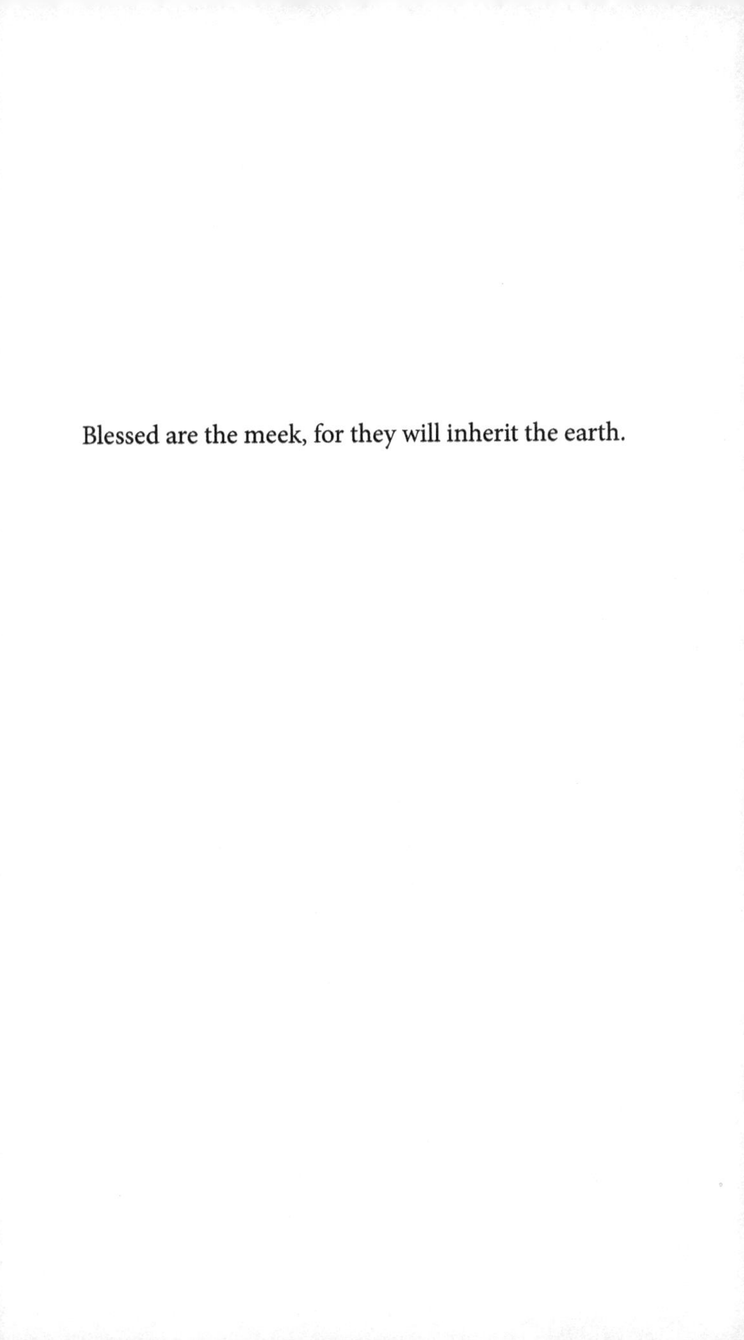
Blessed are the meek, for they will inherit the earth.

1

Eli gripped the Bible, the cover contorting, squeezing the Word of God.

The leather bent underneath his fingers, his grip wet, holding the book like a vise.

He sweat, naked, the folding chair cold beneath his bare ass. The basement was warm, water clinging to the walls, the summer humidity bleeding down into the concrete.

The sweat beaded on Eli's forehead, dripping down over his eyes, down onto his naked chest, onto the concrete floor, a puddle beneath him.

Eli stared ahead, looking up, blinking his eyes free of sweat. His eyes focused only on the Lord, Christ Jesus, his Savior, who had taken on his sins, who had died for his salvation.

The crucifix was massive, eight feet tall. It stood against the back wall of the basement, nailed to it. Eli had done the work himself. He had built it to Biblical specifications, using the best lumber from the hardware store. He spared no expense.

The cross was secondary. Christ was more important, and Christ was true to size, six feet tall, made to order, sculpted to fit this cross.

Eli stared up at him, Christ nude, Biblically accurate. Christ was crucified, the nails driven through him, the sharp metal penetrating the soft skin of his Lord and Savior Jesus Christ. The nails sliding through skin, and muscle, and sinew, holy blood exploding from the body of Christ, pouring like a torrent from his wrists, flowing like a river into the ground—

Eli licked his lips, squeezing the Bible, his left thumb sliding back and forth over the black leather. His heart thudded against his rib cage, his torso shaking, his breath coming in halting bursts. His eyes looked to the holes in Christ's wrists, the nails punching through, he had punched them through himself, to attach him to the cross, the cross to the wall, and he shuddered, goosebumps on his skin, the heat in the room—

THOOMP THOOMP THOOMP

Goddamnit, distracting him, he had to focus—

The ceiling shook above him and Eli's focus shifted, his eyes leaving his Holy Lord and Savior, away from the bloodshed of Christ's crucifixion. Samuel was running around upstairs again, and he had told them, he had told them all, that while he was down here, they were supposed to remain quiet, he was worshiping, he was communing with Christ himself, there was no place for extra noise, no place for distraction, he needed to focus, he needed to worship, to block out—

The sweat poured off him, the concrete beneath him stained. Eli blinked, blinked away the sudden interruption, he'd discipline Sam later, not now, not now—

He took a deep breath and closed his eyes, and then opened them again, staring at the figure of Christ once more. He had blasphemed. Unwelcome behavior. He was a Man of God. He must worship.

Christ peered back at him, his eyes delivering holy pain, and Eli stared, holding the Bible, his fingertips grazing the subtle leather, the texture on his skin. He pressed, feeling the paper bend underneath his touch. Eli looked at the hands of Christ, fingers outstretched in agony, as the nails were driven through him, as his ankles were stacked and staked to the wood, bones cracking, cartilage breaking, as he was hammered to the cross, his feet never to walk again, not in this form, this deific torture the beginning of a transformation, and Eli could see the fingers curl in agony, see his shoulders stretch as he struggled against the cross, in the strong arms of the Romans, see his chest heave and fight as he slowly suffocated, slowly losing the strength to breathe.

The wound at his side, the spear—

The spear entered the side of Christ, the blade razor sharp, the ready blade of Longinus, pierced the dead body, blood and water pouring out, sliding down the side of Christ, a torrent of liquid, sliding down his hip, and over his groin—

Eli squeezed the Bible, his palm sliding over it, his chest heaving, his breath held, his body hot, hotter, cheeks red, sweat pouring from him, his body shuddering, shaking, as waves of pleasure rolled through him, warmth, and heat, everything he wanted, the moment he lived for—and then Eli took a great gasping breath, and the warmth left him, his hand gripped tight on the Holy Word, and then the cold entered, sliding through his feet, up his legs, settling into his guts, infiltrating up into his lungs, and his heart—

He took another shuddering breath, his heart still beating hard, the focus on Christ dissipating, blinking back into reality, back to the world, out of worship. The cold sat in him, back into him, it was always there, the dark cold shame, and he took a breath and held it, forcing back a tear, blinking it away, gritting his teeth, and sat with the coldness in his guts, in his heart, the utter familiarity.

Eli was cold.

Cold, in the heat of the basement, the floor beneath drenched, a puddle of sweat pooled beneath his ass in the metal chair. He looked down at the carnage of his worship.

He looked up, into the eyes of Christ, still filled with pain.

I love you, Lord. I love you. Forgive me.

2

We're better than this.

John Grace pulled himself through the mud, his fingers desperately grasping at the muck. He reached out, his lanky frame stretched out along the ground. He clawed through the mire, his heart beating too hard, too fast, he could barely breathe—

He spit out dirt from his tongue and pulled, dragging his mangled leg behind him. John pushed away the pain ripping through him, his leg broken in two spots, maybe three. He felt his face swelling, his nose broken as well, blood leaking down over his lips. His left eye was half shut, blackened. He felt the jagged corner of a tooth, his tongue rubbing against it.

His heart thudded, but every breath screamed with pain,

multiple ribs broken. Every movement was agony.

The water laid ahead. If he made the water, maybe he could escape. He could swim, even with one leg—

"You knew this was coming, Pastor," said Sheriff Kyle Bronson, stalking behind him, his steps slow. "Don't tell me you didn't." His breath was heavy in the still summer night, the frogs chirping in the distance. Bronson loomed over him, the mud squelching beneath his boots, as he stomped behind John's prone, crawling body.

John ignored Bronson, pulling at the roots, at the mud, the filth underneath his fingernails. He needed to warn Laurie, tell her what was coming. He reached for his phone in his pocket—

—it was still in the car, his hand finding nothing. She needed to know, what Bronson was capable of, what Eli was capable of—

Pain flared in his leg as his destroyed knee scraped along a massive exposed root, the bone catching, the raw nerves exploding and John screamed, twisting until his knee was free, and he blinked his eyes and pulled, his knuckles bleeding as they dragged through the slick mud.

"Dear Lord. May you deliver me from evil. May you grant me the courage to battle against the everyday sins that plague our lives. May you grant all men and women the strength to fight against temptation—"

Bronson stepped on his already broken knee and John screamed again, his voice echoing through the swamp. Bronson eased his weight down onto the bone, slowly grinding up and down on John's leg, and black spots popped into his vision, the pain driving the breath from him, he would pass out—

And then Bronson stepped off, chuckling.

"God ain't listening, Pastor," he said. "If that ain't clear. I think if he was listening to you, none of this would be going down—"

John squeezed the wad of mud in his hand and turned quickly, throwing it into the face of Bronson, the dim evening lit only by the headlights of Bronson's cruiser. Bronson grunted as the mud hit him in the eye.

"You motherfucker!" he yelled, scraping at his face and eyes, and John forced himself to move, kicking with his one good leg, his hands pulling at the ground, and his leg caught on another root, and the pain flared up, but he swallowed it down—

Please God, please Lord, let me live—

John pushed hard through the mud, hearing Bronson struggle behind him. If he could get into the water, into the dark, he could escape out into the swamp. Even with his mangled leg, he could find a way back into town, away from Bronson. Get some help, someway, somehow. The headlights glowed off the softly lapping water, and it was only ten feet away, and he scrambled hard, his whole body pain, tears flowing down his face, mud and blood mingling as they touched his lips, but if he reached the water, there was a way out—

"You piece of shit," said Bronson, wrapping his hand around John's ankle, around the ankle of the mutilated leg, and he pulled, and John did pass out then, black spots coalescing into a field and there was nothing.

*

"Wake up, Pastor."

John woke up, his back against a massive tree, his mangled leg in front of him, bent at an unnatural angle. His leg pulsed in agony, his ribs yowled with every breath, and his left eye had swollen completely shut, along with his nose. Bronson's cruiser lit him, parked to his left, along with John's pickup.

Bronson stood in front of him, staring, holding his billy club, lazily twirling it. But he didn't stand alone.

Next to him stood Eli. It was Eli's voice that had woke him.

Something fell inside John then, something deep, like a porcelain dish off the top shelf of the curio cabinet, breaking into many pieces, never to be fixed.

Eli stood there, regret on his face. He lied before he spoke. Before this moment, John had doubt. A slight doubt, that Eli wasn't involved.

But John should have known. Bronson was an attack dog, on a short lead. He wasn't let off without his master's command.

"What are you doing, Eli?" asked John, every word breaking his body. But he still spoke.

"What's necessary, Pastor," said Eli, kneeling in front of him. "Only what's necessary. Believe me, I don't want to do this. I don't. But—"

"Bullshit, Eli," said John. He stared out of his one good eye. "Don't bullshit me before you kill me."

Eli knelt there, silent. The night air hung heavy, the frogs and insects singing beyond them.

"You're changing the church, John," said Eli, finally. "Into something I can't recognize. Something God can't recognize—letting Ezekiel worship there, letting the Campbell woman into the chapel—"

"The Lord our God doesn't discriminate, Eli, and if you studied the Bible, if you read the Word—"

Bronson stepped up and swung the billy club across John's face, the club hitting him squarely in the jaw with a CRACK, and stars floated in his eyes, his lone good eye swimming. His vision was cloudy, staring at Eli.

Eli watched, and waited. Bronson stepped back behind him. "We warned you, John. We told you, what was permissible. What God would allow. And you didn't listen. You instead ignored us. You dismissed us. You thought you could do whatever you wanted. You thought you could follow the church in Raleigh, like they know anything—"

"They ruled, Eli," muttered John. He forced out the words, through an aching jaw, teeth loose. "And the congregation voted to follow their ruling. You were there. You had your say."

"Narrowly outvoted," said Eli. "It wasn't right. A bunch of new people had their say. Why? Why did their vote count as much as mine? We've been here since the beginning, John, and you—"

"God in Heaven does not grant you more power for your family name, Eli," said John, his voice crawling from his throat. "Maybe one day you'll understand." Bronson moved up to swing the club once more, but Eli held him back.

"Understand what?"

John stared into Eli's eyes, his one good eye, still foggy. Eli stared back in the night, the headlights cutting between them. John saw only resentment. Self-righteousness.

And then only a void.

He did not look to Bronson. A dog had no reflection.

"How long has your family been in Sacred, Eli?"

"We were among the first."

"How long have you worshiped at the Holy Church of Sacred?"

"My whole life," said Eli. His eyes did not change.

"Your whole life," said John. "Have you ever truly listened to my sermons? Did a word ever penetrate? Did you ever take anything I said, and apply it to your life? Or was the practice nothing but a facade? Nothing but set dressing for your life, for your name?"

Eli stared, and then smiled. "Finally some anger, Pastor. We've asked it of you for years, and now, you finally find it."

"I'm not angry, Eli," said John, every breath, every word, hurting. "I'm not angry."

Eli stared, and the smile vanished. "Don't worry, Pastor. The church will remain in good hands. We'll watch over her." He stood then, and nodded at Bronson.

John opened his mouth to speak, but Bronson swung his club, harder now, the CRACK across his skull too loud to hear, to respond, all sense gone from him, a great reeling pain ripping through his head, but Bronson didn't stop.

Lord forgive him.

Bronson beat him, over and over, swinging the club hard, as hard as he could. He ensured John suffered.

He did not die, not then.

Pastor John Grace only died as they dragged his body to the swamp and drowned him in the murky waters.

3

Someone had painted over the rot.

The Holy Church of Sacred sat on a space of cleared land off of Sacred Drive, the trees cleared from the lot whenever the church was built, a hundred odd years ago. The church stood alone, the sun beaming down on it, the white wooden shingles shining in the Georgia sun.

The church was small, the chapel enough for a few hundred people, the offices attached a similar size. No steeple on top, the building barely recognizable as a church.

The grass was dead around it, browning, no amount of water enough to keep it alive in the heat. What wasn't dead by heat had been killed by the traffic, parishioners parking their vehicles on top of it, threatening a large part of the lot to turn into a mess of sand and clay, potholes big enough to lose a child in.

David Ingram pulled in and parked on the lone paved spot, a small sign reading "Holy Church of Sacred Pastor Parking".

"You get your own parking spot," said Jason. "The first of many perks, I assume."

The front tires of the Prius thumped up on the small plot of concrete, and then the back. He looked into his rear view mirror, angled to see the backseat. Solly still slept in his car seat, his head leaning against the middle headrest, his body diagonal. They'd been driving since early that morning, the back of the hatchback stacked with their essentials. The moving truck would arrive tomorrow.

David let Jason's comment slide. David had wanted to see the Holy Church of Sacred first, before they saw the house, even after the long drive. Even with Solly with them. He needed to see it.

He needed to see *his* church.

David had felt a pull, a certain knowledge, that seeing his new church was tantamount, essential, to not just getting a handle on his new mission, but to understand their place in their new home.

He thumbed off the hybrid and got out, the cool interior of the car giving way to the sweltering heat.

"Jesus, it's only May," said Jason, getting out as well.

"We're in Georgia, Jase. It's only going to get hotter."

"I'll wake up Solly, if you want to go inside," said Jason. He ducked into the backseat, and David turned to the church.

As David approached, he smelled the paint. It was tacky to the touch, still drying. Painted for his arrival. But not fast enough, as some of the paint had sloughed off, thin pools and tendrils piling on the dirt around the foundation. The wood siding laid underneath, peeking through, the last bad paint job showing.

And yes, some of the rot.

David took a small breath, and walked up the slim set of stairs that led to the front doors of the chapel. He unlocked the deadbolt and entered, the cold air hitting him, smelling slightly of must and mildew.

There was a cramped antechamber, the carpet a dark red, short, covering the wooden floors. The color was washed out, faded, cleaned and vacuumed a thousand times, stepped on by thousands over the years.

The antechamber was compact, leading quickly into the chapel proper, the red carpet covering the central floor of the aisle, two rows of pews on either side. His eyes weren't on the pews, but on the stage, and the figure of Christ that dominated the back wall of the church. It was a massive figure, too big for this small church, looming over the modest pulpit, on the slight stage.

David's hands ran over the wooden pews as he walked the aisle, his eyes only on the figure of Christ, crucified on a wooden cross, his eyes contorted in pain, blood running from his wounds in his hands and feet. David stared, his eyes studying the vast amounts of detail in the statue, the top of the cross mere inches away from the elevated ceiling. He had seen nothing like it, and he was fixated on it, the blood vivid, the expression on Christ's face—

"Jesus," said Jason, from behind him, Solly toddling next to him, holding his hand. "That is one big Christ."

David blinked. "I can't believe it."

"Did Laurie say anything about that?"

"Not a word."

"Hmm," said Jason. "This place needs some work. I'd rip up the carpet, to start."

David walked past the front pew, no longer enraptured by the figure of Christ. The stage was waist high, and he walked up the stairs, and stood behind the pulpit, weathered.

He went to place his hands, and then saw the bare spots, where the grain and finish had been worn away. Two spots. David placed his hands on them, the natural resting spot for a pastor, as they preached.

"How does it feel?" asked Jason, who had sat in a pew, with Solly in his lap. Solomon looked around absently, his eyes taking in the space.

David looked down at him.

The space was plain, the carpet tired. The wooden pews were cracked, worn, and decades old. The rotten wood, beneath the dripping, tacky paint.

But David's gaze settled on Jason's face, and Solly's. Love beamed from them. And in that glow was God.

David felt his faith, blooming in him. A joy in his heart, a safety, a warmth.

The presence of God.

And that light bloomed everywhere in the Holy Church of Sacred. In the worn pews, the weathered hymnals, the faded carpet. In the pulpit, the hands of the pastor marking the wood with his faith as he worked, innumerable Sunday services. For the wear bore the mark of humanity, coming to celebrate their faith, and to improve themselves.

The faded carpet shone bright red, beaming with life and

energy. The wooden pews stood strong, firm, a testament to the strength of God. The hymnals sang with the psalms within, the music of the Lord filling the space, believers filling the air, their throats opened, pouring love outward, with fellowship, with joy. Rapturous emotion overtaking everyone there, not just a place, but truly a church, a chapel, a sanctuary, a place of God.

David closed his eyes and felt it, breathing deeply, the power of faith filling him, golden ambrosia pouring in, the same faith he felt as a child, as a young man, as a student in seminary school.

As he knelt before God. His eyes shut, and he felt God there. This was his church, and it would reflect the goodness of the Lord, of his faith. He opened his eyes.

David placed his hands over those weathered spots, and felt the last pastor. Pastor John, Laurie's husband, who had tragically passed.

A community in need Laurie had told him, her voice cracking.

David would help them. He met Jason's eyes.

"It feels right," said David, and Jason smiled, despite the unease in his eyes.

And David knew why. He turned to look at it again.

The figure of Christ crucified.

The joy in David's heart vanished, the glow gone.

David had seen countless statues of Christ, but none other felt like this. Up close, the figure was distorted, distended, the exaggerated features strong at a distance now overpowering to his senses. The blood was more vivid, Christ's face warped in agony, his eyes squeezed tight against the pain. The nails were sculpted in exquisite detail, penetrating Christ's flesh. David stared, the sound of the nails being driven echoing in his mind—

He turned away, taking a sharp breath. A tension in his heart eased.

"Bathroom," said Solly. "Daddy, bathroom."

"Let's go," said David. "We can come back later. Let's get to the house, and Solly can use the bathroom there. It's only ten minutes away."

"Just a couple minutes, Solly," said Jason, carrying him. David walked down the steps, leaving the stage. The pews were once again worn, weathered, some risking collapse. The hymnals cracked. The carpet worn.

"There's probably a good hardwood underneath this carpet," said Jason. "Shouldn't be too much trouble to rip it up."

"I'm already mentally compiling a punch list," said David. "I'll talk to Laurie about it. I assume she already knows about the church's needs. It's almost never ignorance."

They left the church, locking the door behind them. The tension in his chest eased further.

Jason was right about the carpet. Some of the pews needed replacing, before they broke and hurt someone. The wooden siding, the rot underneath—another long term project.

But none of that was on top of David's mind.

Christ, crucified, his face contorted in pain.

He would not preach with it behind him.

4

Laurie Grace's blonde hair was stacked high on her head, stiff curls and swoops, piled on top of each other.

The closer to God.

"You're already getting settled in," said Laurie, her Southern accent coming through. "It's good to see."

They sat in the living room, the couch and love seat set up, the television not yet mounted on the wall.

"We're getting there," said David. "We've been working every day nonstop. I think we both work better when the house is set up. Another few days and we'll be mostly there."

"It's looking great," said Laurie, her eyes flitting around the house. She wore a floral print dress. "I can't help but still see it the way we kept it, you know. But that was years and years ago. Y'all have much better taste." She reminded David of his mother. But he couldn't put it together why. Her looks were a part of it, even if his mother was a brunette.

It's her makeup, David. She wears too much, just like Mom.

"It's a nice house," said David. "I'd be lying if I said it wasn't a part of why I accepted your offer."

"Well we're all glad you're here!" she said, smiling.

"Why did you move out of the house?" asked Jason. He sat on the floor with Solly, as Solly played with blocks.

"Oh—" started Laurie, her smile half-faded. "We just—just wanted to have a place of our own. Even though John did preach there for so long—hard to think of a place as your own until you own it."

Jason nodded, but said nothing else, looking back to Solly.

"Our condolences for John," said David.

"Oh, thank you," said Laurie, smiling again, but this one all artifice. It wasn't just the makeup. It was the smiles too, the polite smiles, even when she didn't feel like it. It was easy to see through this one.

"How are you holding up?" asked David.

"Oh, you don't get over it," said Laurie. "You just get through it, right? I'm getting through it. Putting my energy into the church. I hope you don't mind—"

"I wanted to talk about it," said David. "We stopped by on our way in—"

"Oh, how nice! What did you think?" she asked, her eyes lingering on David. The same smile.

David returned it. "It felt right. It felt—felt like a place of God." He took a breath. "But I want to make some changes. Not a lot, and not all at once, but I'd like to update the interior, and fix some of the rotting siding. Buy some new pews, to replace some of the older ones."

Laurie nodded. "We tried to keep up, we did. But there was always something else, that needed our attention, and we're not the richest church, our tithes—"

"It's okay, it really is," said David. "None of these are emergencies. They're mostly small things, and they don't have to be done all at once. There is one thing however, that I'd like to move quickly on." He paused, glancing again at Laurie, gauging her reaction. "The Christ figure, behind the pulpit."

Laurie's smile vanished in an instant.

"I'm sorry, but I don't want it behind me while I preach—"

"No, no, David," she said. She put out a hand. "I agree with you. I—I hate it."

"Then why is it there?" asked David. "Did John—"

"No, no. He wasn't fond of it either. It was—it was an olive branch."

"I don't—"

"The statue was a gift from Eli Parsons. And John using it in the church, was him extending the olive branch to Eli. They argued—well, argued is not a strong enough word. They had a row, is how my pawpaw would have described it."

"You said the community was in need," said David. "Is Eli the cause?"

"Not just him," said Laurie. Her hands were clasped, wringing. "But he is at the forefront. The Parsons were in Sacred at the beginning, and a part of the church at the beginning."

David stared at her. "He wanted to split, didn't he? Go

with the Traditionalists."

"Yes," said Laurie. "He was the most vocal."

"But they lost. I wouldn't have taken the job—"

"No, I know," she said. "And the Church leaders—John spoke to them. And John wanted to stay, and I did, and after speaking to them, we put it to a vote. And the majority wanted to stay. But the Church leaders—" Laurie took a deep, halting breath.

"They didn't have any guidance on what to do afterward."

"No," said Laurie. "Because when sixty percent want to stay—there's the remaining forty, isn't there? And the Church just said, well, if they want to go, they can go. But they didn't want to go. It's their church, too, isn't it? Try telling Eli to leave the church his family helped found." She shook her head. "It wasn't going to happen."

"I still don't understand—"

"They had it out," said Laurie. "And I guess Eli felt bad, because he came back, hat in hand, with the statue. That horrific thing. He had it custom made. Eli's well off, with his landscaping company. And John agreed to replace the cross we had with—with that. To try and make peace."

"I don't like it," said David. "It glorifies the violence of the crucifixion."

Laurie wrung her hands, looking down. She took a breath, and then met his eyes.

"If you want to stay on Eli's good side, I wouldn't."

David took a breath. "Will it make a difference?"

Laurie pursed her lips, but said nothing. She slowly inhaled. She looked at Solly.

"Your boy is beautiful," said Laurie.

"Thank you," said Jason. "Solomon."

"A king's name," said Laurie, she smiled. "Adopted?"

"Yes," said David. "We got lucky. Sometimes it takes years."

"I had a discussion with John," said Laurie. "John was a kind and welcoming man, to all people. But he was afraid of change. Afraid of splitting the community. But I told him, that we could either look forward, or look back. Those were the two choices, and not doing anything, not changing— that was staying in the past. That it was looking back. And he agreed. And it led to more people in the church, people who thought they weren't welcome. You'll meet some of them, on Sunday."

"And Eli?"

"Eli—" started Laurie, and she took a short breath. Emotions swept over her face. She looked down, and David glanced at Jason. Jason was already looking right at him, his face still. Laurie looked back up, and David met her eyes. "I don't know what Eli will do. But I want peace. And that awful Jesus statue is a small price to pay for it."

"I guess that's fair," said David. "If it works."

"Are you ready for Sunday? Do you have a sermon prepared?"

"I am," said David. "It's been ready for a while now. I've been polishing it, but at this point I'd just be moving furniture. Not improving it."

"Good," said Laurie, smiling again. "We're having a potluck afterward, in the meeting room. You'll be able to see everyone, say hi."

"Do we need to bring anything?" asked Jason.

"Oh, no," said Laurie. "At least not this time. You'll have enough on your plate." She laughed. "I didn't even mean to do that. Oh, I should be going. The girls are expecting me at Tom's. Have y'all been to Tom's yet?" Laurie got up, grabbing her purse.

"No, not yet," said David, standing with her, and following her to the door.

"It's a wonderful little diner, local, been here for a thousand years," said Laurie. "You should give it a chance. You have my number, if you need anything. I'll see you on Sunday!"

And then she was gone, out the door. David shut it behind her, and returned to the living room, where Solly still played, and Jason still sat.

David sat down again. Jason helped Solly with a misplaced block, and then looked at him.

"There's something she's not saying," said Jason.

"We knew it'd be hard," said David. "That's partially why I wanted the job."

"No, not that," said Jason. "We're in the rural South. Of course there'll be homophobes. And this Eli—he may be one of them. Probably is. But her eyes when she talked about him—about Pastor John. There's something else going on."

"She reminds me of my mother," said David.

"I'm glad you said it, because I wasn't going to," said Jason. "Is she wearing enough make-up?"

David laughed. "She's trying her best."

"I bet she is," said Jason. "That's part of the problem." Jason sighed. "So that Christ statue—it's staying?"

"For now," said David. "But I don't like it."

They lapsed into silence, watching Solly play.

"Are me and Solly coming on Sunday?" asked Jason.

"Solly and I," said David. "And yes, of course."

"I just thought, maybe it'd be easier—"

"No," said David. "No. We are well beyond hiding."

5

The sirens scared David, a sudden flash of light and noise behind him on the side road that led back to their new home.

He had gotten groceries, the back of the car loaded with bags and bags from the only store within 25 miles of them.

He pulled over, following the procedure in his head, putting on his blinker, slowing, and then easing to the side of the road. He turned off his vehicle, and reached to the glove compartment, hoping his proof of insurance was where he left it.

Damn it.

They had moved stuff around for the drive down, and this was the worst time, of course he couldn't find it, he wasn't even speeding, why did they pull him over—

He looked in the rear view mirror, and the cop was still sitting in his cruiser, and David pulled the entire stack of paperwork and threw it in the passenger seat, quickly rifling through it—

The cruiser shifted back and forth as the cop leaned one way and then the other, climbing out of his car. The huge cop, tall and wide. He had a cop belly, but that didn't change the fact he was a massive man.

The cop took careful, heavy steps, walking up to David's window, and tapped on the window with a curled knuckle—

Damn it, where is it—

He found the paperwork, and then hit the power window button, the window rolling down.

"Sir, can I please see your license and registration," said the cop, his big mustache filling David's vision.

"Sorry, let me find it," said David. "I've got proof of insurance—"

"Not necessary," said the cop. "Registration."

"Yes, of course," said David, his heart still beating hard. *Calm down, David. Calm down, it's just a traffic stop.*

David sorted through the paperwork again, feeling the cop's impatience next to him, throwing old receipts and paperwork to the floor, and there it was, finally—

"Sir," said the cop.

"I found it," he said, taking a breath, sliding his ID out of his wallet, and handing it over to the cop—correction, sheriff—

"Thank you, sir," he said, his voice cold. "Let me run it real quick."

The cop took his ID and paperwork and trod back to his cruiser, the vehicle easing back under his weight.

He hadn't been speeding, as far as he knew. Maybe his tail light was out, maybe—

But the cop hadn't said anything. Had just taken his paperwork and left. Was that normal?

He was suddenly very conscious of the groceries in the back, the cold and frozen food slowly melting.

He thumbed the power back on in the Prius, rolling up the window. The AC wouldn't stop it entirely, but it was nearly a 100 today, it would help some—

TAP TAP

David jumped at the tapping. He hadn't noticed the cop, even as big as he was. He rolled down the window.

"Yes, officer—"

"Power off," he said.

"It's just the battery, my groceries—"

"Power off," he said again, his voice dark, his hand sliding down to his holster. "I won't ask again."

David thumbed off the battery.

The cop said nothing, returning to his cruiser once again.

David sat in silence, sweat pouring down his back and forehead, his shirt soaking through. The cop sat in his cruiser, and David looked in his rear view, side eyeing the sheriff. The AC was long gone, and errant cars sped bye as David sat.

How long could it take to run my ID and registration?

And the minutes crawled, and David felt his face grow hot and—

He's doing this on purpose.

The cop stared at his computer, in his cruiser, idling, the AC running, and David's chest grew hot, but not from the Georgia sun, rage building inside him. The anger slid up into his mind, overwhelming caution, overriding the fear of the cop's size, his gun, his authority.

Overwhelming his faith.

Righteous anger overwhelmed it all, the fury burning through him

Son, your anger will only heap anger back on you—

The anger burned away the memories of patience, of intelligence, he would march down this fucking pig and tell him—

"Sir," said the cop, at his window again, and David stared at him, his face contorted in anger. He breathed smoke through his nose, fire from his throat, nothing about this cop could stop David—

"You're the new pastor, aren't you?"

The question sparked reason in David's mind, and the anger fell from him, in a moment.

"Yes," he said, sweat pouring from his face, beading on his eyebrows. He absently wiped it with his hand.

"Taking over for old Pastor John, huh?" said the cop. "Shame what happened to him."

"I heard it was a car accident."

"Yeah," said the cop. "Brutal." He paused. "I go to your church. Sheriff Kyle Bronson."

"Well, nice to meet you," said David, forcing a smile. "Can I ask why you pulled me over?"

Bronson smiled wide then, as wide as his mustache.

"Oh, it was that New York plate of yours," he said, like he was telling a joke. "Don't have too many of those around here. Had to do a courtesy check, just to make sure. Make sure to get your license plate changed before too long." He paused, chewing nothing. "Sometimes, we get Yankees 'round here, and they're up to no good." Bronson's face filled the window, his eyes hidden by the reflective sunglasses. "But you're up to *good*, aren't ya, Pastor?"

"Yes," said David, still smiling, his face dripping. "May I have my paperwork back?"

"Oh, yeah. Almost forgot," said Bronson, handing over David's ID and registration. "I'll see ya on Sunday, Pastor."

And then he was gone, trodding back to his cruiser, sliding down into his seat once again, the car rocking back and forth as he settled his weight into it. He pulled off, gliding the big cop car around the Prius, and then pulling a U-turn in the middle of the two lane road, heading back toward Sacred proper.

David thumbed on the power, and boosted the AC all the way, his clothes soaked through with sweat, his frozen groceries thawed.

6

David's stomach ached, a hollow anxiety ripping through him.

He stood at the back door of the chapel, the soft chatter of the congregation reaching him. Laurie had led the hymns, had greeted everyone as they had come in. Jason had always balked at serving as pastor's wife, and David wouldn't force the issue now.

He had suggested greeting the assembly alongside Laurie, but she had insisted the pastor at Sacred always remained inside until after their sermon. And David didn't want to upset the apple cart.

David took a deep breath, closing his eyes.

You've done this before.

Yes, but not at his own church. He only had one opportunity for a first impression. He clutched his notes in his right hand, the notebook he'd been developing his sermons in for over a year.

The hornets in his stomach didn't go away with his breath. David held another—

Think of God. He will carry you through.

And David did. He prayed, a soft, gentle prayer, and he closed his eyes, a gentle warmth flowing through him, from the top of his head, down, filling his body with golden heat.

He paused, and heard the final hymn stop, and another brief pause as the crowd hushed, a soft patter from them, through the door, and he didn't wait any longer, swallowing his fear, and he opened the door, and walked through, the crowd quieting. His eyes scanned the chapel, the worn pews full of people. He glanced over them, and then focused on the stairs, one step at a time, and ascended the small stage.

The statue of Christ was on his left, its face contorted, the blood gushing from its wounds, the nails sliding through flesh and bone, the cross and Christ himself gigantic, towering, overwhelming—

David averted his eyes, and put the statue out of his mind, before it took him again, and he turned away from it, and set his hands where John Grace had set his, in the faded wood of the pulpit.

He looked out over the congregation, split in two, like Solomon's judgment.

Laurie sat in front at his right, alongside Jason and Solly. His eyes scanned the crowd there, and recognized no one else.

His eyes passed to his left, and he set eyes on Eli Parsons, dressed in a polo shirt and khaki pants, his face plain, his haircut screaming suburban dad. His children sat next to him, two boys, one a teenager, one younger, and his wife, bookending the kids. Sheriff Bronson sat behind him, dwarfing his wife who sat next to him, a young girl next to her.

David felt a flare of rage as his eyes scanned Bronson, but he pushed it away and looked out over the assembled crowd, the room silent and stuffy, the bolted on AC doing its best to keep out the summer heat, slowly failing.

David took a breath, and held it, and exhaled, and preached.

"Judge not, that you be not judged. For with the judgment you pronounce you will be judged, and with the measure you use it will be measured to you. Why do you see the speck that is in your brother's eye, but do not notice the log that is in your own eye? Or how can you say to your brother, 'Let me take the speck out of your eye,' when there is the log in your own eye? You hypocrite, first take the log out of your own eye, and then you will see clearly to take the speck out of your brother's eye."

David paused, letting the verse hang in the air. "Matthew 7, verse 1 through 5. Christ's words, and they are powerful. Judge not, that you be not judged. For with the judgment you pronounce you will be judged, and with the measure you use it will be measured to you. My mother told me this many times, as a child. I'm sure all of you have heard it many times as well, in some form or another. Judge not, lest ye be judged."

People among the crowd nodded. Some voiced assent, a smattering of "mhmms" and "yeps".

"And it never made sense to me as a child," said David.

"Maybe because I was a smart aleck. But the verb there, judge. We judge all the time. We *decide* all the time. When we buy a car, we judge whether we can trust the salesman. When we drive on the highway, we judge if we can make that gap. When we deal with another person, we judge the content of their character. We judge if its wise to associate with them, to let them get close. Even to love them. All judgment."

He took a breath, feeling sweat bead on his back. His thoughts jumped back to the traffic stop, but he shook them away. He focused on the crowd, the pews, the red carpet, the ceiling and walls. He focused on the presence of God.

"But Christ is not telling us not to judge. He is telling us to hold ourselves to the same standard that we hold others. To pluck the log from our own eye before we remove the speck from our brother's."

David reached to his own eye, and pantomimed. "To pluck the log out from thine own eye. To study oneself, to see the faults, the problems, and to remedy them, before judging another on those same merits." David's voice boomed across the assembly. The hornets in his stomach had vanished, nerves dispersed. The warmth he had summoned earlier was there again, and he belted his sermon to the crowd.

The sunlight beaming into the chapel brightened, contrast turned up, and the faces of the congregation glowed, each face a beacon, each face glowing, brighter and brighter, and then extending into a chromascope of saturated light and rainbow, a spectrum of prism. The broken pews brightened, whole again, the carpet fresh. The world beamed.

"Do you judge the teenager for petty theft, while stealing

wages from your employees? Do you judge your neighbor for infidelity, while dreaming of your own adultery? Do you judge the suffering man on the street for his laziness while you sit in air conditioning?"

The crowd was silent. They still glowed. Their faces were indistinct, scattered stars glowing in the chapel.

"Are you guilty?" he asked. He paused. "For I am. Guilty of all those things, at times in my life. Or of their kin. For we all are human. We all walk with sin as a shadow. And that truly is Christ's message here. That none of us are perfect, none of us like God. And to judge without self-reflection— that, that is truly for God alone. For only he is without sin."

David paused. His heart thudded against his ribs. A bead of sweat trickled down the side of his head, but he did not wipe it. The shining congregation glowed in front of him, silently.

"And Christ's words are not only about self-reflection. About hypocrisy. They are also a warning."

David took a deep breath. He spoke deeply, his voice projecting. "For with the judgment you pronounce you will be judged, and with the measure you use it will be measured to you." He looked into the shining sea, his eyes filled with the glory of God. "For if you do not pluck the log from your own eye, before removing the speck from your brother's— you will be judged. The judgment you visit upon others, will be reflected back upon you. That the log you keep in your eye will blind you to your hypocrisy. And hide you from the judgment that will be visited upon you by God himself."

He took a deep breath, and the light over the crowd faded.

David felt himself again.

"I'm Pastor David Ingram, and I'm honored to be your new pastor here at the Holy Church of Sacred, despite the circumstances. I want to improve the church—to unify the church. For us all to be a place of support, of community, not just now, but far into the future. For Sacred to be a place of God. Thank you all for coming."

David smiled, and briefly bowed his head in thanks to the congregation. He closed his eyes.

The applause started, and David opened them. The congregation all clapped. All except for Eli, and Bronson.

7

The meeting room buzzed, the congregation sitting at the assembled round tables, tired folding chairs creaking under the weight of the parishioners.

David had taken a breather after his sermon, retiring to his office, and changing shirts, his first soaked through by heat and holy furor.

He had preached before, but never in his own church, and he felt empty now, the adrenaline wearing off.

You're not done yet.

The potluck was after, after every service, Laurie had explained, and this was just as hard a job, meeting everyone, shaking hands, and socializing. The pastor was connective tissue in a church, and he couldn't preach his sermon and then retire to his study. This was as much the job as anything.

So David peeled off his shirt soaked through with sweat and put on a fresh one, ironed himself that morning, and joined the crowd.

The room was filled to capacity, almost everyone in the pews now in a metal folding chair. Or waiting in line at the long tables, filled with food, the room filled with incredible smells. David's stomach rumbled, suddenly starving. He never ate breakfast, not before preaching.

Jason sat at a table in the far corner, busy with Solly. Laurie stood near the food, serving as host. He walked to her.

"Everything going well?" asked David.

"I think so," said Laurie. "People are waiting on you to say grace."

"Oh, I'm sorry, I didn't realize. Should I wait until everyone has their food?"

"I don't know," said Laurie. "John always waited." David looked over the people, and no one ate, some chatting, some glancing his direction, obviously waiting on his go ahead. He wasn't John.

"Excuse me," said David, raising his voice. The crowd hushed. "I don't believe in making people wait longer than they should to eat. I'll lead us in grace, and we can all get to the fine food provided by your neighbors and God's love." The crowd silenced.

"Dear Lord," spoke David, his voice loud. "Thank you for this food. Thank you for your love and for your son, Jesus Christ, who sacrificed himself for us. Thank you for this opportunity, for this congregation, and for all you give us. Amen."

AMEN echoed the crowd, and the buzz resumed, as people chatted and ate, grabbing food from the long table, and sitting. David scanned them. He saw Eli and his family, already eating. Bronson and his sat with them.

His stomach grumbled, hungry, but meeting everyone came first, and David started the rounds. Table by table, David stopped, said hello and shook hands, learning names, and making small talk.

He met the Jenkins, who owned the farmer's stand in town. They had sat on the right, with the Graces. A married couple, without children.

The Lincolns, who had sat on the left. A husband and wife, and two children, a boy and a girl. They kindly smiled as he introduced himself. Adam owned the Ford dealership in Marshall, two towns over.

Ruth Simons was a widow, who lived alone, surviving off her late husband's pension and her social security, who explained this to David breathlessly, a paper plate in front of her, with small bites of everything from the potluck. Everyone at Ruth's table lived similarly, senior women with no husbands, all widowed. Some from this table sat on the right, some on the left. An in-road, perhaps.

Eli's table was next. The children still ate, but the adults had all finished. Eli and Bronson were talking as David approached. Eli's older son, a teenager, sat quietly, staring off into the distance.

"Sorry to interrupt," said David. "I just wanted to say hello, as I made my rounds. Eli, right?" David extended a hand.

"That's right," said Eli. His black hair was short, cut simply. His haircut didn't suit his face, and he didn't smile. Eli's skin was sun-damaged. His small eyes met David's, peering into him. David didn't like it.

"Laurie mentioned you. Said your family has been in the church since the beginning."

"We have," said Eli. "It's in our blood."

"I'm glad you're here," said David. "Is this your wife?"

"Oh, yes, pardon my manners," said Eli. "This is my wife, Angie, and my boys, my oldest, Thomas, and Samuel, my youngest."

"Nice to meet you," said David. Angie didn't extend a hand. Thomas looked at him with furtive eyes, but didn't smile. Samuel waved and smiled, not yet ten years old.

"And you've met Kyle already," said Eli, his lip twitching. A smirk?

"Yes," said David. "Not the best of circumstances, but we did."

"Things happen," said Bronson. Bronson didn't introduce his wife, whose eyes looked down, or his small daughter, who played with the food on her plate, and David didn't ask. Uneasiness crept into him here, standing, and he wanted to move on.

"It was nice meeting you," said David. Eli stared at him, and then wore a smile.

"Be seeing you, Pastor," said Eli, and then broke his gaze, his eyes veering off into the middle distance.

David smiled a broad smile and walked away, letting out a cold breath. Something was wrong.

David circled around all the tables, saying hello, meeting everyone. He came back to Laurie.

"Did I miss anyone?"

"Did you talk to Ann? Or Ezekiel?"

"I don't think so," said David. Laurie pointed them out. They both stood, at the edges of the room. Ann, a middle aged woman, stood alone, drinking a cup of tea. Ezekiel ate standing, dressed in jeans and a white button-up shirt, wearing a camo hat.

"They haven't found a table yet," said Laurie. "Both have joined relatively recently."

"We'll find them a spot," said David, but then looked to see Ann leaving, throwing her plastic cup away. "Well, guess Ann will have to wait." He walked toward Ezekiel, who stood next to a wall, his head bent over a paper plate, one hand holding it, the other with a fork.

His face was covered in stubble, his eyes large, dark, almost black, and piercing. He glanced up at David, staring. His eyes seemed enormous up close.

"Hi," said David. "You're Ezekiel, right?"

Ezekiel stared for a moment longer before slowly nodding. "You—you are a Man of God. Like Pastor Grace." He glanced down at his plate, some food still clinging to the ridges of the portioned parts of it. He walked over to the trash and dumped the plate and fork in it, casting it aside, rubbing his hands on his pants, and extending a handshake to David. "And you can call me Zeke." Zeke's voice was a deep Southern baroque, coming out of his throat like barbwire.

"Nice to meet you, Zeke," said David, shaking his hand. His skin was hot. "Are—are you okay?"

"Yes," said Zeke, his eyes the size of saucers. "I was worried. When John left us. But Laurie chose wisely. You are the right man for the job."

"I appreciate your confidence," said David. He realized why Zeke's eyes seemed enormous. It was his pupils. They were dilated.

"Have your tried my venison stew?" asked Zeke.

"Oh, I haven't eaten yet."

"I shot the deer myself," said Zeke. "Please, try it."

"I will."

No wonder why Zeke doesn't sit with anyone.

Zeke leaned in close to David, his pupils a mile wide. "If you need help with anything, you let me know, Pastor." David stared into his eyes, and softly nodded.

Zeke nodded in return, and leaned back.

I guess that's that.

David scanned the room. He had visited with everyone still there, and he went to the food, grabbing a plate, and taking an assortment of everything, even the things he didn't like. He'd eat them all. And as hungry as he was, it wouldn't be difficult. His feet ached, from being on them all morning, and he desperately wanted to sit, and eat, and talk to Jason. To be out of the eye of the congregation.

But he would be the last to leave, especially today.

Laurie was gone from her perch near the food. Had she left?

David didn't care, he was hungry, and he walked over to Jason, who still sat with Solly.

"You haven't eaten yet?" asked Jason. "You're going to starve."

"I had to say hello," said David. "You know the drill."

"I know," said Jason. "Solly is dragging. He needs a nap."

"You didn't have to stay the entire time," said David.

"It's your first day," said Jason. "I wasn't going to leave you here, high and dry." David set his food down, and looked into Jason's face. Jason was tired, much like David, and had watched Solly all morning.

But he was here, anyway.

David leaned over and kissed him once, softly, with gentle love.

He turned back to eat his lunch and was hit by waves of rolling, sudden silence.

The chatter and buzz had died down, and David knew immediately.

Laurie had lied.

The eyes of the assembled stared at them. Some with surprise and shock. Others with revulsion and disgust.

Others with hate.

Eli was the first to stand up, followed quickly by Bronson. Their families followed. He guided them out, even as Thomas held a stare with David.

But he wasn't surprised. They'd been waiting for this moment.

He would have looked up your information, with your license plate. Registered to two men.

More left after them. Almost all that had sat on the left side. A few remained behind from the left, and almost all from the right.

David looked on with sadness.

But fury bloomed in him as well.

At these people, and their prejudices, sure.

But moreso at Laurie, who had lied to him.

David saw Zeke, and caught his eye. Zeke nodded at him, the same soft nod, his eyes shifting to Eli as he left the room.

8

David watched the professor as he lectured. It was his second semester in seminary.

"Revelation is often described as strict prophecy. But is it? How much of the figurative language should we take literally? It's an interesting question, the answer to which changes depending on who you ask—"

The professor turned, to write on the white board. He wrote down chapter and verse, and David started to copy—

A crumpled piece of paper bounced off the back of his head, clattering to the floor. David blinked in surprise, but he already knew who threw it. He didn't look back. It was what Collins wanted.

He did grab the piece of paper off the floor, and uncrumpled it, flattening it on his desk.

FAGGOTS SUCK SATAN'S COCK

It read, in big, bold letters. David sighed, folding the paper in half, and then half again, and then half again. The professor had turned around, and David paid attention.

*

He paused outside the classroom, shifting the books in his backpack, when someone checked him in the shoulder, hard, and he tumbled to the ground, falling on top of his bag.

David grimaced, breathing, heat rising in him. He glanced up to see Collins standing there, along with his two friends. David didn't know their names.

"Why are you here?" Collins asked, his lips curled. "You're not welcome."

David glanced around, saw a few people watching. They had seen Collins hit him. So be it.

David didn't respond, pushing himself up to his feet and throwing a punch straight into Collins' nose, and it broke with a CRACK, and Collins fell, immediately, blood spurting from it, and David mounted him, and threw more punches, one, two, three, four, five, and then Collins' friends pulled him off, and David pushed them away.

Collins laid on the ground, dazed, his face a bloody mess.

*

"They want to expel you, David."

David sat across from Dean Howard, who looked at him with concern.

"Who's they?"

"Basically everyone but me," said Howard, a man in his fifties who passed for forty, with a spark of gray at each temple. "This isn't the first incident—"

"He started it, Dean," said David. "He knocked me down."

"I know, I know," said the Dean. "But—"

"But what?"

"I had to talk admissions into letting you in," said Howard. "You know that. They're looking for any excuse to get you out."

David took a breath, and then went to his backpack, unzipping it, and pulling out one folded piece of paper, and then another, and another, piling them on top of each other, and handing them over to the dean.

The Dean took them, with a confused glance, and then opened them, his eyes scanning the big, bold letters, each filled with epithets and slurs.

"Every class, Dean," said David. "Every class. And that's just Collins."

"Can you prove it was him?"

"Ask anyone in the class," said David. "Even Professor Wills. I'm sure someone won't cover for him. And they saw me get knocked down."

"David, you can't throw punches every time someone—"

"Someone what, Dean? Bullies me? Attacks me? Am I supposed to just absorb the punishment?"

The dean looked up from the slips of paper, meeting his eyes. He said nothing.

"Do you think I haven't been bullied before?"

"No, I know you have."

"I waited until Collins went too far, and I showed not him, but everyone, if they bother me, if they attack me, what will happen."

Howard sighed. "With the notes, I think I'll be able to convince them to make it a suspension—"

"A suspension—"

"You're lucky it's just that," said Howard.

"I was defending myself—"

"I know," said the dean. "I know you were. And I'm not contesting that. But this isn't high school anymore, David. Once you leave here, you'll most likely be in charge of a congregation. Of a church."

David said nothing.

"And I'll tell you, what I wouldn't tell most of the other students—it's not fair. And it won't be. It will never be fair in the church. You will always face more opposition. Regardless of the church you came from, or the church you go to. *You* will always face more scrutiny. You will always face more antagonism."

"I'm tired of it," said David. "I just want to serve God."

"You will," said Howard. "That's why I fought for you. I believe that you will be a great church leader, one day." He stared into David's eyes. "But to get there, you have to be that much better than everyone else."

"Can I go?"

"Yes," said Howard. "Before you go. I'm going to schedule a meeting with a friend of mine."

"In the college?"

"No," said Howard. "A pastor. I think talking to him might help you. His name is Philip."

"I don't know—"

"Talk to him, and I'll try to talk them down from a suspension. Okay?"

David stared at him. "Okay."

9

David went to Laurie that night. She answered the door with a glass of wine in her hand. By the flush in her cheeks, it wasn't her first.

"David," she said, with a slow, slight, smile. "Come in." She led him inside, to the couch and loveseat. A game show was paused on her television.

"Please, sit," she said, falling slowly into the couch.

He wanted to yell at her, to let out the anger he'd felt all day, since the end of the potluck, but her drunken hospitality had disarmed him.

"Can I get you anything? Wine?" she asked.

"Laurie, I—"

"Are you hungry? I could make you a sandwich. I have some chips, too—"

"Laurie, please," said David. "You lied to me. You lied to us, to me and Jason."

Laurie glanced at him then, and then looked down at her glass of wine. "Now, David, I don't think—"

"They didn't know, Laurie. You told me they knew. You told me you told them I was gay. That even if it was a problem, at least they knew." He stared at her. "I kissed Jason, a peck on the lips, and everyone reacted like they were punched in the stomach. And you weren't there. You knew what would happen."

"David—"

"You lied to me, Laurie." David shook his head, and sighed. "Why should I stay?"

Laurie looked up now, her face flush. "What? You can't leave."

"You lied to me, Laurie. You told me—"

"I told you the church was divided, David—"

"That's different, and you know it."

"Is it?" asked Laurie. "And I did tell folk that you were gay. Just not everyone. Because they wouldn't have shown up at all. They would have stayed home, and it's not what I wanted. I wanted them to listen to you speak, like I did, before I hired you. To hear your sermon. To hear God's Word, spoken through you. You're what Sacred needs, David. I told you that before, and I'll tell you again. You're young, you're hungry, you're a damn good pastor, and you have a fire in your belly. And John, may he rest in peace, was a good pastor, but he was old, and he was tired. If I misled you, I apologize, but I don't think I did. This will be a fight, to get people on your side, to make the Holy Church of Sacred whole again. But if anyone can do it, you can."

David took a breath.

"I just want to be a pastor, Laurie."

Laurie took a long sip of her wine, and put it on the table. She smiled.

"Well, I've got good news for you, then. You're the pastor of the Holy Church of Sacred."

David sighed. "I came in here wanting to scream at you."

Laurie raised her eyebrows. "You still can, if you'd like."

"No," said David. "I shouldn't yell. It bothers Jason."

"Well, he's not here," said Laurie. "You sure you don't want any wine? It's a good bottle."

David eyed her. "Maybe one glass."

Laurie winked at him, and got up, pouring him a heavy glass, bringing it to him.

David took a sip of the dark red. It was good.

"See?" she asked. "Even Christ drank wine."

"In moderation," said David. As the wine settled in him, a pleasant warmth followed. The dark knot of nerves in him loosened.

"What changed, Laurie?"

"What do you mean?"

"You told me that you had a realization, and you convinced John to be more open. More progressive. Changing the church."

"Yes," she said. Her eyes settled on her glass of wine, half full.

"What is it something specific? A come to Jesus moment?" Laurie glanced at him, and he smiled. "I'm allowed to make jokes."

"I guess that's fair," she said. Her eyes, back on the wine, the red swirling, the surface moving, a deep red ocean, contained within the glass.

"Well?"

She stared at her wine. Her eyes were distant.

"It was nothing, really," she said, and her eyes went back to him. "I just realized one day that we were part of the problem. That we had settled. Both John, and I."

"Settled?"

"I think it happens to everyone," she said. "As you get older, you settle into a life, into a routine. And you don't want to upset things. Change—it's dangerous. It's scary. So we just kept on keeping on. And we weren't challenging ourselves any more. Challenging our own beliefs."

"That takes courage," said David.

Laurie smiled. "That's kind of you, but I don't know about that. We probably took too long. And John, John was a good man. He sometimes just needed a little push. So I pushed him."

"That's what a good partner does. Holds their spouse accountable."

"Thank you," she said. "You ask Eli, you'd think I twisted John's arm. I didn't. I just talked to him."

David finished his wine.

"Do you want more?"

"No, one is plenty," said David. "I should head home."

"Thank you for stopping by," said Laurie, finishing her own glass.

"Laurie, please," said David, getting up. "Just be honest with me. Even if it'll hurt."

"I'll do my best, David," she said. She stood up. "I was afraid."

"The fear of man lays a snare, but whoever trusts in the

Lord is safe," said David.

"Proverbs?" asked Laurie.

"Yes," said David. "I read them every night." He walked to the front door, and Laurie opened it for him. David left, walking down the front steps.

"Be careful out there, Pastor," she shouted out after him.

David turned, to answer, but the door was already closed.

10

Noises woke them in the night.

Scrabbling sounds, the sounds of footsteps, and paint cans shaking, and voices held back, trying to whisper while still being heard, laced with menace and threat.

David had finally fallen asleep.

Sleeping in the new house felt like his childhood, and David couldn't sleep.

The house was off the highway and there was no traffic after dark. A slim forest butted up against the back of the property, quickly turning into marshlands beyond that, acres of swamp mixed with forest, laced with dirt roads used only by hunters and drug dealers.

But they were miles away, and the only sounds the house heard were crickets, frogs chirping, and the growl of gators echoing across the water, the slim sounds that cut through the trees and reached the house.

David had grown up with those sounds, familiar sounds, not silence, because true silence didn't exist, but the absence of human sound, no car engines, no television speaker, no music droning from a house party down the street, or an apartment two floors up who left their window open and passed out drunk listening to Sublime.

After he had moved to the city, the change had been drastic, and he had slept fitfully for months, eventually growing accustomed to the din of humanity, the din of New York City.

But now, pulled from the constant drone of traffic, the continual bombardment of horns and engines, of yelling, of music, of *noise*—

—the near silence of Sacred was too silent. The frogs chirping, the insects, the birds—they weren't enough to fill the space in David's mind as he fell asleep. He had grown used to it. Sleep had been hard to come by in Sacred.

But he awoke, the sound jarring his eyes open, unsure if what he heard was real or dream, and then there was another sound, the sound of a ball bearing inside a can of spray paint. He looked to the clock, which read 3:13 AM in red letters and his heart raced, and he jumped out of bed.

"Wha?" muttered Jason, always slow to wake up.

"Someone's outside," said David. "Stay with Solly."

Jason woke then, eyes bleary but feet moving. "You sure—"

"I'll take care of it," said David, and he grabbed the baseball bat propped in the corner of the bedroom, just within arm's reach. A Louisville Slugger. He squeezed, wrapping his fingers around the handle, the familiar weight pulled up into the air. Swing hard enough, and it would stop anyone.

Swing hard enough, and they would learn a lesson—

What are you going to do with that, son?

David said nothing, holding the baseball bat aloft, heading out the back door, carrying the bat, rage in his blood, seeing red, anger coursing through his veins, down into his hands, squeezing the handle of the bat, he wasn't bigger, or faster, but the bat would equalize it all.

His dad stopped him, behind him, standing in the frame of the back door, his words firm.

"What are you going to do with that, son?"

David held the bat, his back to his dad, hot breath spitting from his throat.

They stood there, the moment bleeding on, silence lingering. The hot air of late summer hung heavy.

David finally turned, still holding the bat above the ground.

"Tim Barber ripped open my locker. He broke the lock, took everything out, and threw it the ground. He ripped apart my books, my notebooks, *my Bible*—"

"Son—"

"And then he wrote 'Fags burn in hell' across the front," said David. "In big bold marker."

His dad stared at him, standing in the doorway.

"What are you going to do with that bat?" he asked.

David's nostrils flared. "Tim is bigger than me, and he runs with a couple other guys. This will make it fair."

"Give me the bat, son."

"He won't stop—"

"Give me the bat."

"No."

His dad stared at him. "What do you think will happen after you attack him, David? After you hurt him? After you break his arm, or his leg, or his ribs?"

David said nothing. He squeezed the handle of the bat. The heavy weight. It felt good.

"After you swing too hard, and hit him in the head, and kill him? Or one of his friends?"

His dad finally left the door frame, and walked toward him.

"Or—or. Or they take the bat from you, and swing too hard, and kill you? Or cripple you?"

The heat flushed from David's throat, from his eyes. Cold entered him, settling into his gut, into his throat, into his balls. A deep chilling ache.

"Because I'll tell you," he said. "You'll get expelled, and because you're seventeen and in the South, you'll get sent straight to prison. And your life will be gone." He took a breath. "Or the hospital. Or the morgue."

"He—"

"I'm sorry he did it, son. It's not right," he said. "And it's okay to feel outraged. It's okay to feel anger. It's normal. But it's not okay to resort to violence. Because the only one you'll punish is you."

David lowered the head of the bat to the ground.

"He's not the only one," said David, his eyes on the ground. "I'm tired of it. It's not fair."

"It never will be," said his dad. "But ask yourself—every time—is this worth it? Because I guarantee you son, Tim—what was his name?"

"Tim Barber," said David.

"Tim Barber ain't worth it. You're worth ten Tim Barbers. Don't make that trade."

David held out the bat.

"You can keep it. You still might need it. But only to defend yourself."

David stomped through the house.

David stomped through the house, bare-chested, in his boxers, dragging the bat along the hardwood floors, loud scraping echoing through the old house. He breathed fire through his nostrils, anger rising in his gut.

They might have guns—

David pushed the thought aside, all the rationality and logic gone, fire and fury replacing it all, his skin aflame, his eyes burning. He opened a door, the last one between him and the front door, slamming it behind him. They would hear him coming, coming from a mile away, no sounds except for him and the bat and the frogs and the crickets.

They would hear him, and they would run, or they would wait.

He hoped they would wait, whoever it was, and he would swing the bat as hard as he could—

David lifted the bat, at the front door of the house, and he flung it open, throwing the screen door loose, pulling the bat up to his shoulder, ready to swing away—

"Go go go—" said a slight voice, already vanishing in the distance. David saw flashes of camo on shadows disappearing into the dark, sprinting down the road, out of sight in moments.

David exhaled smoke, standing on his front porch, the bat ready to swing.

With nothing to swing at.

"David," called out Jason, from inside the house.

"They're gone," he said, yelling back.

Jason crept up, bundled in a robe, despite the summer night.

"Sol's still in bed," said Jason. "I didn't wake him."

"Good," said David. "Good." He lowered the head of the bat to the patio.

"Good."

FAGS BURN IN HELL was spray painted across the side of the house in big, bold letters.

The mailbox was destroyed, the post broken, the plastic box itself crumpled and deformed.

All four tires of the Prius were slashed, the rubber deflated, the metal rims resting on the ground.

"You think it was Eli?" asked Jason.

They stared at the side of the house early the next day, the sun rising an hour ago.

"No," said David. "I doubt he came himself. If you ask him, he'll say he had no idea."

"Plausible deniability," said Jason.

David nodded. "Solly still asleep?"

"Yes. You talked to Laurie?"

David nodded. "She's going to call Ann. Ann does handy work. Can help with the mail box, at least. Should be here soon. I'm going to start scrubbing."

"I'll help," said Jason.

"I—I'll do it alone."

"David—"

"Please, Jason," said David. "Sol will be awake soon. Keep him inside. He shouldn't see this."

Jason sighed. "He'll need to know—"

"Not yet," said David. He met Jason's eyes. "Please."

Jason stared, and then nodded, walking back inside.

David stood in front of the spray paint, staring at the message. He turned at the sound of an engine approaching, and saw a old, red, small-bodied truck pull up their driveway.

Ann parked her truck and got out. She was dressed in a full brown jumpsuit, stained with splotches of faded paint and grease.

"Pastor," she said, nodding her head. "I see you've been visited by the Sacred welcoming committee."

David extended a hand, and Ann shook it. "Nice to meet you. Wish it was under better circumstances."

Ann nodded. "It was only a matter of time."

David sighed. "I guess—I guess I hoped for the best."

"Hope in one hand," said Ann. "I've got a mix that will take the paint off easy enough, and won't damage the siding. Brought a replacement post for your mailbox, too."

"That's awful kind of you," said David.

Ann smiled. "Just doing my part."

"Can I help?"

"Sure can. More elbow grease is always welcome."

Ann unloaded a jug from the back of her truck, along with some buckets, and they got to work. They scrubbed. The paint slowly came off.

"You left on Sunday before I could say hello," said David, his arm working. "Did you know what was going to happen?"

Ann took a breath. "I mean, it's not rocket science, Pastor. Eli is a bigot, through and through. He's not going to abide you." She scrubbed. "But no, I left because I never stay long. Got some food, and then headed back home. If I left whenever some asshole homophobe made me feel unwelcome, I would've left Sacred a long time ago."

David paused. "Oh. Of course."

Ann glanced at him. "Putting it together, Pastor?"

"Yes," he said. "And you can call me David." He scrubbed. "So your experience with the welcoming committee comes first hand."

"Yep," said Ann. "It was a long time ago. But tactics haven't changed."

"But you've stayed."

"I have."

"Can I ask—"

"Sacred is mine," said Ann. "I was born here. I was raised here. Eli, Bronson, all the other pieces of shit—pardon my language—they don't got no more claim on this place than I do. And I'm not leaving."

"How often do you have to clean graffiti?"

"Not too often," said Ann. "Yours is the first in a long while."

"Did they give up on harassing you?"

Ann scrubbed. "That's one way to put it."

"What does that mean?"

Ann scrubbed. "I don't get graffiti anymore, because they know I'll shoot them, David."

"I don't—"

Ann scrubbed. "This was years ago, when Eli, Bronson, most of them you saw, were all pups. Didn't matter. Same assholes. They came by, middle of the night. I heard the paint cans. Woke me and my girlfriend at the time up. She was scared, wanted to call the cops. She was from the city, didn't understand that the people outside, spray painting 'GOD HATES DYKES' on the side of my house, *were* the cops."

David had stopped scrubbing. He watched Ann.

"What did you do?"

Ann scrubbed. "I grabbed my shotgun, loaded it, and killed a man on my front porch, David."

"You killed him?"

"Two barrels of buckshot in the chest," said Ann. She scrubbed. "He was on my front porch, carrying a baseball bat. Full within my rights to protect myself and my property."

"You killed a man."

"He wanted worse for me," said Ann. "His name was Anson. Worked down at the lumber mill, back when there was still a lumber mill. Ran with a group of rednecks who'd I pissed off at Charlie's, a bar that don't exist no more."

"What did you do—after?"

"I reloaded, David, and fired after the rest of them, as they tore ass out of there. And then I called the police."

"And that was it?"

"Course not," said Ann. "I called the police. His family wanted to press charges, but no matter how much the cops wanted to distort the facts, there wasn't much they could do. Too much evidence on my side. They buried him. His family moved away. And no one has fucking sprayed my house since. Pardon my language."

David took a breath. "Do you—do you think about it?"

"No," said Ann. "Not too often."

"You killed someone."

"Yeah, yeah I did," said Ann. "Where you from, Pastor?"

"A town called Smithville," said David. "Not very big. In North Carolina."

"Thought I heard it in your voice," said Ann. "You never ran into trouble there?"

"Of course I did," he said. "But—but I don't know. I guess I was lucky. My parents, my friends, my pastor—they protected me. It wasn't perfect. And sure, there were guys in high school, in seminary, that didn't want me there. I did my best."

Ann stopped scrubbing, staring at him. "I didn't come out until my mom died. Never knew my dad. All my other family—strewn to the wind." She took a breath. "People like Anson. Like Eli, like Bronson—I know Jesus says I should extend grace to them. That in God's eyes, we are all the same. All flawed, all sinners, to be redeemed by Christ's sacrifice."

David stared into her eyes, bright blue eyes, in her worn face.

"But none of that matters, when they're perched in your home, ready to hurt you. To beat you, to rape you, to torture you." She resumed scrubbing. "The shotgun worked. And no, I don't think about Anson much. A piece of shit, that I scraped off my boot."

David turned, and scrubbed again. They worked in silence. Within an hour, the graffiti was gone, the house clean again.

They cleaned and emptied the buckets, and then they dug up the broken post, replacing it with the 3x3 Ann had brought.

"All you need is a mailbox, to put on top," said Ann. "Home Depot down the way will have 'em. Might have to tell Mercer to deliver to your door for a while. He won't mind."

"Thank you for your help today, Ann," said David. "I would have hated to do this alone."

"Doing my part, like I said. And if you need me, you can call. I can watch the little one for you, if you need the break."

"You're a babysitter, too?"

"I love kids," said Ann. "Especially when they're not mine."

They loaded up Ann's truck.

"I'll see you Sunday, David," she said, getting behind the wheel. He turned to go back inside. "Pastor?"

He turned.

Ann stared. "Will God forgive me? For killing that man?"

David stood still, and then nodded. "I think so."

Ann nodded, with her cold, blue eyes. "Good." She turned the engine over, and reversed out into the street.

David watched her go.

*

"What the hell is that noise?" asked Jason.

"What noise?"

"Listen," said Jason, and they both did, as Solly toddled

between them, kicking his play ball.

It was a mechanical sound, of metal against metal.

David pushed to his feet, his heart already racing, the adrenaline starting to pump. He pushed his way outside in the late afternoon, onto the porch.

He saw the source of the sound. It was Zeke—changing their tires.

He had already replaced one, the torn and ripped rubber sitting in their driveway. The back of Zeke's SUV was parked nearby, the back open, a huge machine on the ground next to it, a cord from it running to their outdoor outlet.

"Hello there, Pastor, sorry to bother you. This won't take too long."

"How did you—"

"Oh, I keep my ear to the ground," said Zeke, ratcheting the lug nuts tight on the second tire. "It ain't right, what they did. And I had a guy, tire guy, who owed me a favor. Got you some replacements, brand new. Lent me his tire changer, too."

Zeke finished ratcheting, and walked to David. David stared into his eyes, and they were cogent, his pupils normal.

"Hope you don't mind," he said.

"Of course not," said David. "It—it's very kind of you."

"You're a Man of God," said Zeke. "Can't believe the behavior of these men. It ain't becomin'. It *ain't* becomin.'"

Jason was out on the porch, with Solly in tow. Zeke nodded toward him.

"Sir," he said. He leaned into David, close. "We need to talk. Just you and me. I'll host. Take you out on the water. Have supper."

"We can talk here, Zeke—"

"Nothing against you and yours," said Zeke. "But this ain't talk for a child's ears. Alright?"

David paused, and then nodded.

"Alright," said Zeke, leaning away. "Give me twenty more minutes, and I'll get you right."

12

David slid into bed, the house quiet, dark.

"He's asleep," he said, his voice low. He settled next to Jason, in just his boxers, and Jason rolled over, nestling himself into David's chest and under his arm. The house was warm, and they slept under only a sheet.

"He's been sleeping through the night," said Jason. "Lately. He should be tired, after today."

"How did the play date go?"

"Good, I think," said Jason. "Sol and little Susie got along. Amy was very nice. We talked a bit. A little bit of gossip."

"Anything juicy?"

"Pretty tame," said Jason. "Sacred can't compete with the city."

"Already becoming a pastor's wife."

"You're the worst," said Jason. "Don't know why I married you."

"If I remember correctly," said David, softly clearing his throat. "It's not fair you're a Christian, with lips like that."

"I didn't say that."

"It was something like that."

"It's not the only reason I married you," said Jason. "But it is *a* reason."

They laid there, silently, softly touching, David's fingers weaving through Jason's hair.

The sound of the country bled into the house. But no footsteps. No harried scrapes of feet on the driveway. No rattling spray paint cans.

"Will they come back?" asked Jason.

"It's possible," said David. "But I don't think they will. I scared them off."

"It scares me, David."

"I mean—"

"Not just them, either. You. When you get like that."

David took a deep breath. "They were threatening us."

"I know," said Jason. "I just don't want—want you to do something you regret."

"I won't."

Silence. Jason's hand moved across his chest, counting his ribs.

"Was this a mistake?" asked Jason.

"We knew what we were heading into," said David. "It was always going to be a risk."

"There's a difference between knowing it, and seeing it, firsthand," said Jason. "Being in it, especially with Sol."

"I know."

"We can go back, any time," said Jason. "I still have all my contacts in New York. If I did the right shows, with the right people attending, we'd be safe for a while—"

"It's not about that," said David. "You said you were okay with leaving the city. You said you could still sell your paintings—"

"And I can," said Jason. "I haven't painted much here, so far, but we're still getting settled in. I'm just saying we don't *have* to stay—"

"I won't find a job in the city," said David. "Certainly not as a head pastor. Maybe a youth pastor, or an associate role." He let out a breath. "I made too many enemies in seminary."

"You make it sound so dramatic," said Jason. "You called out bullies. Punched a guy in the nose."

"People have long memories," said David. "And it's just like anything else. It's about who you know. And those people know people, and they talk. Nobody wants to hire the hothead gay pastor."

"I'm sure you could find something, if you looked hard enough."

"Did I tell you I met Ed today?" asked David.

"I—uh, no, you didn't," said Jason. "What does that have to do—"

"I met Ed today," said David. "An old guy, in his seventies. Thick accent. Dips. Not in the church, but he told me never goes anywhere without chew."

"What a lovely man."

"He came into the church, knocked on my door," said David. "Wanted to introduce himself. Said he talked to Pastor John every Friday. Like clockwork, after lunch. Came in and talked to Pastor John. Asked me if I wouldn't mind keeping up the tradition."

"What'd you say?"

"Told him I'd be honored," said David. "We talked. For quite a while, actually. Ed is a font of discourse."

"I'm sure."

"He told me a lot of things," said David. "Told me he thinks the price of eggs these days is ridiculous. Told me he hates his new car, and the fact he has to learn a computer to work on it."

"I agree with him about the eggs."

"He told me that he don't mind one lick at all that we're gay folk. Says whatever happens in someone's bedroom is their own damn business."

Jason snorted. "I might like Ed."

"But mostly," David said, his voice quiet. "Ed talked about his late wife. Said he missed her. Today was their anniversary. Would have been forty nine years. Ed started talking about her, wouldn't stop. By the end of the conversation, he was blubbering. Crying into my shoulder."

"Aw, Ed," said Jason.

"I don't want to leave Sacred," said David. "Not yet, at least."

Jason leaned over, and kissed David, softly. Their lips touched, caressing each other in the dark.

They kissed harder.

"It is unfair that a pastor has as skilled lips as you do," said Jason. "We have to be quiet."

"No promises."

13

David stood behind the door, taking deep breaths.

The sound of spray paint cans rattling, the sound of destruction. The feelings of rage, bubbling in his knuckles, wrapped around a baseball bat. The look on Eli's face. On Bronson's.

His nerves ate at him, tension and anger and temperance battling it out in his guts, as he waited for Laurie to introduce him once again.

They were out there, he knew. He had peeked, had seen all the people who had retreated from the potluck. Eli, Bronson, and their slew of followers. The ones who'd seen him share a kiss and had fled.

The ones who'd attacked him at night.

They sat there, occupying half the church. Waiting. They

sang the hymns, dressed in their Sunday best.

Laurie did her part, without shift or change in behavior, as if last Sunday didn't happen. No change in tone, or appearance. Another normal Sunday service.

David waited, using breath to banish demons.

And then Laurie was done and he pushed through the bare wooden door into the chapel, and walked up the stairs, his eyes only on his feet, on the faded red carpet, up the stairs, and to the pulpit, away from the torturous eyes of the massive Christ, who perched behind him, in a terrible, permanent agony, lording over him, beaming down on him with the pain of infinite crucifixion.

David placed hands on worn wood and stared out into the congregation, left and right. They all stared back, Eli, Bronson, Laurie, Jason. Ann Campbell, and Zeke, sitting in the back row.

Eli stared daggers, but David met his eyes only for a moment.

"All of us are one in Jesus Christ," said David, projecting his voice, silence filling the space between his words, not a breath or cough interrupting.

"Galatians 3:28. 'There is no longer Jew or Greek, there is no longer slave or free, there is no longer male and female; for all of you are one in Christ Jesus.'"

The congregation said nothing. Eli stared, but did nothing.

"The early Christian church was splintered. Fractured, between Jewish Christians, and Gentile Christians. Christ appealed to all, Jew and Gentile, but after his ascendance, the two were split in where and how they worshiped. And Paul, in Galatians, called for unity. For the Jewish Christians and Gentile Christians to come together. To worship, to unify under the worship of Christ himself. That we all are equal under the eyes of Christ."

Silence hung in the room, David's words echoing. He shouted now. Details brightened, darkened. Sunlight pouring through high windows, illuminating. Shadow darker still, in the corners of the church. Eli's face, drowned in shadow, light and darkness, filling the chapel, and David witnessed.

"'So in Christ Jesus, you are all children of God through faith, for all of you who were baptized into Christ have clothed yourselves with Christ.'" David paused. He raised his hands. "Through faith. Paul writes, time and time again, that through faith, through Christ we are all equal. No ethnicity, no social status, no gender. We are all but faith." He pounded the pulpit, and pointed back at the statue of Christ behind him, its face contorted in perpetual torture. "Christ died for us all to be clothed in Christ, to be transformed, to be seen *only* as faith, through our baptism, through our faith in him!"

Eli stood then, with Bronson quick behind, author and punisher.

David stared, his chest heaving from his sermon, a bead of sweat dripping down his temple.

"How dare you," belted Eli. "That you dare preach such filth in this church. That you twist the words of the Lord. That you pollute this holy space with your sinful ways!"

Eli yelled, spittle flying from his lips. All eyes were on him. David stared back, seeing only shadow.

"And you—" Eli turned to Laurie. "What have you done to us? You have split us in half, you corrupted your late husband, you have defiled this church by bringing an open sinner into our midst! We have been a pure place, a place of God for generations, and you have brought us low within a year's time!"

Laurie sat, her eyes looking up at Eli, and then down, her face betraying nothing.

"Eli," said David. "Please, sit down."

"I will not," he said. "This is our church, and we won't allow it to be corrupted. We will not allow it to be filled with sin!"

David exhaled, his heart racing, all eyes on him. The fury rose inside, a dark breeding of flame and fire in his chest, but he placed his hands on the worn wood of the pulpit, and pushed the rage down.

"I will not argue with you," said David. "And you do not own this church, no more than I, or any one person here. If you will not sit, please leave. Let the rest of us worship in peace."

Bronson moved, to rush the pulpit, and Zeke rose in the back, his body tense, but Eli held out an arm, holding Bronson in place.

"This isn't over, Pastor," said Eli. "We will have our church again." He glared at Laurie a final time, and then he looked to his wife and kids, who stood with him, and followed. The older boy locked eyes with David, a confused look of strange fear, and then followed his father, with Bronson and his family locked in step behind.

They were not alone.

The left side of the congregation stood, one by one, and followed him out the door, walking through sunlight on faded carpet, the glow of God's presence fading in David's eyes, as he watched them depart in silence.

A handful stayed behind from the left side of the congregation. David watched everyone leave, his hands squeezing. The rage in him strained against his ribcage, but he breathed, squeezing the implacable pulpit, the stained wood.

The double doors of the chapel closed shut again, all the departing gone.

David stood, and took in what remained of his congregation. He took a deep breath. He found Jason's eyes, who looked at him with strength. He finished his sermon.

"'For you are all one in Christ Jesus,' wrote Paul," said David, continuing. "Through faith, we are all one in Christ. Through faith, we are all equal. And to judge anyone, viewed as equal, through faith in our Lord Jesus Christ, puts you above Christ. We are here only to serve in faith, as equals."

David looked out at the congregation. He took a deep breath. "I want to thank you for being here. All of you. In faith, we are all equal."

14

Lord, help me.

David knelt, his shirt sticking to his back with sweat, even in the early morning. The church never cooled down, not in the summer, and the temperature rose as the church soaked in the early morning sun.

David knelt, on the stage, facing away from the gruesome Christ, still feeling its presence. One of many that weighed on his mind.

He had woken up early Monday morning, before the sun, and tossed and turned for an hour before abandoning their bed, waking Jason long enough to tell him he was going to church.

And now he prayed.

He prayed without words, in supplication, in meditation,

alone with God.

He breathed, the face of Eli, spittle flying, as he bellowed his complaints, as he called David a sinner. As he led his shadow flock from the church.

The looming figure of Bronson. The dilated pupils of Zeke, as he called David a Man of God.

Ann Campbell and her shotgun, killing for solace.

Solomon's little legs as he ran around and past the chairs of the potluck.

Laurie's face, her blonde hair stacked high, her eyes hiding falsehood. Or just buried in the grief of a husband lost.

A mass of rage, breathed out, ounce by ounce.

A church, split in half, the Jews and Gentiles, both Christian by faith, unable to recognize each other, despite them both wearing the cloth of Christ.

Lord, help me.

"David?"

A voice interrupted, in the past.

David opened his eyes, glancing at the familiar voice, Pastor Stewart sitting on a pew.

"I hate to interrupt," he said. "But you've been there for a half hour. If there's something you'd like to talk about—"

David's heart leapt into his throat, the sour feeling in his stomach a deeper toxin, poison filtering down into his fingertips and onto his tongue, bile filling him. The dark feeling in him, of the shadow he was, unable to process, a prayer and call for help shouted out.

"Pastor—" started David, but his voice failed him, his heart and lungs squeezed in an iron grip of fear. He sobbed then, quietly, too worried to utter his sadness aloud, his body covered in cold sweat, shaking, wracked.

The Pastor's hand touched his back, softly.

"David," he said, his voice as soft, and he led David out of the chapel, and walked him to his office, and let him sit.

"Just breathe," said the pastor. "Just breathe. A deep breath."

David took one.

"And let it out, nice and slow."

David let it out, and the crushing grip on his lungs and heart relented.

"One more breath. Nice and deep. And hold it."

David took a breath. He held it.

"And out. Nice and slow."

David opened his eyes, bleary, and looked into the face of the pastor, his gaze filled with concern.

"How are you doing, son?"

David spread his lips and said nothing, and then shook his head.

"That bad, huh?"

David took another breath and looked up, into the pastor's eyes.

"I—I don't—" and then froze.

Pastor Stewart took a short breath, and the silence sat between them for a moment.

"David," he said. "Whatever you're holding—for someone so young—you can tell me."

"I can't—I can't," said David. He looked up into the pastor's eyes, through tears. "There's no—" and then the grip tightened on him again, and he breathed, forcing air in, and out.

"I won't force you to tell me anything," said Pastor Stewart. "If you want me to just sit with you, I'll do that. But

I promise you—whatever you'll tell me, I've heard much worse." David looked up to his eyes again, and held his gaze. "Or heard the same from others. Probably from someone in the congregation. Someone you've shook hands with during fellowship." He nodded, a slight, knowing gesture.

David inhaled. "Pastor—I'm gay." He let out the words and then a long, tortured breath. David paused a moment, the cold and poison inside forcing more words. "And no matter what I do, there's no changing it, no amount of prayer, nothing I do—it's still there, right there, and I don't know—"

"David," said the pastor. "You don't need to explain yourself. Not to me, and not to God."

David closed his eyes, blinking away more tears.

"Have I ever, in any sermon, in anything I've ever said— have I ever said anything bad about gay people?"

David looked at him, and shook his head.

"No, I haven't," said Pastor Stewart. "I'm careful with my words, especially at the pulpit. And now some, some in our congregation—they may choose to interpret things I've said, or things the Bible says—as a condemnation of gay people. To use those words as a weapon for their own beliefs. For their own hate. But I haven't. And I won't."

David's heart eased, the vice grip loosening.

"If you're gay, it's because God made you that way. I don't believe God makes mistakes, and I promise to support you, and protect you if need be. Alright?"

David nodded.

"I was afraid."

"I don't blame you," said the pastor. "But I'm here for you. And so is God."

"David—"

David opened his eyes, Laurie sitting in the front pew, her blonde hair immaculate, even at nine in the morning, in the rising heat of the chapel.

Her eyes—her eyes were tired, though. She looked at him, her face coated in makeup, but no amount could hide the weary in her eyes.

David took a deep breath, and then pulled a handkerchief from a pocket and wiped the sweat from his face.

"Did you need me?" he asked.

"No," said Laurie. "I came here to think. And then you were here."

David nodded. He forced himself to his feet, his hips straining, and climbed down, and sat next to her in the pew, in the spot Eli had delivered his diatribe from not a day before.

"I've failed," said David, the tortured Christ staring down at them. "Already, I've failed."

"I wouldn't go that far," said Laurie. "There is still a church. We are still a congregation. Maybe even a better one, without Eli, without Bronson. Without his ilk."

David matched eyes with the tortured Christ figure. It did not meet his gaze, staring up in agony to its father.

David shook his head. "I don't want this schism dividing the town. Dividing the church. I want to—I want to unite people."

"I don't think you're to blame for Eli," said Laurie. "I think it's just time to move on. I thought that after John's death, and when you came in, new blood and all, that he would see the writing on the wall." She took a breath. "And maybe he is. And instead of growing up, he's taking his ball and going home."

David looked away from the statue, down at the faded carpet.

"You may be right," said David. "But I have to try."

Laurie scoffed. "Why?"

David exhaled. "Everyone deserves an olive branch."

Laurie shook her head. "Eli doesn't. And of all the things he said in here yesterday, he's thinking much worse. You should have heard his arguments with John. The things he said—"

"Laurie—"

"Just the most disgusting things. And he thinks he's speaking for the Lord, it's just the most absurd—"

"Laurie," said David, raising his voice. "Please."

Laurie stopped.

"It's not about Eli," said David. "It's about the church. It's about all the others who followed him out of here." He took a breath. "It's about me."

"I don't—"

"I don't extend an olive branch for him. I extend it for me, and for the church. The church is a better place if he has every opportunity to be a better man. *I* am in a better place if I extend that grace to every one. Especially to the men like Eli, who do not deserve it, through their faith, through their actions. Do you think Eli is the first man in the church I've encountered who doesn't believe I belong?"

"Now, David—"

"Of course it isn't," said David. "Since I was a child, I have had to battle for my place in God's light. Have had to prove myself worthy of my faith. And I won't exclude other's faith, no matter how much it pains me." David sighed. "I don't *want* to do it, Laurie. I'd love to just preach in peace, and let this church, and Sacred in general, be a place of acceptance. But ignoring the wound won't make it heal."

"He won't listen," said Laurie.

"I know," said David. "But I will still try."

15

David arrived at the coordinates, down a dirt road, the trees close on the side of the Prius, the stand of trees thick, blotting out the sun.

Cell service had died back at the pavement. The Prius had rattled down the clay road, potholes big enough to swim in. It wasn't yet five PM, but the thick tree cover blocked the sunlight.

The clay road ended at a short dock, only a few feet long, extending out into the swamp. David pulled the Prius to the side, hoping he could get it out later, and thumbed off the engine.

When Zeke had given him the GPS coordinates, he'd assumed it was because Maps gave bad directions to his house. But there was no home here, only a dock.

David stepped out, humidity hitting him in a wave, the buzz of mosquitoes instantly overwhelming, and he reached for the bug spray, and covered himself in it, closing his mouth and eyes, and then spitting the small amount he felt on his lips.

He left the Prius, locking it behind him, the chirp echoing through the swamp and then dying, the lights blinking in the gloom.

David walked in the dim, testing the dock, the wood dark brown, stained green. It bent slightly, but held his weight. He checked his phone again. He was five minutes early, anxiety making it a habit. Still no signal.

BRBRBRBRBR

David glanced up, shoving his phone in his pocket. The sound arced over the murky water, and he spotted the light, coming in and out as it passed in and around copses of trees, dotting the swamp.

"Pastor David," shouted Zeke, as his mud boat cut through the green water. "You're early."

"Only a few minutes," said David, still not venturing out to the edge of the dock. He watched Zeke approach, the sputtering engine slowing. Zeke grabbed a spare oar and pulled himself close to the short dock, grabbing a hold with a hand.

"Climb on in," said Zeke. "We got a little trip ahead of us."

David edged out to the end of the dock, the wet wood supporting him, if bent from years.

"Don't worry, Pastor," said Zeke. "It'll hold you. Take the oar." Zeke held out the edge of the oar, and David grabbed it, holding it for stability as he stepped down into the low slung boat, the vessel rocking slightly as he put his weight in it. "See? Easy as pie."

"I'm not much of a sailor," said David, easing down onto one of the planks that served as seats.

"Neither am I," said Zeke. "All I got is this little feller. Gets me where I need to go. You seated?"

"I think so."

"Alright," said Zeke, and the engine sputtered louder, as Zeke tilled them back out into the water.

They slid through it, navigating the murky swamp. David was immediately lost, out of sight of the dock. The water surrounded them, dotted with lily pads, small windows of light where the cypress and tupelo trees didn't cover. The dark water stretched around them. Zeke steered with quiet confidence.

"My car will be okay, right? Parked back there?"

"Yeah, should be," said Zeke. "Farmer from upstate owns that plot, but he don't use it for nothing. Gave me the go-ahead to build the dock."

"It's dark out here," said David. "Don't know how you navigate."

"You learn," said Zeke. "Enough time on the water. The swamp moves, if you pay 'tention. You orient yourself the right way, you know the trees, know the landmarks. You get your bearings."

"How far is it? To your house?"

"Oh, maybe twenty minutes. Be there in no time." The swamp surrounded them, trees darting up in the middle of the water, no clear direction or path the water took, despite Zeke's insistence. David jumped at a loud splash to their side.

"Only a gator, Pastor," said Zeke. "Won't get you. Mostly only small ones out here."

"Mostly?" asked David. "How deep is the water?"

"Oh, not that deep," said Zeke. "You can get out and walk most of it."

"Most of it?"

"There are the gators, and the gator holes," said Zeke. "Plus the water is filthy. Wouldn't get in there, not unless you had to." Zeke chuckled. "Don't worry, Pastor. We won't tip."

"I can swim," said David. "I'd just prefer not to."

Zeke piloted them through the swamp. David sat, listening to the sounds of water, to the insects, to the frogs.

The sound of God's creation.

He took a deep breath, and he listened, his eyes closed.

The motor churned behind him, and Zeke steered them to his home, a bigger dock, using the oar to guide them close and tie off his boat, killing the motor.

"Is that—"

"It's my little island," said Zeke. "Take her in."

It was a small mass of land, sitting in the middle of the wider swamp. Trees jutted out of the water around it, with a massive oak on one side. The setting evening sun beamed down on the house that sat in the middle of the land, a halo.

"My humble abode," said Zeke. "Welcome, Pastor. You can get out, I'll keep the boat steady."

David climbed out. The dock was stacked with crates and boxes, and tipped over coolers. The dock led to the land, and it was dark and mildewed, but some of the boards were more recently replaced, and none of it sagged. Zeke kept it maintained. He climbed out behind him.

"Come on Pastor David," said Zeke, scooting past him, glancing back. "No need to stand on ceremony. Let's get inside, in from the bugs."

The house was small, surrounded by barrels. Solar panels covered the roof. The small front porch had a couple of rocking chairs, stacked crates serving as a table.

"Solar?"

"I've got a gas generator as a back-up, but yeah, solar is my main energy source. Don't got no power lines out here."

Zeke opened the door and walked in, holding it for David.

"Come on in. I'll give you the dime tour."

Zeke led David through the small house. The front door opened into a small hallway, with doors leading off.

"There's my bedroom," said Zeke, peeking his head in, and David followed. "Ain't much, but it suits me." David saw a bed and dresser, both simple. The room was tidy.

"This is my study," said Zeke. The room was sparser still than Zeke's bedroom, a desk and chair, and a small bookshelf. A Bible sat on the desk. "Where I do my Bible study. Look up all the verses you mention."

"And finally, the kitchen, and workshop, too, I guess," said Zeke, leading David into the biggest room of the house. Kitchen table sat in the middle of the room, with a fridge, oven, and a big work bench along one wall, with tools hanging on a peg board. "You can have a seat, Pastor, and I'll get us our food."

"Thank you," said David, and he sat, easing into a wooden chair, none of the four at the table matching.

"You don't mind fried chicken, do you?"

"No, that sounds great."

"Good," said Zeke, opening the fridge and taking out a bucket of fried chicken, and pre-heating the oven. David laughed.

"I had thought—"

"Naw, I leave it to the pros," said Zeke. "Don't get me wrong, I cook sometimes, but mostly it's just me. Sandwiches and cereal, Pastor."

"You can call me David."

Zeke placed the cold chicken on a sheet pan and slid it into the oven. He sat down across from David, shaking his head.

"I appreciate it, Pastor, I do," said Zeke. "But you're my pastor. You earned the title. I'll use it."

"Thank you for your hospitality," said David. "It seems peaceful out here."

Zeke knit his hands together on his chest, and then nodded. "It is now."

"Now?"

Zeke smiled, a small smile, that he hid away, just as quick. "Pastor John saved my life."

David raised an eyebrow. "I don't follow."

Zeke took a long breath. "I sold meth, Pastor. For a long time. That whole wall over there, the workstation—I cooked, every day. And when I wasn't cooking, I was moving it, smuggling it, all across the county, all across the state. So, no, it wasn't peaceful out here. It smelled like dying. Never slept, waiting for other dealers to take me out. Every splash in the water, every broken twig—I thought they was killers in the dark."

The oven creaked as it heated up. David took a breath.

"I was using. Had to, at a certain point, running myself

ragged. Kept me up, kept me alert. Kept me paranoid, too. But it ain't no surprise I got caught. The meth made me reckless. I cut corners, and the cops caught me. Bronson caught me." Zeke took a breath. "But the judge, he saw I used, and said I could either go to rehab, or go to jail. I picked rehab." He didn't make eye contact with David as he spoke.

"I had no intention of quitting. But I met Pastor John there. He volunteered, you know, talked to us. Preached, sometimes. Mostly though, he just listened. He's the first man—"

Zeke stopped, and wiped at a tear with the back of his hand. "He was the first man who listened to me. Maybe that's all it took. But he promised me that I was more than everything I'd done. That Jesus had already forgiven me, for all my sins."

"He was right."

Zeke nodded. "I would've died, Pastor. Either the drugs, or another dealer. He made me understand. I would have run through a brick wall for Pastor John. Nearly did." The room had filled with the smell of fried chicken, and Zeke got up, and pulled out the sheet pan, and then pulled a container of potato salad out of the fridge, and then served both himself and David. He poured them sweet tea.

They ate.

They went out to the porch, with new glasses of tea.

"Sugar is about the only vice I let myself have anymore," said Zeke.

"Among them all, it's relatively tame."

They sat in the rocking chairs, the chirps of frogs and gators and birds intermixing in the dark.

David took a breath. "Your past—is that what you wanted to tell me? What wasn't suitable for children's ears?"

Zeke sat silent in the dark for a moment. "No, Pastor. And you'll have to forgive me, but that wasn't the complete truth. I didn't want your husband hearing it neither. Not that I don't trust him, but less ears that hear it, the better. Least for now."

"What if I tell him?"

"That's up to you," said Zeke. "But that's how it should be."

"Well—"

Zeke took a long swallow of sweet tea, and then took a deep breath. "Pastor John's death wasn't an accident."

"I was told he crashed his truck."

"Yeah, so was I," said Zeke. "So was everyone. Bronson was the one to report it. Found the truck wrapped around a tree. Pastor John's body thrown from it. Dead on impact. Body floating in the swamp."

"Then why—"

"I know the fella who works at the junkyard, where the truck ended up," said Zeke. "He said it don't add up, the state of the truck. He's seen a lot of accidents. A lot of fatalities. Truck didn't look like it was supposed to. And Pastor John always wore his seatbelt. Always."

"Wouldn't the truth come out in an autopsy, then?" asked David. "Medical examination, what have you?"

"I'd imagine so," said Zeke. "But it never happened. Case closed. At least far as I know. It's what Laurie told me."

"Bronson?" asked David. "You think?"

"It's never just him," said Zeke. "He don't do a thing on his own, not anything with the church. If he did it, Eli told him to."

"I thought they were close. Pastor John and Eli. Eli's been in the church his whole life, right?"

"Yeah," said Zeke. "But after everything—after the vote, after Pastor John changed things—" Zeke stopped, paused. Took a breath. "I've never liked him, Pastor. Bronson hates me, always has. Hard to blame him. Sheriff is easy t' read, though. His lies are simple, and you can see right through them. Eli's hiding something. I know it."

David took his own breath. "Have you talked to Laurie about it?"

"No," said Zeke. "You're the first. But the look in her eyes—I know she's thought about it. But what can she do?"

"That's a big accusation."

"And there ain't no way to prove it, neither," said Zeke. "It's all hearsay. Least by the law."

"If it's true—"

"I'll kill 'em," Zeke said, his voice cold. "Both of them."

"Zeke—"

"I know, Pastor. It's ain't godly, to think such things. Or to do 'em."

David shook his head. "I just want the town to be whole again."

"Don't know if that's in the cards, Pastor," said Zeke. "Especially not if it's true. If it's true, there ain't no coming back."

David exhaled, a long breath. He sat in the dark with Zeke.

"I should say, Pastor. My friend at the junkyard, he ain't the only reason I'm telling you." He paused. "Ain't because of him I *know* that Eli killed Pastor John."

"How do you know?"

A long pause, the frogs and insects quieting.

"God told me."

"Zeke, we all pray, and we all feel things, but—"

"It's not just prayer, Pastor," said Zeke. "It's the mushrooms."

David paused, silence between them. "I thought you were clean."

"These are different, Pastor. Nothing like the speed. These let you see God—and the God in things. And sometimes, they let me hear him. It's the damndest thing."

"Zeke—"

"He told me that Eli killed Pastor John. To watch him, and watch him close."

David took a breath.

"I know you don't believe me, Pastor, but that's alright. God told me you're one of his. A Man of God. I saw it myself, when we first met. Don't you worry, whatever happens—I've got your back." Zeke reached out and patted him on the shoulder. "And if you ever need a direct line—let me know."

16

David knocked on the door, taking a deep breath and slowing down his heart.

Angie Parsons opened it a few moments later, her face fighting to maintain an even facade as she recognized him.

"Pastor," she said. "I'm surprised to see you here."

David smiled, his pastor smile. A pleasant, welcoming smile, even when David didn't feel it. Bedside manor, it had been described to him in seminary school. A pastor was warm, and welcoming, and his face should reflect it, even on bad days.

"Hello," he said. "I'd like to speak to Eli, if that's possible."

Angie's face flickered again, the facade crumbling and rebuilt, all in a moment.

"Of course," she said. "He's upstairs, cleaning up after

work. Come in, and I'll go see how he's doing."

Angie backed away and opened the door, and David came into the house, a large, two-story home. It looked to be new construction, built on a big lot, a long concrete driveway leading to a two car garage and the house itself.

"If you'd wait right here," she said, and then she climbed the nearby stairs, leaving David in the foyer, a shoe rack lined with dozens of pairs nearby, along with a key holder and entrance table, covered with baskets and trays.

Small steps pattered down a hallway, and Eli's younger son zipped toward him, sliding to a stop.

"You're the pastor," he said, staring up at David.

"I am," said David. "You're Samuel, right?"

"Yeah," he said. "But no one calls me that, except for Dad. I'm Sam."

"Nice to meet you, Sam."

"Dad said you're evil."

"Did he now?" asked David. "Well, I'm not."

"You don't look evil," said Sam. "But it's hard to tell, sometimes. Sometimes bad guys look normal."

"You're right about that," said David. "But I try my best to be good."

Sam squinted at him, examining him. "I don't think—"

"Sam, go to your room," said Eli, his voice hard, as he stepped down the stairs.

"Dad—"

"Go," he said, reaching the bottom, his face red, wearing a t-shirt and athletic shorts, in bare feet. "No arguments."

Sam glanced at David one last time and ran up the stairs.

Eli waited for him to turn the corner upstairs, watching David. David waited, taking a breath, silent.

"We can talk on the porch," said Eli, and pulled the door open, and gestured outside. David walked back out, onto the wide porch, a two person swing dangling on one side. The humid embrace of the late evening hit him, the cooling sweat on his back dripping again. Eli closed the door, clicking it shut.

"Why are you here?" asked Eli.

David took a breath. "I want you in the church, Eli."

Eli stared at him, the dim shadow of the porch masking his features. "You were there. You heard what I said."

"Every word," said David. "I want you in the church."

Eli exhaled a heavy breath. "I'm not doing this with you."

"Please, Eli," said David. "You're clearly an important man in the community. Your family has been with the church since the beginning. This is an olive branch. I want you in the church, and I want your people in the church. I don't want half a congregation."

"Did Laurie tell you to do this? To come to my house?"

"No," said David. "She told me not to bother. She told me you wouldn't listen. Laurie hired me, Eli, but she is not the pastor of the Holy Church of Sacred. I am."

"Listen—"

"And I know you had problems with Pastor John before his passing—but I am also not Pastor John. If you want input on the direction of the church, I will listen. I want this to be a place for Sacred to worship."

Eli exhaled again, staring at David.

"Then leave," said Eli.

"I—"

"*You* are the problem," said Eli. "You and your kind. John wanted to change the church, and let anyone in, and now

Laurie's made it worse, appointed you—"

David cut through his words. "Do you have tattoos, Eli?"

"What—"

"Do you have tattoos, Eli?" asked David, glancing at Eli's exposed right arm.

"Yes," said Eli. "They're for my sons. Their birth dates."

"What does the Bible say about tattoos?"

"I don't care—"

"The next thing you're going to do is quote the Bible at me," said David. "A book I've read and studied more than you, or anyone else in Sacred. You're going to cherry pick scripture that condemns homosexuality. Over thirty thousand verses in the Bible, Eli, and under a dozen of them mention homosexuality. Roughly the same amount condemn tattoos." David paused. "Are your tattoos a sin, Eli?"

"Don't—"

"No, they're not," said David. "Because we know the Bible was written a long time ago, with very different context."

Eli looked away for a moment, but said nothing.

"Why do you hate me?" asked David. "Have you ever asked yourself that question, Eli? Because the answer isn't the Bible."

"Don't tell me—"

"I don't need you to like me, Eli," said David. "I want Sacred to be a better place, and the church to be a better place. Those people, they'll listen to you."

Eli shook his head. "I will not be preached to by a fag. By some butt-fucking queer—"

"You can't hurt me with your words, Eli," said David. "I heard worse things than that before I was ten years old. I was out of the closet in high school, and no matter what you say, it's not worse than what the dudes in school called me."

"We don't want an olive branch!" said Eli, his voice louder. "We want our church back. We want it the way it used to be, before John decided to change, before Laurie got in his ear. When—"

"The way it used to be," said David, cutting him off. "Back when I didn't haveta look at people different than me," said David, effecting a heavy southern accent. "Do you think there aren't gay people in Sacred, Eli? And I'm not talking about me, or Ann Campbell. I'm talking about the group that followed you out of the church. Someone, probably multiple someones, are holding it back. Killing themselves with guilt and worry, and heartache, and it doesn't have to be that way."

Eli slapped him, hard, a gunshot reverberating in the dark, striking David across the cheek, his face on fire.

The pain was only momentary, ringing for a second before rage flooded through and over, pouring in a torrent out of David's heart, filling his body, sliding over his organs, fire building up his throat into his head, and he tensed, his breath aflame.

He charged Eli, both hands squeezing his face, thumbs sliding into his eye sockets, pushing, pushing, Eli screaming, feebly batting at David's arms, but he could do nothing as both his eyes POPPED, liquid gushing from his skull, orbital nerves dangling in useless sockets—

David stood there, breathing, doing nothing. Eli stared.

"Get off my property," said Eli. "And don't come back."

David seethed, holding his rage inside.

He took another breath, rage boiling, forcing his feet to walk down the steps, leaving the porch. Eli stood, watching him go, saying nothing, his fists balled at his side.

David walked away, back to his car. He paused at the driver's side door, staring back at Eli's house. Eli still stood on the porch, waiting. But David's eyes caught something else.

A light, out of an open window, on the second floor. Eli's older son, Thomas. He'd been listening.

David left, rage ripping at him.

17

The phone rang.

"David!" answered Phil. "How are you?"

"I'm—I'm okay, Phil," said David. "Still settling in."

"That's right, you've got the new job. You had just accepted it, right, the last time we talked?"

"Yes, yes," said David. "We've been here a couple weeks now."

"How's it going?"

"Not great," said David. "That's why I'm calling."

"Oh no, David," said Phil. "What happened?"

"They, uh, they walked out on me. Just under half the congregation."

"They walked out on you? During a sermon?"

"Yeah," said David. "All together. Their leader criticized

me, and then they walked out."

"Organized," said Phil. "That's—that's disappointing."

"Yeah," said David. "They want me out."

"Of course they do," said Phil. "The church has moved on from that. We've settled it. It took us a long time, but we did it."

"Well, it's not settled here."

"David—"

"I went to the leader of the other side," said David. "His name is Eli. I talked to him. Asked him to come back. To give me an opportunity, to win him over. He—well, he hit me."

"He hit you?" asked Phil. "What did you do?"

"Nothing. I did nothing," said David. "I walked away."

"Good."

"He wanted to provoke me," said David. "He wants a fight."

"I'm sure he does," said Phil. "You've grown, David. You're a better man."

"I hope so," said David. "What do I do? Half the church is gone."

Phil said nothing for a second, and David heard him take a breath.

"They won't tell you this in seminary, David. But sometimes, churches, just like people, have cancers in them. And to get them out, you have to damn near kill yourself. Either cutting it out, or poisoning it, you know. But you can't live with a cancer inside you, and neither can a church. And it can take a long time to heal, and it's tiring, and it's frustrating. But your church will be whole again. It'll regrow."

"I just want a normal church."

"No such thing, my friend," said Phil. "No such thing. Listen, you stay strong. I've got to go. We're at the hotel now, about to head to dinner. But if you've got any other problems, call. Leave me a voicemail. I'll call you when I get a minute."

"Thanks, Phil. I appreciate it."

"You're fighting the good fight, David. Don't lose faith. Or your temper."

18

Jason nestled his head into David's chest. They caught their breath. They'd only been official for a few weeks.

"I feel like this guarantees me a spot in Hell," said Jason. "Spoiling a young holy man."

David laughed. "He'll forgive you."

"Oh, he will? What about you?"

"I'm already forgiven."

"Oh, is that right?" asked Jason. "That's fast. Didn't know you had a direct line."

"I do, actually. He said I'm good."

"That's reassuring," said Jason. "I was worried."

"Don't be," said David. "If anything is going to send me to Hell, it's not pre-marital sex."

"What would it be?"

"Probably my temper."

"You seem pretty even keeled to me," said Jason, rubbing David's chest.

"I try," said David. "It's hard sometimes. I've burned some bridges."

"Sometimes anger is warranted."

"It's not godly of me," said David. "And I need to be better."

"If we—nevermind," started Jason.

"If we what?"

"We don't have to talk about it now. I don't want to spoil anything."

"I'll be thinking about it anyway. If we what?"

"If we, you know, stay together long-term—will I have to go to church?"

"I'm not going to *make* you go—"

"But—"

David paused. "But let's say I'm preaching somewhere—in a perfect world, yes, you would attend."

Jason was silent, his hands still grazing David's chest. "In a perfect world."

"In a perfect world, you would want to attend."

"I don't know if that will happen."

"You believe," said David. "I know you do."

"It's not that," said Jason. "And I do. Probably even in a Christian God. But attending a service—it's hard for me to imagine a situation where I feel welcome. Where I feel—"

"Where you feel what?"

Jason breathed. "Where I feel God."

"When do you feel him?"

Jason paused again. "I don't know that I do."

"Not at all?"

"I don't know," said Jason. "Do you?"

"Yes," said David.

"When?"

"When I'm joyous," said David. "When people are their best selves. That's when I feel him. That's when I *see* him."

"You see God?" asked Jason. "Really?"

"Of course," said David. "The few times I've preached. When I've felt a connection to someone in Christ. When people come together for a common good. Everyone glows. Everyone is happy. I saw him in your face, when you laughed earlier." David paused. "You don't experience that?"

Jason took a breath. "Well—I guess when I paint a landscape. When I get caught up in the waves crashing, or a river flowing—I feel—I don't know—wonder. Awe. Is that what you mean?"

"I think it's close enough to count," said David. "And not feeling welcome—"

David stopped.

"You okay?"

"I'm fine," said David. "It's why I'm doing this. I want a place that cultivates that feeling in everyone. That is safe. That is welcoming. So that everyone can feel that joy. Can feel that wonder."

"Are you going to be preaching anytime soon?"

"Students get opportunities whenever a pastor calls in sick. It's always short notice."

"When it happens next—tell me. I want to go."

"You serious?"

Jason leaned over him, staring him in the eyes. "As eternal damnation," he said, smiling, and kissed him.

19

Eli worshiped.

It was hotter now, even in the middle of the night, the sun long since set. The heat had settled in, the humidity clinging to the warmth, and the basement was a furnace.

He had crept down from his marriage bed in the dead of night, the house asleep, the naked lights above casting a bare shadow on the floor.

Eli looked up at the nude figure of Christ, his eyes filled with pain, up and down the figure, his eyes seeing the massive nails penetrating the soft skin of Jesus, his chest, his stomach, tight with exertion, stretched to the limit, as he suffered. Down his hips, bones pressed out against the skin and muscle, strained at the force of the crucifixion.

Eli's eyes moved downward and he forced his mind

blank, staring, only sensation, only pleasure, no thought, squeezing the Bible, held in his hand, the leather rubbing across his skin, sweat dripping from his body—

Eli struggled.

He closed his eyes.

He had walked out of the service, they had walked out. They had demonstrated their principles, that they wouldn't take part in a service with a sinner leading the church. They had done the right thing, the godly thing. He had rejected the homosexuals and their agenda. They had made a righteous display, and showed the people of Sacred the moral right.

It was the right thing. Laurie had hired a sinner to preach to them, an evil scourge to lead the church down into Hell, and they had rejected it soundly, as they should.

It was the right thing.

But he could not worship.

He feebly held the Bible, the pliable pages bending in his hand. He could not worship, no connection, no feeling, no pleasure.

Eli stared up at the figure of Christ, focusing. He let all thoughts, all concerns, all bleed away, flowing out of him, an arterial spray, thoughts of David, of John—

John struggled, flailing in the murky water. His hand grabbed a hold of your forearm, wrenching at you as he drowned, as his lungs filled with the bog, and you held your breath with him, waiting for him to stop, his body broken from the Sheriff's brutality—

Eli focused on the figure of Christ, his body contorted, struggling to breathe, nailed to the cross, the bloody spray of Roman spear, of hammer and nail, of Christ's grunts and groans, as he suffered and suffocated, the hard wood of the cross holding him taut, his spine, his hips, all strained against the structural strength of both judgment and sacrifice.

Eli squeezed the Bible hard, worshiping. He stared—

His palm rang with sudden pain as he slapped David across the face on his front porch, challenging him to strike him back. Skin on skin, his palm against David's face, a sudden strike, the force, his hand whipping across his cheek, blood rushing to the surface, the thrill, the aggression, finally released, the contact, touching another man—

Cold filled Eli, a dark burning intensity spreading like wildfire inside him, in his fingers, his toes, burning into his stomach, his lungs, and settling into his chest. Tears flowed to the surface then, a deep, harrowing sorrow filling him, and he wept, naked, Christ staring down at him.

Eli shook, face in hands, tears pouring from him, his bare ass against the cold metal of the chair, the tortured body of Christ looming over him, his eyes filled with torment, blood pouring from his wrists, his ankles, and his side. The Bible was held against his face, the leather against his cheek, to hold back his woe.

He wept soundlessly, covering his own mouth, holding back the sound of pain and guilt, to not wake the house.

Eli wept as Christ watched.

The tears stopped, Eli taking giant, gasping breaths, forcing his heart rate back down.

He wiped his eyes, and stared up at the figure of Christ, so elegantly sculpted, for worship, for worship. He suffered for him, he died for him.

They did the right thing. They had walked out on the sin

of Laurie, of David, of the world.

Eli focused, staring at the suffering of Christ.

Nothing.

Nothing.

He threw the Bible across the basement, and it landed on the unfinished floor with a soft thud.

Tears threatened to come again, but he forced them down and away, into the part of himself that wasn't there.

Eli fell from the chair, onto the floor, past the puddle of his sweat, and crawled to the feet of the figure. He fell prostrate, bent over, naked, his legs below him.

He placed his forehead on the bare floor, pressing hard, until it hurt, until the pain was all he felt.

I'm sorry, Lord. I'm sorry.

20

"This feels wrong, David."

"Is there any other way to take it down?"

"Not easily. I have no idea how they made it, and Jesus is separate from the cross, but doing both is even harder—"

"Then you have my permission," said David. "Take it down."

Ann revved the reciprocating saw, vibrations in the air, and brought it down on Christ's legs, right below his knees.

David stood on the stage of the church and watched as Ann sliced through the sculpture, the blade chewing through the material.

"Don't know what the hell this is made out of," said Ann. "But the saw is getting through it. It's like wood and epoxy, and something else? Who the hell made this?"

"I don't know," said David. "Laurie told me that Eli had it commissioned."

Ann pressed the saw as it bucked back against her, and it grinded as it cut the remainder of the lower legs, feet and shins falling to the floor.

"That wasn't so bad," she said. "It'll be tougher with the body, where it's thicker."

David stared up at the figure of Christ, into its weeping eyes, its face distended in agony, as Ann revved up the saw again, cutting through its thighs. The sharp blade cut through the wood and lacquer, through the skin and sinew, the church warm in the mid-day.

David locked eyes with it, the pain and horror of the crucifixion present in its gaze. Ann cut, and the face contorted in agony, they as Romans cutting through its flesh, Christ's body mutilated, cut and chopped into pieces, falling to the floor, sprays of wood and pulp, of gore and blood, onto the faded red carpeting. It begged David, pleading with a stare, to end its suffering, to let it die, its muscles tight, as breath wouldn't come, the heavy weight of the body too much to bear, tears flowing from Christ's eyes, Ann working through the thighs, the blade fighting her, her finger holding the trigger down as it chewed, as it chewed.

Shhunk.

The blade cut through the remainder of the thighs, and they tumbled, heavy pieces of Christ falling to the carpet, landing with a dull thud.

David only stared into the eyes of Christ, the face deformed, distorted into an inhuman shape, bent and pulled, as Ann cut into its stomach, the reciprocating saw spitting out streams of wood and pulp and dust, holy remnants of a broken God, and David stared into its eyes. The face changed, moving in the heat of the church. It melted and reformed every moment, screaming in silence. Its eyes pleaded, begged, begged to a Father that wouldn't listen.

Ann cut, her saw chewing through the tense muscles of Christ's stomach, a model's abdominals on this Son of God. The saw cut through the skin, the muscle, the fat, through organs and bone, through the other side, Ann's taut arms holding the saw steady, guiding it through the body of Christ with expert precision.

The hips of Christ fell to the church carpet, Jesus only whole from the belly button up, but Ann was already working taking a single rejuvenating breath before revving the saw again, taking it across Christ, below his armpits, above his nipples, the blade sawing through them, the blade sliding back and forth, too fast to see, the teeth biting into the form of the Holy Son.

David still stared into its eyes. The face had changed more, the eyes whole, but the cheeks sunken, the mouth wide, wider still, opening up, as if Christ was a great snake, unhinging its jaw to swallow the world. Christ would pull himself from the cross, and slither across the ground, its legs gone, and coil its form around David, trapping, constricting, and stealing his breath, their eyes still locked together, and then Christ would wrap his lips around David's head and swallow, forcing him down his gullet while he still lived, David struggling inside the body of Christ.

Ann cut, and the last of Christ's torso fell to the ground, only his arms, shoulders, neck, and head left. She moved to his arms.

David stared into its eyes, and the face of God was

no longer God, but now it was Sheriff Bronson, his smile curved into a sneer, as he held David at a traffic stop, and Ann cut through the arm at the shoulder, moving quickly, and cut the hand nailed to the cross, removing it, finally easing the weight of the crucifixion. Bronson sneered as the arm fell to the carpet.

Ann went to the other arm, and cut through it quickly, Bronson's face resolute, even as he was butchered, reveling in the pride of pain.

The second arm, removed at shoulder, and then the hand from cross. The arm fell, Christ only a disembodied shoulders and head.

Its face was no longer Bronson, no longer Christ, David staring into the eyes of Eli now. His face was not contorted in the pain of disfigurement, nor in the sneer of pride, but in elation. He was joyous as Ann revved the saw and cut through the last connection point, behind the head, removing it from the massive cross.

Eli's mouth curled in pleasure, his eyes closed, and then the head of Christ fell to the carpeted floor, leaving only the massive cross.

His gaze broken, David breathed, his mind sliding out of a torpor. The statue laid in pieces at his feet. Ann looked at her handiwork.

"Still feels wrong," she said. "Are we doing the cross, too?"

David cut his gaze away from the pieces of Christ on the floor, and looked up to the huge cross. It was naked without Christ, without its pair, designed for each other. It was never meant to be seen alone, divots and dents in it where Christ's body had been nestled. The remnants of the bolts and glue that had kept the sculpture and the cross together, still there, garish.

Christ had hidden its flaws, the imperfect cut, the uneven paint of the cross. Without the body there, they were plain to see.

"Is it even possible?" asked David.

"It's bolted through the drywall into the stone or brick, or whatever the hell is behind the wall. The church is old, probably frankensteined together over the years." Ann stared at the anchor points of the cross. "They sunk them in way too deep. I could maybe get them out, but it'd be easier to break through the drywall, cut them off at the insert point, and then patch it all, and re-lathe it with some mud." She sighed. "It'd take some work. Probably all day. But I'll do it. Give me the word."

"No," said David. "Leave it. It's honest."

"It's ugly," said Ann. "But I like ugly." She glanced at the pieces of the statue. "I'm glad it's down. I know I shouldn't say it, but I hated that thing. Its eyes—"

"It's gone now."

"Eli won't be happy," said Ann. "If he commissioned it."

"We have to move on," said David. "I tried to invite him and his people back, but he—he rebuffed my offer."

Ann raised an eyebrow. "He didn't deserve that. He's a piece of shit."

David exhaled. "It's not just him. It's all those people he leads. Some of them could be brought back."

"You say that," said Ann. "The reason I didn't come, for the longest time, was because of Eli, Bronson, their people. With them gone, there might be people who attend."

David looked at the eyes of Christ, the head sitting on

the floor, staring up at him. He glanced away, quickly.

"What should I do with the pieces?" asked Ann. "I have a wood chipper. It'll make short work of 'em."

"No," said David. "Will you help me load them into my car? I have a use for them."

Ann paused. "Okay."

They loaded David's car.

*

David drove.

He had told no one Eli had slapped him, not even Jason. He had left, his cheek pink, slowly returning to its normal color.

No mark, no legacy.

He hadn't swung back at Eli. It was what Eli wanted, a fight, on his own porch, where he could do whatever he wished.

David had left, but his anger had stayed with him, simmering.

David drove, and came to a stop at the end of Eli's long driveway.

He left the comfortable confines of the car, and emerged into the Georgia heat, sweltering. He popped open the trunk of the hatchback, and grabbed the pieces of Christ, blocking the end of the driveway, from each side of the road. It would be the first thing Eli saw when he arrived home.

Righteous anger flowed through him as he worked, unloading the pieces. No one passed him on the road, and there was no movement from Eli's house. He worked in silence, the sun beating down on him.

David placed the head and shoulders of Christ in the middle of the driveway, staring out into the road.

Its face was its face.

David left, fury in his fingertips. If Eli wanted to cut ties with the church, David would swing the blade.

21

David didn't wait behind closed doors before his sermon. He sat with the congregation, in a half empty chapel, the left side barren.

He sang hymns, and joined in fellowship, and listened as Laurie spoke. The church was hot, hotter than ever, deeper in summer, the AC failing, even with Ann's intervention.

Christ did not stare down at him. Only a bare cross, pockmarked with its former inhabitant.

David rose quietly as Laurie introduced him, with applause ringing through the church. David took the pulpit, resting his hands on worn wood. He stared out into the congregation, the audience quiet. Everyone still sat in their normal spots, leaving the left side bare. He thought to reorganize them. But no, not yet. Perhaps still some would return.

"Jesus preached. A scribe stood up, asking, 'Which commandment is the most important one of all?' and Jesus replied. 'The most important is, Hear, O Israel: The Lord our God, the Lord is one. And you shall love the Lord your God with all your heart and with all your soul and with all your mind and with all your strength. The second is this: You shall love your neighbor as yourself. There is no other commandment greater than these.'"

David looked over his congregation. "Which is most important? Jesus replied with only two. Love the Lord, with everything you have. And love your neighbor as yourself." David paused. "Only two." He raised two fingers. "The Greatest Commandment. Another thing quoted to me by my parents, many times. Love your neighbor as yourself, David, is what they would say. And again, as a child, I didn't understand. Loving God, a simple thing. At least to a child." He paused, took a breath. "But loving a neighbor, as I loved myself? It felt nebulous, and strange. How do I fulfill that commandment?"

David shook his head. "And here, here is where I think the scripture verbatim perhaps fails us. Because if the word care is used instead, it becomes a simpler commandment. Both to understand, and to follow."

David looked out, to the sun, that beamed through the high windows of the church, illuminating the faded carpet, and the worn pews. The tired eyes of a sweating congregation, waking up early on a Sunday morning. David's heart yearned for the Spirit to seize him, for his vision to be filled with God's grace.

But there was nothing.

David continued.

"And if we look elsewhere in the Gospel, I think we see ample understanding and definition of what Christ meant. For in Luke, Christ repeats the same commandments, but then is asked for clarification. A lawyer asks him, 'And who is my neighbor?'"

David waited, waited for his sight to see God's glory, projecting as he preached. But nothing came. He locked eyes with Jason, with Solly, with Ann, and Laurie, and even with Zeke, sitting in the back row.

But nothing came. Zeke locked eyes with him, his face betraying something.

"I'll take this moment to explain one other thing. In both instances, men interrupt, asking questions. A scribe once, and a lawyer the other. Men trying to catch Christ on his proclamations. Trying to find a loophole. Testing Jesus. But what they don't understand is Christ himself is a scholar. He had studied the Old Testament extensively. When asked the most important commandment, he was quoting both Leviticus and Deuteronomy, compounding them into the greatest commandment. Many don't understand that Christ is not summoning new commandments from God. He is *choosing* the most important from the Bible at the time, and emphasizing their importance over all others."

David boomed, projecting, preaching.

But nothing came, his vision the same.

His thoughts went to the broken figure of Christ. Of the contorted face of the statue, of Bronson, of Eli.

Of the ringing pain of Eli's slap, the gunshot strike echoing into Thomas' open window.

"And so, a lawyer asked Christ, who is my neighbor? And Christ answered, answered with the parable of the Good Samaritan. The story of a man who is beaten and left for dead by robbers, and is passed by a priest, by a Levite. Finally, a Samaritan comes by, and helps him. Nurses him, and brings him to an inn, and cares for him, and pays for further care. After finishing the story, Christ turns the question back on the lawyer, asking him which of three proved to be a neighbor. His answer was simple. 'The one who showed him mercy.'"

David breathed, forcing the air out. He reached for God, but found only the summer heat of the chapel.

"You shall love your neighbor as yourself," said David. "You shall care for your neighbor as you would yourself. You would feed them. You would clothe them. You would pull them to their feet when they have fallen." David exhaled. "And who is your neighbor? The world. Your neighbor is not only the family that lives next door. It is not only the couple that lives around the block, or your co-worker. It is not only a member of your fellow congregation. It is anyone and everyone. All should be loved as you love yourself." David's voice boomed, carrying the words of God and Christ, delivering it to the half empty chapel.

His eyes scanned the audience again, but they were just themselves, peering up at him, listening. No shine, no glow, no feeling of God sliding into his backbone—

David's eyes caught a face, in the back row, near Zeke.

Thomas, Eli's son. He had slipped in. He was listening.

David felt the breath of God then, the gentle glow enter his heart, and then slide into his vision.

The faded red carpet flashed bold crimson.

The worn pews shined with a fresh dark stain.

"We do not have the luxury of choosing between neighbors." David's voice carried, louder now, echoing in the hot chapel. "We do not pass by the wounded man on the street, the unhoused on the corner, the child suffering quietly, the criminal who wishes to change his ways, the addict suffering from their substance!"

"We love them as we love ourselves, we care for them as we care for ourselves!" yelled David. "And if you reject that? If you think surely there are exceptions, surely there are times and places when you can find a loophole in the greatest commandment? Then you reject the teachings of Christ entirely. Then you reject God."

David stared out at the congregation, and their faces glowed, shining again.

"The lawyer spoke to Christ. He said, 'The one who showed him mercy.' And Jesus said to him, 'You go, and do likewise.'"

David breathed, exhaling a huge breath.

"Go, and do likewise."

*

The potluck was smaller, but all attended.

All except one.

David looked for Thomas, Eli's son, but he wasn't there, gone after David's sermon. David scanned the room, hoping he'd missed him, but no, he was gone, back to Eli.

As David scanned the crowd, Zeke appeared next to him. David jumped.

"Man, Zeke, we need to put a bell on you," said David.

"I'm sorry, Pastor, didn't mean to frighten," he said. "Are you alright?"

"All things considered, I think so."

"You looked lost up there for a second."

David paused. "It's—it's hard to explain."

Zeke leaned in. "Do you need to speak to him? You know?" Zeke cast his eyes upward.

"Zeke—I don't think—"

"You should come again," said Zeke. "We should go hunting."

"I'm not much of an outdoorsman."

"It's not about the hunting, Pastor" said Zeke, smiling. "It's about the ambiance."

22

Eli found the body of Christ at the head of his driveway.

He threw his flashers on his Superduty and opened the tailgate, heat rising in his chest, anger and embarrassment flooding in, and he grabbed the pieces of Christ, bundling them in his arms like firewood, the legs, the feet, the pieces and parts of his Savior, and placed them in the bed of his truck, slowly lowering, he didn't want to jostle the Lord.

He grabbed the head last, looking into the eyes of Christ, holding the head with delicate fingers, his hands probing the gaping wound of Christ—

Save me, Eli.

Eli blinked away the interjection and lowered Christ's head into the bed of his truck and flipped up the tailgate. He glanced back and forth down the street, no one was watching, no one saw.

Not right now, but the neighbors had driven past, had seen the statue torn and broken, guarding his driveway.

Eli shook away the thought again, and climbed back up into the cab and turned down the drive.

He had come home for a late lunch, and his eyes scanned quickly for Angie's SUV, but it was gone, it was Wednesday, she had lunch with the gals, and relief flooded into him, a sudden shame having to carry Jesus into the house.

How dare he, how dare he do this to our Lord and Savior, cutting him into pieces—

Eli keyed off the engine and climbed down, sweat clinging to him, he had to hurry, even if no one was watching. He needed to hide this, hide this poor broken Savior from the world's eyes.

He let the tailgate open and grabbed the pieces of Christ as before, piling them into his arms with clammy hands, the jagged edges of the parts scraping against his forearms.

He threw the front door open, and hurried to the door to the basement, pulling the pieces close to himself, struggling with his keyring, snaking the right key, sliding into the heavy deadbolt he'd installed, for no one to see what was below.

He unlocked the door and hurried the pieces down, first his legs, then his arms and body, and finally Christ's head, cradling him in his outstretched arms, feeling the eyes of Christ on him, the suffering eyes of Jesus appraising him.

Please, Eli.

Another interjection, and Eli shook it away. Eli hurried, locking the basement door behind him, and a part of him eased, a measure of protection between the world's eyes and him, a deadbolt that guarded against all intruders.

Only God and himself.

Eli carried the head downstairs, the other pieces lying on the floor in front of the intact Christ, the naked Christ, the dying Christ, and Eli couldn't look at him, not in the light of day.

He stared down at the pieces, and anger flared again in him, now that he had time to think. David had done this, had retaliated the one way he knew would hurt Eli the most, and Eli squeezed his fists, he would show him, this deed wouldn't go unpunished—

Please, Eli. Please.

The words again, like honey, and Eli couldn't ignore them, couldn't shake them away. He looked to the source of the words. He looked into the eyes of the disembodied head of Christ.

Eli. Please.

The voice begged, pleaded, and alarm rose in Eli's guts, his stomach tensing, his lungs spasming.

He ran upstairs, leaving the basement, locking the door behind him.

*

Sunday morning, Eli went to the hardware store. He scoured the glue section, looking for the right type of adhesive, finally grabbing a few different tubes. One would surely work.

Angie had asked him, asked him what they would do for Sunday service, if they weren't going to Holy Sacred, and Eli had told them they would worship quietly in the house, until they had figured out a suitable replacement, and Angie had nodded, not asking any more questions.

Eli had a worship in mind.

He came home, the house quiet, and went downstairs, the hardware store plastic bag filled with glue. He looked at all of the packaging, and picked out a contact cement.

Eli, you've returned. Please, help me.

The voice rose again, and Eli nodded, saying nothing, not knowing what to say.

He worshiped.

Eli laid out the body of Christ on the basement floor, the feet, the legs, the hips and then torso, the arms and the head, the assemblage of the Lord.

He started at the legs, layering the contact cement onto each foot, holding them to the calves, sliding the pieces back together as best he could. Some of the sculpture was gone, shredded to pieces, torn from Christ when they had cut it apart, but he did his best to repair his Lord.

He held them together, gingerly, letting them set, and then worked on the arms, sliding them into the torso, more contact cement, more worship. He held them with reverence, the pieces of God, and there was more gone here, they had butchered him, they had butchered him.

He glued the arms back to the torso, slices of material missing, his flesh gone. They would hold, they would have to.

Eli cradled the arms of the Lord, holding them tight to the torso, lining up the shoulders, the sinew, the muscle, the bone, putting the Lord back together. He breathed silently, his body tense, on hands and knees.

His knees ached, the pressure, but he held strong for

God, the cement bonding them together again, and he let go, holding his breath, and the arms stayed, first one, then the other. He left them, and with the legs now set, he would join them to Christ's hips.

Eli grabbed Jesus' waist, his fingers settling into his hip bones, and slid them down to the thick thighs of Christ, connecting them again. He layered contact cement, covering the stumps with a dense layer of material, and pressed them together, the excess glue oozing out, and he wiped it away with a towel, sliding off the excess liquid, holding the two tight. The house was silent, and it was right, they all worshiped. He worshiped.

First one leg, and then the other, moving with purpose, with slow strength, the way of the Lord, and then the hips were attached to the legs. The torso next, to the shoulders, his fingers grazing the belly of Christ, the defined abdomen, and he layered more cement, and pressed the torso to the shoulders, not disturbing the arms, pushing the stomach and torso into the shoulders, wiping the excess, settling into a ritual.

Eli held them until they bonded.

The lower half and top half of Christ. And then only the head remained.

He took a breath and wiped the sweat from his eyes, his shirt and pants soaked, and he knelt again, his thighs trembling from the strain. More contact cement, the massive tube empty, and he threw it aside and grabbed a second, slicing off the top, and layered more on, never enough, he must be covered to be repaired. The bond must be strong.

He held them together, the two halves now one. He knelt, and pressed them, the silent basement filled with

God's peace.

His sweat dripped to the floor, and he didn't wipe it now, running down his chin, there was only the head left, then Christ would be whole again, *must* be whole again. The sinner, the false pastor, he would see, see that he couldn't remove Christ from the church, no tool, no blade, nothing could harm the Lord Our God.

He cradled the head of Christ, his face in agony, suffering from sacrifice, exquisite holy pain to redeem humanity, redeem us fallen. He slathered on the cement, thick translucent slime covering the neck stump of God, and Eli covered it all, and then pressed it onto the shoulders, pushing the two pieces together, making Christ whole again.

Eli held Christ's body, letting the cement bond, counting down seconds, the glue was quick dry, and he looked at the body again, taking it all in, giving it more minutes to set. Not all of the limbs lined up perfectly, never could again, not after the butchery of the sinner, but it would do, it would do. It had been perfect, looked perfect, had been solace every time he stepped into Holy Sacred, but this was still perfect, because it was Christ, mended.

He sat on the metal folding chair, soaked in sweat, and stared at his Lord. Eli panted, catching his breath, his legs sore and knees aching, and he waited.

Waited until the bond was set, and then he stood up, and took a hold of Christ. He would stand him up, once again, the final step, the final test, and grabbed Jesus by his hips and pulled him to his feet, the weight not insubstantial, and Eli leaned him against the wall, giving him support—

An arm fell, the left, THUNK, tips of a finger cracking off as it hit the concrete, and then the right arm fell, the glue failing, and then the bond at the hips, both legs tumbling, and Eli scrambled, trying to holding him together, his hands searching for purchase, and soon Christ was back in pieces, falling, and Eli reached, and grabbed the Lord's head, and it was all he held, everything else back on the floor.

He sighed, tears threatening the corners of his eyes, his work gone in an instant, and he stared into the sorrowed eyes of Christ.

"I'm sorry, Lord, I'm sorry," he muttered, words barely audible, his breath short again.

I forgive you, Eli.

"What do I do?" asked Eli. "I could use another glue—

No. You know what must be done.

"I do? Lord, I've tried to make you whole—"

The church, Eli.

Eli froze. "Of course," he said. He nodded, staring into the Lord's eyes. "Of course."

23

The house shook as the door rattled, loud knocks reverberating through the walls.

David looked out the window, Eli standing at the door, his face full of plain indignity. Jason was out, taking Solly on a play date with another family from church.

Eli was alone. No Sheriff's cruiser in the driveway or on the street.

David took a breath, heat coursing through him, and walked to the bedroom. He grabbed the bat, holding it aloft in two hands. He squeezed the wood once, twice, and then walked back to the front door.

He softly leaned the baseball bat against the wall, within reach of the open door. He opened it, Eli in full view, bristling on his front porch.

"Hello, Eli," said David. "Come to apologize?"

"How dare you—"

"Why are you here?"

"You know why I'm here," said Eli, his voice loud. "After what you did—"

"I didn't do anything," said David. "I did my job."

Eli's eyes flared, and he tensed, as if he was going to swing at David, but he held back. David still stood in his open door, the handle of the baseball bat within a foot's reach.

But Eli did hold back. He took a hot breath. "You desecrated a statue of Christ."

David stared at him, a gentle smile on his face.

"What did you think would happen, Eli?"

"Excuse me?"

"You left the church," said David. "You slapped me, on your front porch. All I did was ask you to come back, and you spit in my face. What did you think would happen? Did you think I would roll over and show my belly?"

"You—"

"You what?" asked David. "Fag? Sinner?" David paused. "Is that all you have?"

Eli stared, his fury burning hot.

"After speaking with Laurie, it was clear you insisted on that statue in the church, and John did it to appease you. I think it's an affront to God, and I only kept it to try and keep you in the church. But you left. So it went with you. And I gave you it back. What more do you want?"

"An affront?" asked Eli. "It's a work of art, it looks—"

"What do you worship, Eli?"

"What the hell kind of question—"

"What do you worship?" asked David. "Answer me."

"I worship our Lord, Jesus Christ, and his father, God in Heaven, and the Holy Spirit."

"No, you don't," said David, plainly, his voice from the pulpit.

"You can't—"

"You worship suffering, Eli," said David. "You worship pain, and trauma, and sacrifice. You worship torture. You worship blood, and death. I knew it the moment I saw that figure of Christ. But I hoped, that if you listened—if I had the opportunity to preach to you, to teach—that I could make you understand. That I could show you that Christ is more than the last moments of his life." David stared. "I had hoped. Perhaps foolishly. You can keep that statue. It glorifies suffering. It's gone forever. Put it up on your wall, if you want, so you may worship at home."

Eli stared at him then, his face turning red, and he blustered, trying to get words out, but failing.

"What do you want, Eli? If you're going to be angry, please don't do it on my front porch."

Eli took another deep breath. "I want my church back."

"I don't know what that means."

"I want my church back," said Eli. "I want you to leave, and start a new church. In Sacred, if you want. But I want the building, I want the name. I want the legacy."

David stared at him, coldly. He shook his head. "It's not mine to give, Eli."

"You're the new preacher, damned if it's true—"

"It doesn't belong to me. Or Laurie, for that matter, even if she's the administrator. It belongs to everyone who belongs to it, to the congregation, as a whole. To Sacred. Which outweigh you and your followers."

"They're not—"

"Followers?" asked David. "What are they then? They followed you out. I hoped to appeal to some of them, as time went on, to return. I hope they listen—"

"They won't. I'll make sure—"

"Sounds like you should be starting a new church, then, Eli," said David. "You can preach, with all your training."

"You motherfucker. Lording it over me, lording it over everyone—"

"No. Just you."

"You've taken my church from me. Taken God from me," said Eli. "I won't stand for it. You'll pay for this."

David pursed his lips, and pulled the bat out from behind the door, his hand wrapping firmly around the handle, the familiar and comforting heft of the weapon. He moved slowly, and Eli's eyes focused on it, staring at it, before looking back at David.

"Is that right, Eli?" asked David. He pulled the bat next to him, the tip grazing the wood of the deck, a soft *tap tap* as it touched the deck, ringing, wood on wood.

How easy it would be, to swing away.

The echo of Eli's slap across his cheek still rang in his ears.

"There's no one else here, Eli," said David. "Jason and Solomon are gone." David peeked around Eli's shoulders, looking out into the driveway. "No neighbors. No Sheriff. Just us."

Eli eyed the bat again, as David shifted it, raising it into the air.

"David—"

"But that's not true, is it?" asked David. "Because God is

watching. God would see me beat you to death on my front porch. He would see me lie to the police about you starting a fight with me, and me ending it. He would see me cry crocodile tears as I described the incident to Jason." David stared into Eli's eyes. "Which is why I won't hurt you, Eli. God is watching."

Eli stared, his eyes wide.

"But I want to." David shook his head, squeezing the handle of the bat, the worn wood a soft comfort. "I want to, so desperately. I've had to hold back my violence my whole life, Eli. Against people like you, who don't deserve the Lord's grace, or my kindness." David exhaled, and dropped the head of the bat to the wooden deck. "But still, I give it."

Eli said nothing, exhaling.

"If you wish to return to the church, Eli, we will welcome you back with open arms. Me, and God."

Eli narrowed his eyes and quickly turned, walking down the steps, back to his truck. David watched him.

The worn wood of the bat's handle spoke to him.

24

Tommy read in his room, the door closed. He heard footsteps come up the stairs, soft padding on the carpet. Mom.

"Tommy, it's dinner time," she said, her soft voice barely audible through the door.

"Can I just eat in here? I don't want—"

"Come on, Tommy, you know how your father is."

"Mom, please."

A moment of silence. "I'll send him up here, Tommy. Come on. I made cheeseburgers and fries. Just eat dinner, and you can go back to your room."

Another beat of silence, and then she padded away, and Tommy sighed, and got up, following her downstairs. Sam and his dad were already at the table.

Mom came in, placing a plate in front of Dad, then both

Sam and him, and herself last.

"Thank you, honey," said Dad. "Smells great. Looks great."

"Thanks," she said, smiling. "Do you want to say the blessing?"

"Let me do it, Dad," said Sam, teeth missing.

"You think you can handle it?"

"Yeah, I can do it," said Sam. "Can I? Please?"

"Okay," said Dad. "But this is serious."

"I know," said Sam. "Everyone, bow your heads."

Tommy glanced at Sam, and his father, and mother, and then did, closing his eyes. The voice of his brother belted out from beside him.

"Dear Jesus, thank you for this food. Thank you for my mom, and my dad, and my brother Tommy. Thank you Jesus for everything you do for us. And Jesus, please let us have a church again. Amen."

"Amen," said Tommy, a barest mutter, with his dad and mom echoing.

"That was good, son," said Dad. "And don't worry, we'll have a church again. We will. God will see to it."

Mom eyed him. She looked at her plate, and then back at him. "Eli—"

He smiled. "I've been planning something with Kyle. We'll have a church again, I promise. Don't you worry your pretty little head. Soon."

Tommy stared at his dad's smile. It held something Tommy didn't like. "Dad, why can't we just go to Holy Sacred again?"

His eyes turned to Tommy, anger flaring in them. "Are you kidding me, Tommy?"

"What was wrong with Pastor David? I liked his sermon. He didn't say anything crazy."

His father stared at him. He shook his head. "That's how it starts, Tommy. You're young, you don't understand. You can't take him at his word."

"Why can't you just give him a chance, Dad?"

The table was silent. Eli glared at him. Tommy's heart beat hard. His hands sweat.

"He's evil, Tommy. Right down to his heart." Eli put down his burger. "All of them. They're not human. They were put here on Earth by the Devil, to test us. Now, they look human, and they may even act human, but inside, they're just creatures. Creatures of sin. You can't trust them, because they don't think like we do. If they want to claim that they don't choose to be gay, well—well I'll take them at their word. Because if they don't choose it, that means that what they are is sin. And despite whatever Ingram says, it's just sin in sheep's clothing."

Tommy closed his eyes until he was sure he wouldn't cry. He looked at his father again.

"Dad—"

"I won't hear no dissent on this, Tommy—"

"Dad—"

"Go to your room. No dinner."

Tommy stared at him.

"Eli, please," said Mom.

"No," said Eli, silencing her with a stare. "Your room. Now."

Tommy left the table. He held back his tears until he closed and locked his door.

25

David stood in the chapel, bat in hand.

He strode through, heat coursing through him, electricity flowing through his veins, belching fire.

Eli stood at the pulpit. He preached, preached hellfire, but David strode forward, the bat in the air now, raised to strike.

He swung, destroying pews, wood shattering, but not wood, flesh, blood, bile, venom, gore, water expelled from the side of Christ, and the bat flew with ease, great force with no effort, David swinging with the force of God, the bat destroying the chapel, the pews, the walls, the great stained glass. They all broke, made of wood and glass, of bone and blood, and he swung, he swung, with fury and rage uncontained, and Eli stood, and preached, spitting, waiting, and

David charged at him, and swung—

A knock at David's office door woke him. He blinked his eyes open, awake in his chair.

Thomas Parsons stood at his door, slightly hunched, hands in his pockets.

David blinked the sleep from his eyes. "Thomas? I'm—I'm surprised to see you."

He stood in the door, meeting David's eyes for a moment, and then looked back down, glancing left and right down the short hallway. They were the only ones in the building.

"Thomas? Can I help you? Would you like to sit down?"

Thomas looked up again, nodded, and sat down in one of the seats opposite David's desk. He seemed a bundle of raw nerves. He sat, his hands resting on the armrest, but they shook, trembling against the fake leather upholstery.

"I'm not supposed to be here," said Thomas. "And just call me Tommy. Only my dad calls me Thomas."

"Tommy," said David. "Does your father not know you're here?"

"No," said Tommy. He stared at his hands, at his fingers. "He'd kill me." Tommy took a breath. "He hates you."

"I saw you at the service," said David. "I assume he didn't know you came."

"No," said Tommy. "I lied to him. Told him I was going for a walk." Tommy's eyes still darted, down, left, right, up to meet David's, and then gone again.

"I was glad to see you," said David. "Is that why you're here now?"

"Yes. No," said Tommy. "I don't—" He took a breath, eyes darting. He raised his hands to his face, covering his eyes, and they shook, fingers trembling, shuddering until they reached his face, a soft burial.

"Tommy—"

Tommy took a shuddering breath, and cried, his face in his hands. David let him have his tears, grabbing a tissue box from a nearby shelf and sliding it over to Tommy's side of the desk, within reach of him. Tommy cried.

David watched him, a desperate hope and fear both growing inside. Hope for this child's future.

And fear for the fruit of these tears.

"It's alright, Tommy," said David. "It's okay. Let it out."

Tommy cried. "He'll kill me. He'll kill me. He'll kill me. He'll kill me." Tommy repeated, sobbing, his tears drowning him. Tommy shook, repeating the same phrase.

"He'll kill me."

"Who will kill you, Tommy?"

Tommy paused, and then coughed, hyperventilating.

"Take a breath, Tommy. Slow down. Blow your nose. You're safe here."

Tommy coughed some more, and snatched tissues from the box, and blew his nose, and then did it again, coughing more, stealing breath in between them. He slowed down enough, and blew his nose again. He inhaled, and exhaled. David waited on him.

"My dad," said Tommy, finally. "He'll kill me."

"Why?" asked David. He already knew the answer.

Tommy looked up at him, their eyes meeting, and then Tommy looked away, and then back up.

"I'm—" he started. "I can't—" and then coughed again.

"Tommy," said David. "Look at me."

Tommy coughed, and grabbed another tissue, wiping his face, red and blotchy. He looked up, again at David.

"You're gay, aren't you?"

Tommy exhaled through his nose, and then nodded at David through bleary eyes. David nodded back. He pushed himself from his chair, and moved to David, kneeling.

"Would a hug be okay, Tommy?"

Tommy nodded, and David hugged him, embracing him. Tommy hugged him back, squeezing him tightly, crying again, weeping into David's shoulder.

David held him.

Tommy let go, and David returned to his chair. Tommy blew his nose again.

"I didn't know what to do," said Tommy. "I just thought something was wrong with me—"

"Nothing's wrong with you," said David. "You're perfectly normal, despite what your father might say."

"I'm afraid."

"I know," said David. "I know. And that's okay too."

"I don't know what to do."

"You don't have to *do* anything."

"I can't be gay," said Tommy. "I can't, he'll send me to a camp—"

"Tommy," said David. "There's nothing wrong with you."

"I just don't—"

"See a way out?" said David. Tommy glanced at him. Nodded.

David nodded back. He took a breath. "You are who you are, Tommy. You're gay, and that's normal."

"I don't know any gay people," said Tommy, his voice quiet.

"That's not true," said David. "There are gay men here. And that's true everywhere. If you listen to your dad, you might believe you're the odd one out. But it's not true." David paused. "How old are you?"

"Fifteen," said Tommy. "I turn sixteen in four months."

"Can you handle two more years of this?"

Tommy met his eyes. "I don't know. Sometimes, I just want to scream. When you and Dad argued on the porch—I wanted to be there. I wanted to help you. He doesn't—"

"Listen, Tommy," said David. "And this is hypocritical on my part, because I came out when I was a teenager. Younger than you. I told my pastor. I told my parents. They supported me, and I told my friends, and they also supported me. They protected me. And even then, it was still hard. I still was attacked. Bullied. Still had to defend myself. And as I've gotten older, I've realized how lucky I was." David exhaled. "Because you shouldn't tell anyone else. And as much as I appreciate you coming to service, you shouldn't do that either. Your father—"

David paused, and looked into Tommy's eyes. The fear in them hadn't left.

"—you're right to be afraid of him. I don't know what he would do. And until you're an adult, with rights, and the freedom to leave—you should prioritize your safety."

Tommy nodded, and sighed. "I feel like a freak."

"God created you in his image, like everyone else," said David. "They do their best to twist the Bible, Tommy. To twist God's love into hate. Don't let them hurt you. You'll hear hateful things for the rest of your life. But anyone who insults you for being gay—they're not Christians." David looked at him. "Do you have any other questions for me?"

"I don't know," said Tommy. "I didn't have a plan in mind. I wanted to tell you. Tell somebody. I've kept it inside for so long."

David took a business card off his desk, and wrote down his cell on the back. "That's my cell. Call me anytime, and I mean, any time. Understand?"

"Yes," said Tommy. "Thank you, Pastor."

"You can call me David."

Tommy stood up, and then went to David again, hugging him a final time, squeezing hard, before leaving.

26

A few slim trees stood out in the dark.

A few slim trees in the dark.

"You ever fired a gun before, Pastor?"

They sat in a small tree stand in the early morning black, the summer humidity clinging to them. They wore camo, David's jacket and pants borrowed from Zeke, sweating in them.

No animals within sight, nothing at all, except for shadows and trees, Zeke's slight body pushed up against him.

"Yes," said David. "Many times. But only at the range."

"Never hunted?" asked Zeke, his voice hushed.

"No," said David. "Never liked the idea of killing an innocent animal. Even if I ended up eating it."

"Well, I grew up not getting meat with my dinner unless

daddy had money for ammunition. Changes perspective."

"I guess it does."

"And well, nothing innocent about what we're hunting today," said Zeke. "Invasive. Dangerous. Doing the area a service."

"You said it was a boar. I've seen stories on the news—"

"Most of it is overblown," said Zeke. "Sure, they're a pest, but they're not killers. Mostly just run away when they see you. But this one—old man Johnson says it's a big 'un. He reckons it's three hundred pounds. Maybe more. Tore through a fence, and multiple traps. Just broke 'em, with sheer force."

"Are—are these rifles enough?"

"Oh, yeah," said Zeke. "These'll take down anything under a thousand pounds, I'd guess. But don't feel too bad about killing this 'un. No different than killing a rat."

"I've never killed a rat, either."

"Really?"

"Really," said David. "There's a difference between defending yourself, and hunting. Setting an ambush. What we're doing. At least in my head, there is."

"You're a pastor, a Man of God," said Zeke. "I don't expect violence to come natural."

"You might be surprised then," said David. "I raised hell, when I was younger. Even more recently. Got into fights."

"Really?"

"Yeah," said David. "Defending myself. Or at least I thought I was. Even now—sometimes it's hard."

"I imagine, being a gay guy, you've got enemies at the gates. Tough, living your life that way."

"Couldn't say it better myself," said David. "But it doesn't excuse it. And Eli, his behavior—it tested me."

"What, leaving?"

"No," said David. "I asked him to stay. Went to his home. He hit me. Slapped me."

He hit you?" asked Zeke. "What did you do?"

"Nothing," said David. "I left."

Zeke looked away, out into the dark woods. The morning sun had filtered up over the horizon, but not yet risen, and the outline on the bark just visible.

"Don't know if I coulda done that," said Zeke. "Just walked away. Right now I want to jump down and whoop his ass. Laying hands on a Man of God."

"It was on his property," said David. "He wanted to provoke me. He wanted a fight. I shouldn't have gone. It was a mistake."

"You did the right thing," said Zeke. "That man can't recognize it. God left him. When I look at him—I don't see no God in him at all."

The sun slowly rose.

David noticed Zeke's belt buckle. He had worn it every time he'd seen him.

"You wear that hunting, too?"

Zeke looked down at it. "It's my security blanket, Pastor. Makes me feel safe."

"Really?" asked David. "A belt buckle?"

"It has a secret," said Zeke. With a slight smile, he tugged at it, and pulled a short blade from it, razor sharp. He winked at David. "Just in case. It's saved my life before."

"Fair enough."

Zeke looked out over the forest.

"Keep your eyes and ears peeled, Pastor," said Zeke. "As

the sun rises, the big hog will be moving through here. There's tracks all through, and it's been wallowing in the creek just a hundred yards that-aways. We're downwind, so the hog won't smell us. It's eyes and ears aren't great, so we should see it and hear it before it us."

Zeke pulled a baggy from his small rucksack, filled with dried brown bits. He opened it, his fingers pushing through the pieces, before grabbing one, and sliding it into his mouth.

"What's that?" asked David.

"Prayer 'shrooms, Pastor," said Zeke. "Want one?"

"I—no," said David. "No thank you." David paused. "I don't know how I feel about them. About you taking them."

"They're safe," said Zeke. "If that's what you're worried about. They let me talk to God, Pastor."

"You say that," said David. "But if they're just hallucinogenic, it's all in your mind. You're only talking to yourself."

"He created everything, right?"

"Yes."

"Well, he created these," said Zeke. "And I ain't against normal prayer. I pray all the time. But I never feel the Lord more than when I take these. Never feel more connected. Multiple times, I almost lost my faith. But every time, a little session with the Lord, and I was strong again. After Pastor John died—I didn't know what to do. But I took some, and sat alone, and spoke with God. We talked for a long time. And he told me to be patient. That I had yet to find my purpose in life. That I would meet a Man of God, and I would be his shepherd. Me—a shepherd for a Man of God."

David studied him.

"You think that's me."

"I do," said Zeke. "And if the Lord Almighty has that as my purpose, I intend to fulfill it. That's why I asked you out here. Part of my purpose."

"To kill a hog?"

"No," said Zeke. His pupils dilated, even as they spoke. "To shepherd."

"I'll pass," said David. "I don't think—"

"Shh," muttered Zeke, a quick noise that silenced David. Zeke listened, the sun just over the horizon, the light filtering through the forest canopy, the ground barely visible. David listened, and heard nothing.

Zeke opened his eyes, and cocked them to the side, and David followed them, and soon he heard the sound, the rustling sound, soft at first, and then louder.

Then he saw the creature, the feral hog, as it wandered into view. It was a massive thing, over six feet long, thick throughout its entire body, covered in brown, coarse hair.

It wasn't alone, a small group of other pigs following along behind it, but none near the size of it.

"Target the big one. Watch me. Aim under its shoulder, and behind. We fire at the same time. Understand?" Zeke's words in his ear, half gone before they got there. David nodded, slowly pulling up his rifle to his shoulder, and aiming at the big hog.

It was crossing in front of them left to right, getting closer, weaving in and out from behind tree trunks, but following its tracks. Zeke had laid their ambush perfectly.

David aimed, tracking the movement of the hog. He hadn't fired a rifle in quite a while, but Zeke had gone over the gun at his home, and it was quite simple.

Safety off.

Aim at what you want to destroy.

Squeeze the trigger.

David followed the path of the hog, aiming below its shoulder, and back, at the heart and lungs.

Zeke did the same next to him, and together, their rifles moved, the barrels floating through the air, and the hog was right in front of them, and Zeke's left hand, which supported the barrel, popped up three fingers. David's eyes stayed on the hog, letting his peripheral pick up Zeke's digits, as they dropped. A countdown.

Three.

Two.

One.

BANGBANG

They fired almost simultaneously, two loud barks of death, high powered lead landing in the hog, the rest of the pigs sprinting at the sound, disappearing back the way they came.

The enormous hog stumbled only for a moment, and then fell, not thirty yards from their tree stand, and laid still.

Zeke exhaled, a long breath, and then smiled. "Let's go confirm."

They climbed down from the stand, the forest already heating up as the sun rose, Zeke leading the way toward the downed hog. The pig was even bigger as they approached. It laid on its side, the thick body nearly four feet high, massive tusks emerging from a gaping, open mouth, tongue lolled to one side.

Zeke pulled a knife from a sheath, a five inch blade, razor sharp, and approached the creature. He circled around it, toward its head, and went to cut its throat, his hand on a massive hoof, when it screamed—

RRRRRAAAEEEEEEERRRRGGGH

And jolted to its feet, knocking Zeke back, massive force hitting him hard. Zeke fell, his knife flying out of his hand.

"Zeke!" yelled David, as the boar charged at Zeke, tusks jutting out, a foot long, rearing back to gore him. David ran without thinking and wrapped his arms around the neck of the pig, and pulled, wrenching on the taut muscle of the creature. It pushed forward for a moment more, to attack Zeke, but David had knocked it off balance, and it struggled, its feet unsteady, two bullets in it.

David pulled with all his might, his heart and lungs straining at the incredible force, stronger than anything he had touched.

"Zeke—please—" he mustered, his lungs without breath, and Zeke scrambled to his feet, grabbing his knife from the ground and sprinting at the beast, stabbing it in the chest, over and over, quick strikes. One, two, three, and one hit its heart, and the fight left it, and it fell, with David on top of it still, his arms around its great neck.

He laid on it, half on the ground, his chest heaving with exertion.

Zeke stood in front of it, breathing hard, the knife covered in the boar's blood.

"You saved my life, Pastor," said Zeke. "You were like Jacob, wrestling the angel."

David pushed himself to his feet, off the corpse of the pig. "I don't think the angel of God looked like this."

"No, but still mighty impressive," said Zeke. "God gave you the strength, Pastor. I see it." Zeke looked at the animal. "I'll have to butcher it here. Too big to move."

"Is there anything I can do to help?"

"Yes," said Zeke. "But a fair warning. It will be messy."

David stared down at the creature. "I understand."

"Grab a leg, and hold it open. Don't look if you don't want to see it."

David grabbed a rear leg of the hog, and held it, as Zeke worked, grabbing a pair of gloves from his pack, and sliding open a huge skinning knife. He worked fast, with precise cuts, taking apart the animal.

David did not avert his eyes, even as Zeke split the skin, cutting around organs, pulling it off the flesh.

David watched, and Zeke was right. It was not a boar.

It was an angel, hunted, ambushed, shot, killed, and now butchered.

Zeke cut deeply, expertly, the angel, removing the skin, cutting around anus and testicles, peeling back flesh, removing organ by organ, without cutting inside, without spoiling the meat, blade cutting through muscle and connective tendon, pure flesh of God cut apart by the blade of the hunter, removing intestine and colon, stomach and gut, lungs and heart. The creature lulled from side to side, David holding it open, as Zeke sliced, peeling back the skin.

The sun rose as Zeke worked, the light of the Lord shining down on them as they field dressed this creature of God. David swallowed back the bile as it rose in his throat, staring. He watched.

Zeke cut, blood covering his hands, gore gushing onto the packed mud of the forest. He sliced, and then the organs were let loose, sliding in a mass onto the dirt. Piles of intestines, kidneys, liver, lungs and heart. Zeke did not pause, pulling the skin, slicing through gristle, pulling it off, and its wings, and Zeke went to cut, with a massive force—

It was just a hog. A wild boar, and Zeke cut off its hooves, and its head. The body was ready now, to be butchered.

He had finished.

"Easy as pie," said Zeke. "Sorry for the blood. Can't be helped."

David took a breath. He blinked, and looked away from the boar. From the pile of guts, flies already landing.

"No, it's okay. You're right," said David. "Can't be helped."

27

David preached.

"What is strength?" David asked, his hands on worn wood. He looked out into the congregation. None of Eli's followers had returned.

"That is what I want you to ponder today. What is strength?"

David let silence linger for a moment.

"Keep that question in mind." David paused. "Blessed are the meek, for they will inherit the Earth. The beatitudes, from Christ's Sermons on the Mount. All worthy of discussion, and don't worry, I'll get to them all, over time. But today, we will focus only on blessed are the meek. Matthew 5:5."

The chapel was stifling, many fanning themselves, sweating through their clothes. Multiple box fans blew from the stage, to keep the air moving, but David's clothes were damp with sweat.

"Meek." David looked over the crowd. He spotted several new faces, along many familiar. "What does that word mean to you? In modern times, meek has become a pejorative. An insult. A meek person is passive, with no ambition. Submissive, a doormat. Someone who is walked over, pushed around." A pause. "It always confused me as a child. A common trend among my sermons. Things I misunderstood, both as a child, and even as an adult. But it always confused me. In the middle of the Beatitudes, he isolates the meek. Says they will inherit the Earth. Was he making a point, about those who suffer, who are walked over? No, not at all."

David looked out over the congregation, and God's grace rose in their eyes, and in their face. The light brighter, the carpet new, the pews strong. The new faces—they glowed brighter still, allowed to shine.

"Alternate translations do not use the word meek. They use the word gentle. Blessed are the gentle, for they will inherit the Earth. Gentle here, meekness, here, are not words demonstrating weakness. They are words demonstrating strength. Demonstrating intentionality. Of control, of endurance." A pause. "Control of one's self. Of gentleness. Of humility. Of strength."

"Demonstrating meekness is all of those things. Above all, meekness is acceptance. Acceptance of the world, and of its people. About the things you can't control, and allow for Christ to control. The Lord doesn't expect us to get along with everyone, or for everyone to get along with us. But he expects us to accept those facts. To be peaceful with those people. Not to lash out, not to reject Christ. To be meek."

"So, I ask again, what is strength?"

God's grace filled David's vision. The heat filled the chapel, but David didn't feel it, cooled by God's love. The new faces, they would blossom, allowed to flourish now in a church unmarred. The church would grow again, and more would come, and more would return, and Sacred would be whole again, the Holy Church of Sacred led into the future by his Holiness.

The chapel doors slammed open.

The light of God's grace disappeared, vanished in an instant, and David blinked, momentarily stunned by the darkness.

Sheriff Bronson stood there, a shotgun held in two hands, flanked by two sheriff's officers, also holding pump action shotguns. In uniform.

Behind him was Eli, holding a rifle, followed by more men, all wielding weapons. Most firearms. Eli, and his followers.

Fear and anger in equal measure filled David, seeing it all happen before it happened. He should have known.

A panicked silence filled the congregation. Jason grabbed Solly, holding him close, and they locked eyes for a moment. And then with Laurie, where there was no fear. Only anger.

"Can I help you, Sheriff? You're interrupting our service," said David, his hands on worn wood.

"It's not your service anymore," said Bronson, yelling loudly, his shotgun gripped firmly in his hands, his forearms flexed.

"What does that mean?" asked David. He'd make them say it aloud.

"We're reclaiming our church," said Eli, stepping in front of Bronson, walking toward the front, cradling his rifle.

"It's not yours, Eli," said David. "I've said it before. I'll say it now."

"Might makes right," said Eli, his face plain. A bead of sweat fell down from his temple. "You did this. This is your fault."

"What if we don't leave, Eli?" asked David. "Are you going to gun us down? What are you doing?"

"I'm taking back what is ours—"

"You still don't understand—"

"Shut up," said Eli, and he lowered his rifle. "I have the gun. I make the rules. This is my church. Not yours. Leave."

David didn't move, the barrel of the rifle leveled at him. He eyed the congregation. The fear in Jason's eyes. He saw Ann Campbell, her jaw set. Zeke, in the back row.

He had stood up, his hands reaching for a sheath on his belt, palming a blade. David locked eyes with him.

No David said with his eyes, softly shaking his head. Zeke stared for a moment longer, and then put away his blade, blinking away from their shared stare.

"What will you tell them, Eli?" asked David. "When you shot a preacher in the middle of a sermon?"

"Shut up."

"Do you think this is an act of strength?"

Eli raised the rifle to his shoulder.

David raised his hands above his head. He shook it.

"You can have the building, Eli. I don't want to see anyone hurt." David looked out at his congregation. "Please, stand. Leave peacefully. Return to your vehicles. Go home." He looked at Eli. "Is that what you wanted?"

Eli's nostrils flared, and he lowered his rifle.

"Any are welcome to stay," said Eli. "Provided they stay true to the Lord's Word."

"Hear that?" David asked the congregation. No one answered, and they stood up, one by one. All of them stood, and filed out, slowly walking, moving past the broad figure of Bronson, who hadn't moved from the center of the aisle, his boots sinking into the faded red carpet.

Jason met David's eyes once again. David nodded, and Jason understood. *Get out, with Sol.*

Jason moved, helping Laurie up, and ushering her down the aisle, behind everyone else. David watched them leave.

"Well?" asked Eli.

"Can I get my things?" asked David. "They're in the office."

"Don't worry. We'll return them, at the head of your driveway," said Eli. "Get out."

David kept his hands above his head, walking away from the pulpit, with a final glance at the worn wood. He left the stage, down the steps, toward Eli, walking slowly.

The congregation filed out in front of him. Ann shared a glance with him, and then left. Zeke the same, venom in his eyes. Jason, Sol, and Laurie were already outside, past Bronson, past the dozen or so men lined up beyond them.

David walked slowly, his arms above his head, covered in sweat. He stared at Eli as he walked. He recited.

"Woe to you, teachers of the law and Pharisees, you hypocrites. You are like whitewashed tombs, which look beautiful on the outside, but are full of dead men's bones."

"Shut up," said Eli. "You're done preaching." David walked past him, reciting loudly. He preached.

"In the same way, on the outside you appear to people as righteous but on the inside you are full of hypocrisy and wickedness."

"I'll shoot you!" said Eli, from behind him, yelling. David did not turn. He stared at Bronson as he passed. He preached.

"And you say if we had lived in the days of our ancestors, we would not have taken part with them in shedding the blood of the prophets."

Eli screamed in rage from behind him. David preached. He waited for a gunshot. He passed Bronson, who stared.

"You testify against yourselves that you are the descendants of those who murdered prophets. Go ahead, and complete what your ancestors started!"

David passed the rows of men, all holding weapons, all watching him. He was the last to leave the chapel. He preached.

"You snakes! You brood of vipers! How will you escape being condemned to Hell?"

28

They sat in David and Jason's house that night. David, Jason, Laurie. Zeke leaned against the wall, unable to sit still.

The summer sun had finally gone down, but it hadn't taken the heat with it, and the house's AC struggled, churning against it. They all sweat.

"What do we do?"

They all asked it with their heart. Their church had been taken from them.

"I've spoken to church leadership in Raleigh," said Laurie. "They—they'd prefer us not to get law enforcement involved."

"Law enforcement is already involved," said Jason. "Bronson was there, with other sheriff's deputies."

"I explained that to them," said Laurie. "They meant

state or federal officials. They don't want a black eye on the church. There have been several high profile cases of churches splintering off, despite not owning their buildings. They don't want any more if they can help it."

"What did they suggest, Laurie? Besides their preference for no law enforcement?"

"They said they'd be sending a senior church official," said Laurie. "Within the week, he'll be down here. He'll meet with us, with Eli and his, and try and sort it out."

David exhaled through his nose, standing, casting his eyes to Solomon's video monitor. He slept peacefully upstairs.

"It's their building. Their deed," said Laurie. "I'm honoring their wishes."

"We can take it back," said Zeke, still leaning against the wall. "They can't watch it all the time. Couple of men, at the right time, could do it. It'll be ours again."

"No violence, Zeke," said David, turning back.

"It's only taking back what's ours—"

"No violence. None. Let them have it."

"We can take it back—"

"And then what, Zeke?" asked David. "We catch them in the middle of the night, with a couple of men. We strong arm them, catch them unaware, and take it back. Okay. And then we have to hold it. We post our own guards, and they try and do the same. Except next time, someone gets shot, or stabbed, or beaten." David shook his head. "And our church becomes a war zone, and our chapel becomes a charnel house."

"We can't let them have it," said Zeke. "It ain't right."

"We do nothing," said David, his voice low.

"What?" asked Zeke.

"We do nothing." David spoke slowly. "We let them keep it. If the church can intervene, so be it. But we don't raise a finger toward Eli. Let him have the building."

"We can't just let him—"

"We can, and we will," said David. "We will not escalate. It will only destroy what's left of the church. We must take the high road. We must turn the other cheek."

"What will we do?" asked Laurie. "No service?"

"No," said David. "We'll worship here."

"Here?" asked Jason.

"Here," said David. "We'll have service in here. We'll set up chairs. If we move all the furniture, we can fit the congregation inside."

"David—"

"Christ preached in all manner of places. He made all of them places of worship. Preaching here makes no less of God's word. Do you think we can get the word out before next Sunday, Laurie?"

Laurie smiled, with no joy in it, and nodded.

"It's not ideal."

"When we worship in it," said David. "It'll be transformed."

Silence hung in the room for a moment, and then a soft cry came from the monitor. Solly had woken up. Jason sighed and met David's eyes.

"I'll calm him down," said Jason, and went upstairs.

David, Laurie, and Zeke stood there, in silence.

"He won't be satisfied," said Laurie, breaking it, her voice low and cold.

David met her eyes.

"Eli," said Laurie. "He won't be satisfied, with just having the church."

"What more can we give him?"

"He wants you outside of God's light, David," said Laurie. "Can't you see that, when you look into his eyes?"

"I don't know what I see," said David. "I see—a sad man."

"Don't pity him," said Zeke. "That's a dangerous road to hoe."

"Everything in me wants to take the church back," said David. "I take a few steps inside, and the wrath is right there, ready for righteous anger."

"But this *is* righteous, Pastor," said Zeke. "He's treading in Christ's home. He's trespassing, right now."

"No, Zeke," said David. "If there is any other way, than it is only wrath. It is only self serving anger, a rage only to convince oneself of truth. Of being right. And you saw it in Eli's eyes, Laurie. When he barked and spit inside of the Holy Church of Sacred, carrying his rifle. Pointing it at me. For the line between us is narrower than you might think. And it feels so, so good. But on the other side will not be a righteous victory. It will only be suffering."

Zeke stared at David, his eyes glancing to Laurie for a moment, and then back to David.

"We should stop him now," said Zeke.

"I said—"

"I know what you said, Pastor," said Zeke. "But I'm not talking about taking back the church. I'm talking about Eli."

David stared at Zeke, Zeke's eyes dark in the dim light of the house. Almost completely black.

"You don't—"

"I can do it," said Zeke. "He's only one man. Make sure

he's isolated. Take him out. Sheriff might catch me. Doubtful, but possible. I'll take the fall. Without Eli, they'll fall apart."

David stared at him. "You can't be discussing murder here, Zeke."

"Not murder, Pastor. A killing. Different thing entirely."

Laurie said nothing, only listening.

"No," said David. "He's not worth your soul."

"You say that, Pastor," said Zeke. "But maybe he is."

Jason returned downstairs, stepping lightly.

"Solomon is back asleep," said Jason. He looked between them all. "Are we really having service here next Sunday?"

David looked at him, and took a deep breath, exhaling. "Yes," said David. "We'll need chairs."

"There's a rental place, out by the highway," said Laurie. "A friend of the family. I'll get us some chairs. How many?"

"A hundred should do," said David. "I think we can squeeze them in."

Laurie nodded again, the smile gone. She stared down, at the floor.

"If you need me, Pastor," said Zeke. "You know how to get in touch." Zeke broke contact with the wall, and walked toward the front door.

"Zeke—" said David, stopping him.

Zeke stopped. "Yes, Pastor?"

"No violence. None," said David. "Do you understand?"

"Yes, Pastor," said Zeke. "I understand."

He left. Laurie stared at the floor.

Solomon slept.

29

Zeke read the Bible, copying down scripture.

He heard the boat engine long before he saw it, the sound echoing through the dim swamp.

Zeke pushed himself away from his small desk, moving neither fast nor slow, knowing the time he had. He dressed, wearing dark camo, and grabbed his rifle. He climbed a ladder to his rooftop, and then walked to the heavy branch of the thick oak that grew adjacent, hoisting himself on top of it, and walking the bark back to the trunk of the tree, sliding across branches to a hidden tree stand, dark in the shadows of the oak's copse.

He waited.

The boat approached, a thick beam of light in front. It docked. Zeke's eyes confirmed what he suspected. The Sheriff, and his two deputies. They carried shotguns, eyes scanning the swamp.

Bronson climbed onto the dock, his two deputies following. He moved slowly, the boards of the dock creaking. Zeke watched, his rifle ready.

"I wouldn't step any closer, Sheriff," said Zeke, calling out from the darkness.

Bronson slowed, and then stopped. His eyes looked up, searching for Zeke in the shadows. He didn't find him.

"Where are you, Zeke?" asked Bronson, calling out. Zeke didn't answer. Zeke waited, holding. Bronson stared out, still looking. "Should have never let you into the church, Zeke. John was a fool. Thinking white trash like you could ever change. You're a drug addict piece of shit, and you always will be."

It would be easy to level his rifle. To shoot them all, and be done with it.

"What do you want, Sheriff?" shouted Zeke. "Why are you here?"

"I want you to stop supporting Ingram," said Bronson, calling out. "I want you to leave his church."

"He's my Pastor—"

"Don't call him that," said Bronson. "He ain't no pastor."

"He's a Man of God, Bronson," said Zeke. "So it makes sense you don't recognize it."

The deputies still scanned the trees, looking for Zeke. Zeke didn't move.

"I can make your life hard, Zeke," said Bronson. "I can put pressure on you, and you know it. I can even find some evidence that you've returned to your old ways. You don't want that, do you?"

Zeke said nothing.

"But then again, I could make your life easier," said Bronson. "We could be—let's call it, business partners. You start up again, you give me a percentage, and life is easy. And profitable."

"I'm not going back, Sheriff," said Zeke. "Christ has saved me—"

"Don't lie to yourself, Zeke," said Bronson. "And don't lie to me. It's only a matter of time. Life will get hard, and you'll look for the easy way out. Might as well not waste any time."

Zeke took a breath, opened his phone, and hit a button. The lights in his house kicked off, leaving the island in darkness, except for the beam of light from the Sheriff's boat. He closed his phone.

Zeke leveled his rifle, and fired, an explosion in the dark. The light on the boat went out in an explosion of glass. Bronson and his deputies dove into the water with three splashes.

"You told me, Sheriff, when I first came to church service," said Zeke, his voice echoing in the dark. "You told me that God wasn't on my side. You told me that God would never support a sinner like me, a piece of white trash like me." Bronson and his deputies stood in the murky water, hiding. "Let me ask you, Sheriff. Do you think he's on your side right now?"

Bronson said nothing.

"Leave," said Zeke. "Go home in the dark. Pray that God finds mercy for all of you."

30

Solomon ran around the house, his little feet padding across the carpets, over hardwood. Ann chased him, staying just out of reach of him, Sol squealing with joy as she brushed him with a fingertip.

"Almost got you," she said, following him around the house. They had eaten, and watched a Disney cartoon that Ann didn't know, but Sol loved, and then Solly had started running, and Ann had chased.

They went in circles, over and over, until Solomon stopped, panting, melting in a puddle, falling onto the couch.

"Story, story," he said.

"A story?" asked Ann.

"Yes, yes," said Sol. He grabbed a big cardboard book

from the floor, and handed it to her. "This one."

Ann held it, the cover a massive cartoon dog, illustrated beautifully.

"You ready?" she asked, and Sol nodded, leaning up against her, and she opened the book, and she read. The story was of a dog, a dog that lost its family, who was searching for it.

Ann read, slowly, flipping the pages, asking Sol questions when appropriate. Sol paid rapt attention, pointing at the pictures, at the dog. Ann continued, and soon, Sol was asleep.

She closed the book, and set it aside. Sol moved slightly, but still slept. Jason had said he hadn't napped today, so he'd most likely fall asleep on her.

Ann scooped him up into her arms, and his eyes briefly opened, and then closed, and she took him upstairs, and laid him down on the bed, turning on the monitor as she left.

A snap outside, and Ann froze, in the middle of the stairs, and crept down, her footsteps silent, and she glanced out the window, toward the sound. She'd installed heavy floodlights around the house, motion activated, and they hadn't tripped. Only the small light outside the front door was on, illuminating the front yard. Nothing. No disturbance.

She'd asked if she should bring the shotgun. Jason had told her no, that had been their answer, even if the look in David's eyes said yes. Ann hadn't brought it, but her fingers itched now, at the wish for it.

She took a breath, and returned to the couch, finding the book she'd brought, a non-fiction book about propagating orchids. She'd always killed them, but wanted to try again.

Her thoughts drifted as she read.

Sonja had wanted kids. Ann hadn't been sure at the time, and had told her that. And now—well, Ann knew she didn't want kids. Babysitting was perfect. Spend a few hours with a kid, have some fun, and then leave before any true responsibility reveals itself.

But if she had left with Sonja—

Don't, Ann. Don't do this—

But if she had left, maybe she would have felt differently. Maybe she would have softened, time with Sonja, in the city, an easier life—it would have removed her armor.

Without the threat of Sacred. With the smaller prejudice of a progressive city. Would they have children now?

They'd be teenagers, in high school. A different challenge.

But you didn't leave with Sonja, Ann. You stayed. You won. You showed all who would drive you out that you weren't weak.

Would defeat have softened her, as well?

The gentle distant song of insects had returned. It did not exist in the city. Nor the feeling of place, or of carving safety into a world. A desperate rising pain in her chest appeared, and threatened tears—

Read your damn book, Ann.

She took a breath, and read, her eyes attempting to focus. She read, but her eyes closed—

The sound of Sol crying woke her, coming from the monitor.

She looked to the video, and he was there, curled in bed, crying. She hurried upstairs, and comforted him.

"Where's Dad and Papa?" he asked, through tears.

"They'll be home soon, honey," she said. She hugged him, rubbing his back, a circle of warm pressure on his small body, and he quieted, and laid back down. She stood, waiting, watching, and he fell asleep again. If she had gone to the city, she would not be here, comforting this child.

She went back downstairs.

As she settled into the couch again, reading, there was another noise outside. Ann hurried to the window, once again.

Still nothing.

A few days passed. Laurie had called. Told David she wanted to speak.

But not about chairs.

Laurie greeted him at the door, the same pastor's wife smile on her face as the first time they met.

Before they had faced down shotguns together.

Laurie's slim smile remained, as she welcomed him in, and sat him down, and fetched him a glass of water.

"Laurie—"

"Please, David, have a drink first," she said. David took a sip.

"Laurie," said David. "You wanted to talk."

"Yes," said Laurie. She pursed her lips, her eyes glancing at him, and then away, out the window, and then down again, at her hands. Blue veins ran across them, her fingernails pointed, shaped, bright red.

"Well?"

Laurie took a small breath. "When John brought Zeke into the church, we were all suspicious. Even me. He had quite the reputation. A criminal record. A hermit. Dangerous."

"Yes," said David. "But it was the right thing. We must welcome all into the church, for Christ sacrificed for all of us. Saints and sinners alike."

"Yes, yes," said Laurie. She wrung her hands together, slowly, rubbing a thumb into the palm of her other hand. "I was suspicious. But Zeke has proven himself to be a committed member of the church. Faithful, and supportive, and—"

"What are you getting at, Laurie?" David stared at her.

Laurie met his gaze, her eyes still.

"Do you believe what he said? The other night?"

"About what?"

Laurie's eyes remained on his.

"About Eli."

"What do you mean? Killing him?"

"Yes," said Laurie. She inhaled, a short breath. "Would he do it?"

"That's the question you have?"

"Yes."

David looked away. "Yes, he would. If I asked him, he would kill Eli." David paused, and looked back. "But I will not ask him to murder anyone, Laurie."

"He's right, though," she said. "Eli won't be happy with just the church. He wants more than a building. It's just the beginning. He'll come for us next."

"So the solution is to kill him?" asked David. "To ask a member of the faith to solve our problem?"

"Ezekiel is a weapon of the Lord."

"You sound like Eli."

Laurie stared at him, her eyes filled with sudden rage. "Do not compare me to that man." She looked away again. "If you want to kill a snake, you cut off its head. Without Eli's leadership, most of his followers will rejoin the church. Bronson will lose his direction. Some will leave, certainly, but we will have a whole church again. It is worth the sacrifice."

"The sacrifice of what?" asked David. "Of Zeke, if he's caught? Of our ethics? Of our faith, of our goodness?"

"Yes," said Laurie. "Yes to all of them."

David shook his head. "No, Laurie. No, I will do no such thing."

"David, we have to consider every option—"

David stared at her, the venom in her eyes. This was no thought experiment. It is why she brought him here.

David stood up, walked a few steps away. His eyes took in the framed photos, of John and Laurie, in front of the church, with members of the community, of years of service to Christ the Lord. His eyes caught a photo of them with Eli and Eli's wife, with only Tommy, as a young boy. They all smiled.

"Why did you hire me?"

"What?" asked Laurie.

David turned, staring down at her.

"Why did you hire me?"

Laurie met his eyes for only a moment, and then looked

away.

"You're young, driven, smart, caring, faithful. You were available on short notice, willing to come down here—"

"Stop lying to me, Laurie."

"I'm not lying," said Laurie. "You are all those things."

"But that's not why you hired me," said David. "You hired me to hurt them—"

"David—"

"To you, I'm just a weapon. No different than Zeke. Eli split your church, and you hired me to replace John, knowing nothing would insult Eli more than having a gay man as his pastor—"

"David—"

"I am not a weapon, Laurie!" said David, loud now, the framed photos rattling, his lungs stronger than his heart. "I am not an object, to be used, to be swung in a battle, to be broken upon the shield of an enemy! My identity will not be a prop—"

"You're wrong, David," said Laurie, her voice cold. "You are a weapon. And so is Zeke. And so am I. When you fight a war, you are a weapon. No matter what your leader says. You are not a soldier in God's war. You are merely a weapon." Her face was sunken, gray, devoid of life, of joy, of anything. "And Eli did more than split my church. He killed my husband."

She looked into his eyes, anger bristling for release, but she did not raise her voice.

"And I was forced to smile like a pastor's wife, at his funeral, and speak about my husband, who I loved and still love, while his killers stood nearby, snakes, filled with cold blood and venom, who spoke of his legacy and of the church, and I had to hug them. Embrace them. Feel their murderous hands." Her hands squeezed into fists. "Let Zeke kill Eli. If he suffers, even better. And if it is wrong, if it is against Christ's wishes, against God's wishes—well, I will ask him at Heaven's gates how my husband died."

Her fists squeezed hard, the blue veins popping.

"Do you have proof, Laurie?"

"Of course I don't have proof, David," said Laurie. "But I am no idiot. John was a safe driver, to a fault. He would stop at green lights, for God's sakes."

"Zeke told me he suspected Eli and Sheriff Bronson."

"He's no idiot, either," said Laurie. "And knows Bronson better than most." She shook her head. "If I must live my life staring at my killers, than they would have to hear the Word preached from a gay man's lips."

"I changed my life for this, Laurie," said David. "I'm in danger."

Laurie looked up again. "God brought you here, David. If that wasn't clear before, it certainly is now. Eli is evil. He must be stopped. Because this isn't his church, no matter where he sits."

"I will not engage in open warfare."

"I saw your eyes, David," said Laurie. "When he came into the chapel."

"We will worship in peace, Laurie," said David. "If we hurt Eli, we will have already lost."

Laurie smiled then. "What exactly have I won, David?"

Her smile died.

"If God brought me here, Laurie," said David. "Then I will follow his wishes. He will show us the way. I'll show you, on Sunday."

David kept her gaze for a moment longer, and then left, walking toward her front door.

"David."

He turned.

"The chairs will be there on Saturday," said Laurie, a meek smile on her face.

32

The phone rang.

"David—"

"They took the church, Phil."

"What? What do you mean, they took it?"

"Eli, his people—they came in with rifles and shotguns, in the middle of my service, and they strong armed us. They took the church."

Silence from the other end.

"I don't believe it," said Phil, finally. "Call the police, if you haven't already—"

"The police were the ones taking the church, Phil. The county sheriff was there, with his deputies. With shotguns."

"The state police then, the feds, you have to call someone. Did you call the church?"

"Yeah, we did."

"And?"

"They're sending a rep to investigate. Asked us not to involve the police."

"They what?"

"They said they've had problems with ownership rights to churches. They don't want the police involved."

Phil took a deep breath. "I don't know about that. This is too much, David. You can't—"

"We're honoring their wishes. For now."

"I—" Phil stopped, with an exasperated sigh. "I don't know if I agree with that. Are you okay? Did anyone get hurt?"

"I'm fine," said David. "Pissed as hell, but I'm fine. And everyone got out peacefully."

"Praise God for that," said Phil. "This was Sunday?"

"Yes."

"What are you going to do, now?"

"We're going to have a service in my house. Pile everyone in."

"That's great, David," said Phil. "That's a great idea. It's not convenient, but I hope it works."

"Me too," said David. "I'm trying. It's hard."

"Well, let's see what the church does. I hope they get the authorities involved. Be patient. Don't antagonize those men. They sound dangerous."

"Like I said. I'm trying." The statue of Christ appeared in David's mind. The pieces of it, arranged on Eli's driveway.

"I hate to say this, David—no, nevermind."

"What, Phil?"

"Have you thought—thought about leaving? I know you

just started the job, but you know what they say—quit early, not late."

"The people here, they need a church they can believe in. A pastor they can believe in."

A long silence, from the other end.

"You're there. You have a better idea of the situation than I do. But retreat is always an option. Don't forget that."

"I won't," said David.

"This is bad timing. But me and the missus are on a road trip. I'll have my phone on me, but connection might be spotty. Still, leave me a message, and I'll get back in touch when I can. Okay?"

"Okay."

"Stay safe, David."

33

"Swing your side to the left—no, your other left," said Ann.

They carried the sofa around the corner of the door, into the garage. David's hands were slick with sweat, and they slipped for a second.

"Do you need a break?" asked Ann.

"Let's just get it in there," said David. "It's the last big thing."

David propped the base on his knee, took a big breath, and then shifted the couch onto his chest, and swung his side into the garage, through the door frame, avoiding smashing his fingers against the inside of the jam. Ann held the other side, and carried it through, and they backed it into the last big space in the garage, David carefully setting it down.

He wiped his forehead on the sleeve of his t-shirt, hands

on knees, catching his breath. Stars behind his eyes co-alesced, into a looming darkness. He shook his head.

"You gonna make it?" asked Ann.

"Yeah, I think so," said David. He panted. The couch, the loveseat, the television and entertainment center, the book-shelves, along with all the books—they'd carried them all out into the garage. "Water."

They returned inside, past the stacks of chairs in the front hallway, in the kitchen, in every spare space on the first floor.

David poured them glasses of water. They drank.

Their first home church service was tomorrow.

"We could do always do the rest early tomorrow," said Ann.

"No," said David. "We need to know how many we can fit in here. I don't want to have to worry about that *and* my sermon tomorrow."

"You don't have it written?"

"I have the broad strokes," said David. "I've had writer's block lately. I'm hoping some pressure will force the words out."

"I can do this, if you want to write—"

"No," said David. "Frankly, this is helpful. It lets me focus on practical matters."

They drank.

"Do you think this is going to work?" asked Ann.

"I think people will come," said David. "The service re-mains the same, in the chapel, or in our home."

"I didn't mean just that," said Ann. She eyed him. "No one would blame you if you left, David."

David took a sip. The sound of Sol playing in the back

yard filtered inside.

"He can't win, Ann," said David. "We like Sacred. We do. But it's more than that. It's more than the church. It's more than Eli, or Bronson." He met Ann's eyes. "You've stayed."

"Yeah, I have," said Ann. "Sometimes—" She trailed off.

"Sometimes what?"

"Sometimes I regret it," she said. "I wonder if I've been too stubborn."

"It's your home."

"It's true," she said. "But is that what kept me here?" She paused. "Do you remember what I told you? About Anson, the mill worker?"

"You killed him."

"Yes," said Ann. "I mentioned my girlfriend at the time."

"She was there with you." David paused. "Did she see—"

"No," said Ann. "I kept her inside. I tried—I tried to protect her. I proposed to her, not too long after."

David raised an eyebrow. "*You* proposed?"

"I thought I was the settling down type at the time," said Ann. "Maybe I am. She accepted. On one condition."

Ann stopped.

"That you leave Sacred," said David.

"Yes," said Ann. "And I agreed. I loved her. I loved her more than Sacred. I think—I think I can still say that. I loved her more than I loved Sacred."

"But you stayed."

"But I stayed," said Ann. She took a drink. "We started the process. We decided we'd move to Atlanta to start, and then play it by ear. And you know that feeling? It hurts, like an empty hollow gnawing on your guts—telling you to stop. Telling you something's wrong."

"Yeah," said David. "I think everyone has it. Your doubts, your fears, eating away at you. I usually try and push through it."

"I couldn't," said Ann. "It got to the point where I couldn't breathe. Was having panic attacks. I broke down. Told Sonja I couldn't leave. That I still loved her, but I couldn't leave Sacred." Ann exhaled. "She left. Atlanta, then Portland. Found a nice woman. Got married."

"It's hard to leave home."

Ann shook her head. "I mean, you're right, but that's not it at all. That's what I thought at the time. That I was afraid to leave home. That my body wouldn't let me. But that wasn't it." Ann narrowed her eyes. "It was a retreat."

"From what?"

"From everything in this town that I hate. It was giving them a victory. Letting them win." She sighed. "I hate the idea of that, more than I loved her. I couldn't—I couldn't do it."

"You seem to have processed it," said David. "You're in a better place."

"I'm still in Sacred," said Ann. "I won." She smiled. "You ready to place some chairs?"

"No time like the present."

They finished their water, and filled the house with chairs. One by one, they set up chair after chair, as close as they could.

One hundred chairs, delivered, and the living room was full, the chairs spilling out into the kitchen, into the dining room, into the hallways. Anywhere with even a small portion of a view, a chair went.

"That's eighty nine," said Ann. "We could squeeze another five in the front, maybe, but you'd be right on top of them when you preached."

"Leave them out for now," said David. "We'll see how many show up. At worst, the more able bodied can stand in the back. We can fit more standing than sitting."

"We had over a hundred at the last service," said Ann. "Before Eli showed up."

"Some won't come, not without the church," said David. "They want the chapel. A building."

"You're right," said Ann. "But maybe we'll get some new people."

"I hope so."

"Faith, right?"

"Right."

"Um—how do we get through here?" asked Jason, with Solly in tow, looking at rows of chairs filling the front hallway.

"We can take them up for now," said David. "We'll put them back as need be tomorrow. But we know how many can fit."

They stowed the chairs again.

"Thank you for your help."

"I'll see you tomorrow, David," said Ann, walking down the steps of their front porch. "Good luck with your sermon."

"I'll need it," said David. He smiled. "I'm glad you stayed, Ann."

Ann smiled. "Say it enough times and maybe I'll agree with you."

34

The fans blew loudly, cranked to max speed, the doors and windows of the Ingram's house open. The house was noisy, filled with chatter, with box fans, with the scraping of chair legs on the wooden floor.

"Does everyone who need a seat have a seat?" asked Jason. "I'm looking at you, Betsy. No shame in wanting to sit. It's hot, and it's a long service.

"Oh, Jason, I don't need—"

But Bill Elsing was already on his feet, and gestured Betsy to please take his seat, and she demurred once, but he insisted, and she sat.

The house was full, all one hundred seats full, with more standing, leaned against walls, crammed into corners, and up against bookshelves. Children sat on adult's laps, or on their shoulders. A slight breeze blew through the house in the early morning, the fans helping keep the temperature down.

Mark Collins had brought big blocks of ice from his store, and they sat in front of fans. Even so, everyone inside fanned themselves, the air holding the heat.

Laurie started the service. They sang the hymns everyone knew.

"If you don't know them, hum the best you can," said Laurie. "No one will know the difference." The crowd laughed. They sang. They hummed.

Laurie read the verse.

"Matthew 16:15. 'But what about you?' he asked. 'Who do you say I am?' Simon Peter answered, 'You are the Messiah, the Son of the living God.' Jesus replied, 'Blessed are you, Simon son of Jonah, for this was not revealed to you by flesh and blood, but by my Father in heaven. And I tell you that you are Peter, and on this rock I will build my church, and the gates of Hades will not overcome it.'"

David rose from his seat and Laurie sat where he had.

"I know some of you can't see me," said David. "But everyone can hear me, right? If you can't, yell out."

The house was silent, aside from distant road noise and the whirring of box fans.

"Alright," said David. He stood in front of them, chairs less than a foot away. They'd stacked them even denser than the day before. The people sat on top of each other, standing stacked in all the spare walking space, standing out of view in other corners of the first floor. He stared out at the people, wiping a drip of sweat from his brow. He had removed his coat, rolling up the sleeves of his white button-down, still sweating.

"Christ preached in many places after his baptism. In temples and synagogues. In the open air, in nature. And in the homes of whoever would have him, as he and the disciples traveled the ancient world." David paused. "But the physical location of his preaching was always secondary. For before Jesus was known as our Messiah, he was only a man challenging the religion of the day. He preached. He searched for believers, and he found the disciples. Men who believed in him, and in return, he believed in them."

"Christ had walked with his disciples from the Sea of Galilee to Caesarea Philippi, known as Banias now, in modern day Israel. This is where this exchange took place, where he confirmed Peter's declaration of him as the Son of God, as the Messiah. And in return, Christ declared Peter the rock upon which his church would be built."

David looked out over the crowd, at the sea of faces, who had crammed themselves into his house, to worship together. To hear his sermon. His heart soared.

But there was no bloom of light in their faces. No explosion of color. No rush of God's grace.

"But is that true? It depends on who you ask. Some say it was literal. In Catholicism, Peter is considered the first Pope, because of this scripture. Others take it as metaphor. That Christ is referring to himself, to this statement of him as Messiah. Some others even say that it is referring to the physical location of the time, of a physical rock."

"Me? I always took it as a simple affirmation of Peter's faith in him. I'm not alone in that. Peter believes that Christ is our Savior, and upon that rock, upon that belief, upon that faith—that is what Christ established his church. It is our belief in Jesus that empowers the church. It is what *creates* the church. It is the foundation of it. We say to Christ with our faith 'You are the Son of the living God' and he, in return, makes us the foundation of his church."

David waited for the grace of God, to return, the familiar rush of God's power, but it wasn't there. He stared into the faces, and no light, no bloom of life or color, but instead—

Instead there was blood. Their faces turned to suffering in his eyes, mouths open, eyes wide, agony stretching their faces, pain distorting their features.

Flashes, their faces, agony, Eli, the fixed trauma-filled eyes of the statue of Christ, Ann chopping it into pieces, the dead boar, slaughtered, an angel butchered—

David squeezed his eyes shut, and pulled a handkerchief from his pocket, wiping his face.

The visions were gone. He blinked again, and they remained gone.

"But that is not all Christ said. 'On this rock I will build this church, and the gates of Hades will not overcome it.' Will not overcome it. Christ did not build his church in a vacuum. He built it in a time where religion had been established, long, long established. I refer back to the location of this conversation, at Caesarea Philippi. A location also referred to as the Gates of Hell."

"Because this location was a pagan worship site, with a myth that the cave there was a portal to Hades. A gateway to Hell. So when Christ spoke these words, he was speaking both figuratively and literally. For he knew that outside forces would batter at his church. But he also knew that the faith and belief of his followers would hold strong. That oppression would come, but it would not matter. The church would hold strong."

The eyes of the congregation watched him, and David looked back at them, hoping the bloom of God's grace would return. He took a halting breath, and held it. He waited for the colors to pop, for his home to explode into the light of God, the vision of his glory.

But there was nothing.

He blinked, and in a flash he beheld suffering, and he blinked again, and it was gone. He squeezed his eyes shut.

He opened them. The people of Sacred, again. He coughed, clearing his throat.

"I will leave you with this. Christ never saw a church built while he lived. He never owned a building, a temple, a sanctuary. He preached in homes, much like this. And when he spoke of building a church, he did not speak in terms of physical space. He spoke in terms of people. Of faith. Of believers, of supporters, of fellowship." David looked out over everyone there, the fans whirring. "If we are to build a church in Sacred, it will be upon those same things, regardless of where we worship."

David took a mighty breath, and let it out.

"Please, bow your heads." One by one, they closed their eyes and did so. "Make all our words fit for your hearing. Make all our deeds acceptable in your sight. Sanctify all our thoughts and desires. And grant that, being pure in heart, we may see you; through Jesus Christ, your Son, who lived and died that we might have life. Amen."

"Amen," the congregation echoed.

35

Tommy stared up at the bare cross.

He sat in the front row, in his normal spot. He sweat, dripping down his forehead, his back, his clothes sticking to him. The chapel was scorching hot, service starting an hour later than normal. His dad had always wanted service to start later, and now they did.

His mom had led the early parts of the service, of hymns and welcome, and the reading of scripture. Exodus 15:2-6.

"The Lord is my strength and my defense; he has become my salvation. He is my God, and I will praise him, my father's God, and I will exalt him. The Lord is a warrior; the Lord is his name. Pharaoh's chariots and his army he has hurled into the sea. The best of Pharaoh's officers are drowned in the Red Sea. The deep waters have covered them; they sank to the depths like a stone. Your right hand, Lord, was majestic in power. Your right hand, Lord, shattered the enemy."

She read it to the assembled congregation. Tommy glanced backward, but no one else had arrived since they'd started.

The church looked empty. It wasn't. There were over fifty people there, give or take. Tommy hadn't counted, but when full the chapel held over three hundred. They all sat in their normal spots, on the left side. No one had migrated over.

Tommy hadn't wanted to come, but hadn't dared utter it, or even feign illness. His dad would have none of it. They had taken back the Holy Church of Sacred, and he wanted everyone there.

Tommy sat, sweating, his eyes looking up at the bare cross. His stomach hurt, nerves bundled up, squeezing inside him. He had texted Pastor David.

I don't want to go he had sent.

David had responded *Go. I know it's unpleasant. But it'll keep him from lashing out at you. If you feel overwhelmed, bring your Bible. Study.*

Tommy had wanted to respond in a thousand different ways, in all the ways it was unfair, that the God David had shared in a few short weeks was everything Tommy wanted. He wanted to scream, to rebel.

Instead, Tommy texted *Okay, I'll try* and so he sat, waiting, the chapel sweltering and quiet, the subtle movement of people sitting behind him, the sniffling of Sheriff Bronson, his allergies flaring up.

The sound echoed, the scuffling of shoes, the whispers of people behind him, the sniffles of Bronson, and the flipping of pages of the hymnal. A child cried, hushed by his mother.

It had never echoed like that before.

Less people, now, to absorb the sound. Hollow.

A sudden terror filled him, a cold fear flooding his heart, a vision of his father, covered in blood, bursting through the door, into the chapel, dragging the body of Pastor David, a blood trail seeping into the worn red carpet, his father with a look of victory and pride on his face, of him dragging the body to the cross, and nailing the corpse of the pastor there, hammer and nail. Blood spilled from the body, and his father didn't stare at his work while he did it, no, he stared at Tommy, his eyes maniacal, filled with hatred and glee in equal measure—

The door opened, and his father emerged, dressed in a blue polo, embroidered with the logo of the church on the breast, and he didn't drag the body of Pastor David, no, but he held something else.

He carried in open arms the head of Jesus Christ.

The chapel was silent. Tommy's heart thudded in his ears, the face of Christ staring out at him, at the crowd. His dad climbed the steps to the stage, the stage dully thudding with each footstep. He placed the head of Christ on the pulpit, and it stared out, decapitated, disembodied. He stood, staring, next to the pulpit, next to the head, in eternal pain.

"We are at war," he said. He stared out over the chapel, already sweating. His eyes passed over Tommy.

"This is the work of David Ingram. This is the work of Laurie Grace. Of all the sinners who tried to take our church from us. We leave for a matter of weeks, and they destroy Christ. They cut off his head, and leave it in my driveway."

"So I took it upon myself to gather some allies. Sheriff Bronson. Vic, Davis, Tyler. Others as well, you know who you are. Many of us have been a part of the church since the beginning, or for many years and have seen it fall into sin. And inviting a sinner like David Ingram to be a pastor was the last straw, with this terrible massacre of our Lord Jesus Christ."

"We took it back last Sunday," he said. "But the fight is not over. Angie read that scripture for that very reason." His father pulled note cards from his pocket, sweat dripping down his face, down his arms, streaks of moisture across the cards, drooping from the damp.

"Exodus 15:3. The Lord is a warrior; the Lord is his name. Exodus 15:7. In the greatness of your majesty you threw down those who opposed you. You unleashed your burning anger; it consumed them like stubble."

Tommy's stomach turned, and he opened his Bible. He thumbed through it, to the verses Pastor David had sent him. He read.

But the fruit of the Spirit is love, joy, peace, patience, kindness, goodness, faithfulness, gentleness, self-control; against such things there is no law.

"The Lord is a warrior," said his dad. "And nothing can stand against him, or against his command. And we may have the building, but Sacred is still filled with sinners."

For he himself is our peace, who has made us both one and has broken down in his flesh the dividing wall of hostility by abolishing the law of commandments expressed in ordinances, that he might create in himself one new man in place of the two, so making peace, and might reconcile us both to God in one body through the cross, thereby killing the hostility.

"Christ suffered for us, sacrificed for us," said Eli. "He died for us, was tortured for us. And this is how he is repaid." He gestured wildly toward the head of Christ. "He is decapitated! He is ripped from the cross!"

Put on then, as God's chosen ones, holy and beloved, compassionate hearts, kindness, humility, meekness, and patience, bearing with one another and, if one has a complaint against another, forgiving each other; as the Lord has forgiven you, so you also must forgive. And above all these put on love, which binds everything together in perfect harmony. And let the peace of Christ rule in your hearts—

"I call for you all to defend our town of Sacred—" said Eli, yelling, sputtering, sweat dripping down over his eyes and mouth, spraying it into the air. He read from the card in front of him, but stopped, pulling it closer. He took a breath, and a silence settled into the chapel. Tommy looked up from his Bible, the silence broken only by his father mumbling.

Eli's head snapped to the left, staring at the head of Christ, his lips moving silently, and it snapped back, and he switched to the next note card, dropping the previous, fluttering to the stage floor. He wiped his forehead with the sleeve of his polo shirt, the shirt soaked through.

He took a breath, his chest shaking with the pounding of his heart. "We cannot rest until the war is won. Until the town of Sacred is ours again, until the chapel, the heart, is part again—"

He stopped, staring at the card, trying to figure it out. It sagged in his hand, the sweat smudging his writing. The silence swallowed the chapel again. Tommy heard slight mumbling behind him, some grunts and whispered chatter.

Another glance to the head of Christ, his father's mouth moving without noise, another note card fluttering to the stage floor. He cleared his throat.

"We will be a true community once again," he said. "We will cast out the sinners from within. By the power of your arm they will be as still as a stone—until your people pass by, Lord, until the people brought pass by. You will bring them in and plant them on the mountain of your inheritance—the place, Lord, you made for your dwelling, the sanctuary, Lord, your hands established. The Lord reigns, for ever and ever."

Tommy heard no words now, as he stared at his father. He barked, reading smudged words from his note cards, one by one, fluttering to the ground. Anger and rage poured from his mouth, smoke and fire, the tongues of retribution, of justice, of a holy war. Tommy understood none of it.

Tommy looked down to his Bible again, but shut it. His father preached, the head of Christ looking out at them.

This wasn't God, or godly, and his heart screamed at him, a deep anguish, and Tommy stood then.

His father stopped his sermon, again, staring.

"Tommy, what are—"

Tommy stared, eyes burrowing into his father.

He left, walking past his mother, past Sam.

"Tommy! You come back here!" his father bellowed behind him. Tommy walked, and as he walked, the pain relented.

The rest of the congregation stared in confusion, and his father bellowed, but Tommy left.

The heat of the summer sun did not compare to the interior of the Holy Church of Sacred.

36

They sat in David's office. "That was quite the sermon," said Smallwood. "Despite the environment."

"We made do with what we had," said David. "It wasn't an option to not have a service."

Smallwood nodded, writing on a notepad. "What happened with the chapel?"

"Didn't Laurie tell you?"

"Yes," said Smallwood. "But I'd like your perspective."

"They took the chapel by force, armed," said David. "Last Sunday, in the middle of my sermon."

"Eli Parsons is his name?"

"Yes," said David. "And his followers, including the Sheriff, and his deputies."

"Why did they do this?"

"Because they didn't like that the Holy Church of Sacred has a gay pastor."

"Are you sure—"

"He might give other reasons among them, but that's first and foremost," said David, staring at Smallwood's scratching pen. "It's like people saying the Civil War wasn't about slavery."

"Was there any other prior antagonism from him?"

"Yes," said David. "He marched out of a service. He slapped me, when I asked him back."

Smallwood scribbled some more.

"And you did nothing else?" he asked. "You didn't provoke him?"

"Does that matter?" asked David. "He's trespassing on church property. He threatened the congregation with shotguns and rifles—"

"I'm just asking—"

"I provoked him by existing," said David. "Write that down, too."

Smallwood put down his pen.

"Pastor—"

"I don't think this is that complicated, Mr. Smallwood."

"I'm not your enemy, Pastor."

David paused. "I'm tired. I'm frustrated. The Church says they support us. They have sent you, to kindly ask about the men holding our building hostage. I don't want a report. I want action."

Smallwood pursed his lips. "Thank you, Pastor. I'm doing my best. We are doing our best. We're in a tough spot—"

"You're in a tough spot?" asked David. "I'm preaching in my house." David stared, his shirt sticking to his back. "Do you have any other questions?"

Smallwood closed his notepad. "No."

*

Eli wiped the sweat from his face. He was soaked through. He hadn't brought a change of clothes, and now they had the potluck, in the back room that was only mildly cooler.

"Eli," said Bronson, filling the door frame.

"What is it?"

"A rep from the church is here," said Bronson. "He wants to talk to you."

"Where is he?"

"Out with the rest of folks," said Bronson. "He was at the service."

"Shit," said Eli. "Bring him back here."

Bronson vanished, and then reappeared a few minutes later, the church rep trailing. He was dressed in simple clothes, soaked through with sweat. He carried a small notebook. Bronson dwarfed him.

"Eli Parsons," said Eli, extending a hand. The rep took it.

"Travis Smallwood."

"Please," said Eli, gesturing toward a chair opposite the desk, worn pleather, a chair as old as Eli. Travis slid down into it. He opened his notebook, pulling out a pen. "How can I help you?"

"Your perspective on this whole thing."

"Have you spoken to Ingram?"

"I will," said Smallwood. "Please, just tell me your side of the story." Eli read his eyes, trying to find a sense of his thoughts, but it betrayed nothing. Bronson stood awkwardly at the door, and went to leave.

"Kyle, don't go too far," said Eli. Bronson nodded, standing outside the door. Eli took a breath. "There's been a Parsons in the Holy Church of Sacred since the beginning, Travis. Can I call you Travis?"

"Sure," he said, still scribbling notes on his pad.

"There's always been a Parsons in the church. And in the past few years—"

"Ingram was only hired a couple months ago, correct?"

Eli paused. "Yes, roughly," said Eli. "But this goes further back. "A few years ago, our old pastor, Pastor John, well, he started to change the church. I suspect it was his wife's doing, getting into his ear. I haven't agreed with the direction of the church lately, and John, well, he and I argued about it. And after his tragic death, I had thought—well, I don't want to sound hateful, but y'know, God doesn't close a door without opening a window. I thought a new pastor might be more amicable to my way of thinking."

"But instead Laurie and the church hired Ingram."

"Yes."

"And you have a problem with his lifestyle."

"It's not my only problem with the man," said Eli. "But it starts with that—it doesn't make a lick of sense to me, how they could allow a sinner like that to be a pastor—to be around kids—"

Smallwood scribbled more notes. "Please, continue."

"Well, we thought it against God's will to do such a thing, so we walked out. All of us."

"When was this?" Scribbling.

"A few weeks ago."

"And then you took back the church? With guns?"

Eli swallowed. "Well, yes." Eli coughed. "Well, it's more than that. There was a Christ figure at the back of the church—"

"Yes, I heard your sermon," said Smallwood. He closed the notebook. "Thank you for speaking to me, Mr. Parsons."

"That's it?" asked Eli. "Well? Do I talk to someone else?"

"To what?"

"I don't know, to convince them we deserve the building—"

"I don't decide such things."

"Who does?"

"The council will decide."

"He's a sinner! He's a faggot—"

"I commiserate, Mr. Parsons," said Smallwood. "I disagreed with the church's ruling, and I myself wanted my church to split off. Neither of those decisions went my way."

"And you just rolled over and took it?"

"I prayed," said Smallwood, looking into his eyes. "And I still pray. It's all I can do."

"That's not true—"

"Thank you for making the time, Mr. Parsons—" Eli glanced at the door, and Bronson was already inside, and the looks he gave him told him everything, and his hands were clasped around Smallwood's shoulders, clamped tight, keeping him sitting.

"What is this—"

"You're going tell the church exactly what they want to hear," said Eli, staring into Smallwood's eyes. He looked back, confused, struggling for a moment. "I wouldn't fight the Sheriff too much, he's a pretty tough guy." Eli stared.

"You'll tell them exactly what they want to hear. Whatever they need to hear to let this stay exactly the way it is."

Smallwood exhaled, not looking back at Bronson looming over him. He looked only at Eli.

"Are you threatening me?"

"No, of course not—"

"I would hope not, Mr. Parsons. Because maybe threats work to establish your foothold on this building, but they won't work on me. I will tell the council the truth, whatever that may be. Please tell your gorilla to let me go."

Eli's heart yearned for pain, to break this man upon the cross, but instead he glanced at Bronson and he let go. Smallwood left, without a glance backward, leaving the church, leaving them alone.

Bronson's eyes bent in anger. "We should have—"

"We couldn't do a thing," said Eli. "We can't have a church rep going missing. They'd track us down."

"We could still—"

"Shut up," said Eli. "Shut up. We have time still."

Bronson left silently, huffing and puffing. Let him be pissed.

Another enemy.

Eli needed to worship, but his Lord was still in the chapel.

He would need to keep him close by.

The phone rang.

"Hello?" An answer, with slight crackling.

"Hi, Phil. It's David."

"David! Sorry if the connection is bad. I'm traveling with Debbie. We're heading toward the Grand Canyon. Our service is spotty right now. Enough about me. How'd it go?"

"It went well," said David. "Big turnout. All the seats were filled, and the rest had to stand."

"That's great news," said Phil. "I told you they'd stick by you. Did you decide on a sermon?"

"Yes," said David. "Matthew 16. Upon this rock. Peter's affirmation. About how building a church starts with believers. Reaffirming that a building does not make a church. Its congregation does."

"Ah, yes," said Phil. "Smart. Did they receive it well?"

"I think so. I think so," said David. "I got compliments afterward. Even from the church representative."

"They sent someone?"

"Yes," said David. "He attended both services, and will be interviewing everyone involved."

"Well? What else did he say?"

"I don't know. I hope he does something. I hope—I hope the Church does something."

"He can't possibly side with Eli. They've stolen Church property."

"You know that doesn't necessarily matter."

The phone broke up. Silence.

"—the building back. And your church will be stronger for it."

David paused.

"I don't know, Phil."

"What are—" Another break. "—Not telling me?"

"I didn't feel it yesterday," said David. "Not at all."

"Feel what?"

"God's grace, Phil," said David. "The feeling. I mentioned it before."

"You can't let Eli's actions affect your feelings about the Lord, David."

"It hasn't, Phil. But there were over a hundred people in my house yesterday, and it should have been brighter than ever. It wasn't. It was replaced by violence. By suffering."

The phone broke up again.

"—was that, David? I'm sorry, I'm losing you."

"I said the feeling. It wasn't there at all. It was replaced by suffering. By pain."

Silence.

"—sorry, David, its—" Silence. "—keep losing you. You can't lose faith, David."

"I haven't lost faith," said David. "I just worry."

"Worry about what?"

"Worry about what I have faith in."

Silence.

"Sorry, David, I keep losing—" More silence. "I'll call—"

And then silence again. David looked at his phone. The call had dropped.

38

The ravine was an open wound, bleeding out into the world.

Jason swiped the brush over the canvas, a swath of red, the dark orange-red of the clay of the ravine, splitting the space between the pine trees.

He sweat, the sun beating down on him, even in the early evening. The light was everything, a pre-dusk light, the clay turning bright red, juxtaposed against the dark green pines, the sky a vacuum of color, white clouds serving as backdrop.

Jason painted, letting the finer details of the world bleed into his eyes, down his arm, and into his hand, onto the canvas. He hadn't gotten away from Solly and David, had no time to paint at all since they had moved, and he needed it.

He had scouted the area around Sacred, had seen the ravine, the red bright, even on Google Earth. The ravine was a scar across the land, a small parking lot off the highway, blink and you'd miss it.

David brushed the red on his palette, a touch of his orange, darker, deeper, pushing the clay in his landscape to the edge of reality.

He brushed, brushed, and then paused.

The sound of rattling spray paint, David's bat scraping across the floorboards—

Jason blinked away the thought. Blinked away the vision of David's face, contorted in anger, a different man—

He breathed, pushing away everything but the ravine, and the trees, and the sky, and he brushed the deep unearthly red onto the canvas, smooth, invisible brush strokes, the artist gone, the landscape divorced from its creator—

"I can't see the brush strokes."

"I'm sorry, were you talking to me?" asked Jason, wandering over toward the man who had spoke, a not quiet question into the air. He stood alone by the painting, Jason's painting, one of the dozen or so paintings he had on display for the gallery. The night was winding down, his show almost over, and he had taken to wander, taking in each of his paintings, all over again.

The man looked back, slightly surprised, but smiled, his face lighting.

Well, hello.

"Oh, no," he said. "Just thinking out loud. Can you see the brush strokes in this?"

Jason smiled, and moved in, studying his own piece, one he had spent dozens of hours on, examining it.

He saw the brush strokes.

"They are there, but they're very difficult to see," said Jason, finally. "If you look at the rest of the pieces, I think it's plain the artist is doing his best to keep them hidden."

"Well, it's working," said the man. "I can't see them at all."

"Do you like the piece, though?"

"I love it," said the man. "They all—they feel like they aren't of Earth. Or maybe—maybe the best version of it."

"That's very kind," said Jason. "Hi, I'm Jason Walker."

"You're—you're the artist," said the man, smiling. He exhaled a small breath. "Well, your work is incredible. I'm David."

"Nice to meet you," said Jason, extending a hand. They shook, skin against skin. "And thank you. And yes, I do my best to make the strokes invisible. I still see them, though."

"Isn't that how it works, though?" asked David. "The artist always knows the art better than anyone."

"Are you an artist?"

"Only as a hobby," said David. "I'm a student."

"What do you study?"

David looked down for a moment. "General Theology. I study at New York Seminary."

"Seminary school?" asked Jason. "You're going to be a priest?"

"Pastor," said David. "Maybe. I'm not sure yet."

Jason looked, realizing they were alone in the gallery.

"I think the show is closing," said Jason. "It was nice to meet you."

"It was," said David. "Say—do you want to get coffee sometime?"

"Strange, you out here all alone," and Jason was back in the present, next to the blood-red ravine, his canvas half-covered in front of him. He turned, and saw him, Bronson, the

sheriff, pacing toward him, his billy club in his hand, slowly twirling.

Ice settled into Jason's heart, the back of his knees aching, a dark pain in his guts. The silence around them was stark, Bronson's footsteps echoing in the setting sunlight.

"You're a painter, huh?" asked Bronson, his footsteps louder, coming up right behind Jason. Jason didn't turn. "I thought that was a stereotype, y'know? That all you fags were artists."

Jason took a short breath, to keep his heart inside his chest.

"It's real pretty, though, I'll give you that," said Bronson. He paced behind Jason, never stepping in front of him. Jason stayed still, waiting. "Real pretty. Never come out here, myself. Guess when you live here, you forget about it."

Bronson stepped, lapsing into silence. He breathed, swinging his billy club. Jason heard it, the soft whistle as the club swung behind his head.

"For a long time, Sacred was a good place," said Bronson. "Back when I was a kid. Things were the way things were supposed to be. We went to church, to football games on Friday, out at the high school. There weren't no queers, no addicts, no fucking homeless begging for money at the stop light. I don't know what it was, but it changed. It wasn't only Pastor John, but he was a part of it. The news, telling kids being gay was cool, or some horse shit. People getting soft."

The billy club whistled. Jason said nothing.

"Now, we've tried talking to David. Letting him know the score. But he's got it in his head he's doing God's work. That God himself brought him here, to set things right. And I know the type. Stubborn, dug in. Eli got mighty pissed off about it. But I told him, I know the way. Told him, let me talk to the other queer. See if I can talk some sense into him."

The billy club whistled.

"Do you feel God out here, faggot?"

Jason said nothing. The billy club went silent, and then jarred him, the end poking him hard, in the shoulder.

"Answer me."

Jason took a breath, tears welling in his eyes, staring at his half-finished painting.

"Yes."

Bronson took a heavy breath behind him, and the billy club whistled.

"That's funny," said Bronson. "Thought you artist types hated God. But I've got news for you." Bronson leaned close, his hot breath on the back of Jason's ear.

"God ain't here," said Bronson. He leaned back. "I know he ain't, because you're here. And God don't abide no homosexual. He is blind to you, and to your kind. When you eat, when you drink, when you pray, when you're fucking each other in the ass—he ain't there. You're an abomination. Hell, even Pastor John said so, back before his damned bitch got in his ear and convinced him otherwise."

The billy club whistled.

"God ain't here, and he ain't watching," said Bronson. "So anything—anything I do out here with you—he doesn't care."

Bronson stood behind him, the billy club twirling.

"You hear me, you piece of shit?"

The billy club tapped him again, hard, and Jason jumped. Tears flowed down his face, his teeth gritted.

"Yes."

"So, you do whatever it takes. You convince the other faggot to leave Sacred. Go back to the city. Don't come back."

The club swung hard toward his face, and then stopped an inch away, and Jason flinched. Bronson laughed, pushing the end of the club toward Jason's cheek, pressing hard into his skin, the cold end of the club pressing into his face, his cheek gnashing into his teeth and gums.

"This is my only warning," said Bronson, and he pulled the club away, and stepped in front of Jason, and grabbed the canvas off the easel, and threw it into the ravine, the piece sailing into the chasm. "Next time—next time that will be you."

Bronson swung his club, knocking the easel over, and then grabbed Jason's palette, covered in paint, smashing it into Jason's face, and then rubbing, covering him in red, in green, in black, in blue, in white, his face smothered in paint, the wood of the palette cracking from the force.

Bronson held it there, rubbing it back and forth over Jason's face, Jason's lips pressed against it, paint in his mouth, in his eyes, in his nose, and he couldn't breathe—

And then Bronson let go, and walked away, his footsteps echoing in the still early evening air.

Jason spit the paint from his mouth, and washed out his eyes with his bottle of water.

The sun set, and the dark red scar of the ravine remained, even in the darkness.

39

"I'll kill him."

"David—"

"I'll kill him."

David paced, the blood boiling underneath his skin. Jason cleaned the paint off his face in their bathroom.

"He threatened you," said David. "He threatened us."

Jason turned, and walked out of the bathroom, and hugged David, squeezing him tight, holding him in place.

"You're burning up."

David exhaled once, squeezing his fists tight, and then let them go, and held his husband.

"This isn't the church," said David. "This is you."

"He's the Sheriff, David," said Jason. "He'll shoot you. He's allowed to shoot you. You can't attack him."

"Jase—"

"Hold me, David. Just hold me."

David did as he was told.

"It's my fault," said David. "This is my fault."

Jason held him. "We don't have to stay. We can go back to New York. There is no shame in retreat. We'll be safe there."

David said nothing, deep emotion brewing inside, a well of darkness and fear, hatred and pain.

"I can't let him win."

Jason let go of him and sat down on the foot of the bed.

"Win what, David?"

David stared at his husband's face, specks of paint still visible, red and yellow and brown and green.

"Win what?" asked Jason. "This dead town? That rotten church? Let him have it. We can't play this game."

David squeezed his hands into fists and closed his eyes. There was only darkness behind them. A great shape. He opened them.

"He's doing something to me."

"What?"

"When I preach, I don't feel the same—I don't *see* the same—"

"David, calm down—"

"He worships the same God as me, Jason. He worships the same God as me!" David found himself yelling, and he looked at Jason's face, and he saw fear.

"David, please. Sol is sleeping—"

David took a breath. "He'll still be here, if we leave. He'll still be here. Still worshiping, in that rotten church—"

Jason pushed himself off the bed, and grabbed David, wrangling him, squeezing his swinging arms tight to his body.

"Stop it. This isn't the man I married."

Jason held him tight, and nestled his face into David's neck.

"We can leave," he said, quietly. "And you can be you again. You find God again. Look at me." Jason let go, holding David at arm's length. "We can leave. It will be a nightmare, but one we wake up from."

David stared back at him.

"I don't want to be afraid of you," said Jason. "We have to protect Solly."

His son's name penetrated David's heart and he nodded. He closed his eyes and there was nothing there and he opened them and stared into his husband's beautiful gaze and he embraced him, and kissed him hard.

"You're right. We have to protect Solly." He took a deep breath. "One more service. I'll say goodbye. Okay?"

Jason kissed him. "Okay."

40

The oven timer went off, the shrill beep echoing through the house. Laurie set down her wine glass and took a peek at the cookies. Light brown, slightly set. She closed the oven door, and set the timer.

One more minute.

She'd made enough cookies to know what they needed. She knew her oven, and the recipe.

She picked up her glass, and took another drink.

Man, those cookies are smelling good.

John's voice reached her from the living room.

"Almost ready," she said, into her wine glass.

Almost ready.

The timer dinged again, and she didn't check them, grabbing the sheet pan with a towel, and sliding it on top of the oven. The already overwhelming smell of freshly baked cookies exploded in the room, wafting into the rest of the house.

Golden brown, perfectly set edges. A slight spread, with just enough chocolate chips. Just the way John liked them.

Laurie gave them three minutes to cool, and then plated them, piling them onto a dish, taking them into the living room, right on the coffee table, right in front of John.

Sunday night, after a long day of service, of preaching. Cookies, and catching up on any television they'd missed from the week. Usually a comedy. John would laugh, a cookie in one hand.

Laurie took another swallow of wine, a deep red, always red.

They had told her not to look at the body. To save her the trauma, the horror, of seeing John in such a state. Of broken bones, and bloated flesh. She had listened. She had wanted to remember John as he had lived, not as he died.

But she regretted it now.

John's soul was gone, she knew, but she should have taken those extra moments with what was left of him, no matter his state. Even broken in death. She would choose them, over nothing.

Laurie picked up her glass, for another swallow, but it was empty, and she filled it, the last of this bottle.

She sat down in the living room again. The cookies were still there.

A last moment with John was not the only reason she regretted it. A part of her wanted to see what Eli had done to her husband. To see his sin.

Eli had insulted her on his way out of the Holy Church

of Sacred. Laurie hadn't heard a word. The look on his face was all she saw, the rage, the false righteousness, the disgust.

She had studied his face then, and remembered it.

Laurie smiled, a grim smile, and drank her glass of wine.

He deserved more than that expression, more betrayal, more suffering. More punishment.

But she had done what she could. She had meted out the revenge of her station and role. All she could do.

She hoped God would deem fit to handle the rest.

Laurie drank the last of her glass. The grandfather clock tolled. It was past midnight. She'd lost track of time.

She reached for the plate of cookies, pressing a finger into the surface. They were room temperature now, all trace of the oven gone from them.

Laurie grabbed the plate, and went to the kitchen.

She dumped them into the trash.

41

Eli paced in his basement. The sun had not risen yet. Christ's detached head sat on a small bookcase, stolen from upstairs.

Eli paced, his stomach on fire, his heart cold.

Sit, Eli.

Eli wrung his hands together, his palms clammy, wiping them on his pants. He paced.

Eli, sit. Please. You cannot worship like this.

Eli stopped, taking a breath. He sat. Christ was right, he must sit. He must worship.

"He walked out on me," said Eli. "He walked out on me."

He is still young.

"Tommy's been rebellious before, but nothing like this. He's a teenager, I expect some pushback. But this? Embarrassing me in front of the entire church?" Eli buried his face in his hands. "I was already struggling like hell. The damned heat, I was sweating like crazy. And he walked out on me. And I try and talk to him, and it's like talking to a brick wall."

Thomas is not the real problem, is he?

"He ain't helping, that's for sure," said Eli. "But you're right. Of course you're right. Tommy—it's just salt in the wound. I expected more people. I expected people to see the light. We took the building—"

Look at me, Eli.

Eli looked up, staring into the eyes of Christ. Framed in pain.

"I did what you told me to do," said Eli. "I took back the church. They had their damned service in the house, and still, they had more people attend. No one came back. Not a one. Heck, there were some I would have sworn were on my side, and they didn't attend."

Christ said nothing.

"Less and less people by the day. Is everyone in this town on the side of the sinners? Even that fella from the church. He says he's on my side. Wants the church to be pure again, but then says he's going to help Ingram. I don't understand it. Telling me to pray. It's ridiculous. He can't speak to you like I do. None of them can. None of them understand. Not even Bronson."

The building is not enough.

Eli stared. "The church? But what else is there? Even with Bronson, I don't know what else we can do. We've tried to apply pressure, but I'm worried about what that Smallwood man is going to say—"

Christ is the culmination of the law. Do you disobey me?

"No, of course not. I would never—"

The building is not enough, Eli. I need your help. Sacred needs your help. Please. Please.

Eli looked up at the statue on the wall, on the oozing wounds of the crucifixion, of the strained lungs of Christ.

Down here, Eli.

Eli looked back at the head of Christ.

You can have me back. You can worship again. But not until Sacred is ours. Not until the sinners have been cast out.

The eyes of Christ pleaded with him. They begged.

"Your word is above all others," said Eli. "Above the laws of man. That's what the Bible says. I must please you before others."

Yes.

"They must be removed from Sacred."

Their worship precludes yours, Disciple. While they worship fully, you cannot.

"Disciple?"

Yes. You have followed my commands. You believe in me. You are mine. And I am yours.

"Yes. I will remove them. I will drive them out."

Yes.

The pain in Eli's stomach eased. His heart warmed.

"But what about Tommy? I can't do your work while my home carries rebellion."

You must instill humility in him. Have him anoint your feet, as Mary did to Christ. Wash them, anoint them with oil, and bestow them with a Holy Kiss. Have him pledge obedience.

"I don't think he'll submit," said Eli. "He's—"

A true disciple will instill discipline within his family. Do you understand?

"Yes, Lord."

Go, Eli. We will worship once again.

Eli stood with purpose, with drive in his heart.

Please, Eli. Not yet. You must bow.

Eli stopped, pausing. He took a breath, and then lowered himself to the floor, to his knees.

42

I waited patiently for the Lord; he turned to me and heard my cry. He lifted me out of the slimy pit, out of the mud and mire; he set my feet on a rock and gave me a firm place to stand.

Tommy copied scripture. Pastor David had told him it was how he studied, and how he journaled. He would copy out scripture, and write his thoughts down afterward. He had recommended Psalms.

Be patient, Tommy. You have many more years ahead of you. It may feel like a prison now, with your father your warden, but blink and you'll be free David had texted him.

Tommy wrote in his journal, a composition book he had stolen from school.

I'm trying to be patient. To put my faith in God, in Christ. I'm sixteen, and in less than two years, I'll be an adult, and can do what I'd like. I can leave Sacred. I can be who I want, without fear.

His pencil scratched across the page, the scribbling interrupted by the sound of footsteps. The front door had opened and shut not too long ago, and Tommy had ignored it. Since Sunday, he'd seldom left his room.

His dad hadn't said much to him, only staring with withering looks and condescension. Tommy had expected an argument. Something.

But there had been nothing. Only his father disappearing into the basement, carrying the head of Christ down the stairs.

But footsteps now plodded up the stairs. His father's steps, too heavy for anyone but him.

Tommy waited. The steps paused, and then turned toward his bedroom, and he held his breath, closing his notebook, and his Bible. Maybe he was going to Sam's room—

Thoomp, thoomp, thoomp, the carpet absorbing his dad's heavy feet, and then they stopped at his door.

The doorknob twisted, his father not knocking, the door locked.

TUNK TUNK TUNK and the door shook with his dad's pounding fist.

"Open up, Tommy," said Dad.

"I'm studying," said Tommy. And he was.

"I don't care what you're doing," said Dad. "Open up. I need you downstairs. Now."

"Dad, I'm busy—"

"I will knock down this door," he said, his voice loud. "Don't make me do it."

"Dad, please—"

"Now," he bellowed. "Three, two—"

Tommy scrambled to his feet, and unlocked the door. He stared his father in the eyes for a moment, his dad's full of furor.

Like when he had preached at the church.

"What do you need?" asked Tommy. The back of his knees ached, and he forced his legs still. A twitch surfaced in his right calf, and he forced it to the floor.

"Downstairs," he said, staring. "Let's go."

"I was—"

"Now," he said, and grabbed the back of Tommy's neck, squeezing, pulling and then pushing him ahead of him. Tommy held his breath, letting his father guide him, his clammy hands on the back of his neck, squeezing, memory—

A memory of them at the mall, Tommy a young child, his father guiding him through the crowd, steering him the same way.

Tommy breathed shallow breaths, holding it as he could. His father pushed him to the stairs, and they went down, his father's footsteps heavy behind him. The front door stood in front of him, and something inside screamed for him to run, to break free of his father's grasp and throw the front door open and not look back, to pump his legs, to run until his heart exploded—

Tommy hit the bottom of the steps.

"Kitchen," said his dad, his fingers still gripped on the base of his neck, and he turned him, and Tommy didn't resist, through the living room, past the couch, and where was Mom, where was Sam—

They reached the kitchen. It was empty, except a single

chair, the kitchen table gone, the single chair, with a metal basin at the foot of it.

"Dad, what—"

"You will wash my feet, and anoint them with oil, and cover them in holy kisses." His father spoke in stark coldness, the words looming over him.

"I'm not washing your feet," said Tommy, looking down at the empty chair. "What are you—"

His dad let go of his neck with a final iron squeeze, and then circled in front of him. He sat down in the chair, his feet bare. He placed them beside the basin. He looked up at Tommy.

"If you want to remain in this house, you will wash my feet. If you wish my forgiveness for what you did on Sunday, walking out on my sermon—you will wash my feet."

"Dad—"

His father's voice filled the house. "She began to wash his feet with her tears, and she dried them with her hair, kissing them many times and rubbing them with the perfume. Then Jesus said to her, 'Your sins are forgiven.'"

"I can't—"

"Fill the basin with water, Tommy. Now."

Tommy swallowed down bile, cold sweat rising on his palms, behind his knees, and everything told him to *run, Tommy, run* but he didn't, and grabbed the basin, taking it to the sink. He filled it with water, and returned to the front of his father.

"On your knees," he said.

Tommy took a halting, deep breath, and lowered himself to his knees, to the cold stone tile of the kitchen floor, setting the basin down. A sponge sat there, clean, unused.

"Wash my feet, Tommy," he said. "Obey your father."

Tommy didn't look up, focusing only on his father's feet. They were the feet of a middle-aged man, of a man who had once worked hard on them, but now lounged in loafers, sitting in an office while others toiled.

The sponge, simple, yellow, and Tommy squeezed it as it entered the basin, and then squeezed it again, before wiping it across the bottom of his father's left foot.

"Good," said Dad, staring down at him. "Honor thy father and thy mother, Tommy. You are my child. You obey me. It is commanded by God."

Tommy paused. "Dad—"

"Don't interrupt me. Keep washing. I want them clean."

Tommy inhaled, a short breath, and scrubbed the bottom of his father's foot, stopping to dip the sponge in the basin once again. Small water dripped to the kitchen floor. He scrubbed more.

"For God commanded, 'Honor your father and your mother,' and 'Whoever reviles father or mother must surely die.'" His father's voice washed over him. Tommy's heart thudded, shaking his body, and his legs trembled underneath him. His veins were acid, his body on fire. He washed his father's feet, finishing the left, scrubbing the top of it, dipping the sponge.

"The eye that mocks a father and scorns to obey a mother will be picked out by the ravens of the valley and eaten by the vultures." He paused. "You will not disobey me again. Do you understand me, Tommy?"

Tommy said nothing, forcing a breath in and out, holding back tears.

"Say you understand, Tommy."

"I understand," he said, words catching in his throat. He washed his father's feet.

"Ingram is evil, Tommy. Right down to the core. It was right for us to take back the church. The Bible spells it out, in black and white and red. There's no question as to what he is, and what he plans to do. To pervert the Word of God."

"He just—"

"I won't hear it, Tommy!" yelled his father. "Wash."

Tommy washed his father's feet, dipping, scrubbing, cleaning.

"They're not human, Tommy. They're full of sin, sent by Satan himself, to try and twist the Word of God." He took a mighty breath. "Or do you not know that wrongdoers will not inherit the kingdom of God? Do not be deceived: Neither the sexually immoral nor idolaters nor men who have sex with men nor thieves nor the greedy nor the drunkards nor slanderers nor swindlers will inherit the kingdom of God."

"It's a mis-translation, Dad—"

"You shut your mouth!" he yelled. "Wash."

Tommy washed his father's feet, dipping, scrubbing, cleaning, finishing the other foot, dragging the wet sponge across his father's skin, removing any last trace of dirt or filth.

"And I don't care what the church council votes for, or what the people in Sacred vote for. It doesn't make it right, it doesn't make it good! We know that the law is good if one uses it properly. We also know that the law is made not for the righteous but for lawbreakers and rebels, the ungodly and sinful, the unholy and irreligious, for those who kill their fathers or mothers, for murderers, for the sexually immoral, for those practicing homosexuality, for slave traders and liars and perjurers—and for whatever else is contrary to the sound doctrine that conforms to the gospel concerning the glory of the blessed God, which he entrusted to me." Tommy finished washing. His dad looked down at his feet.

"Now anoint them with oil."

"I don't—"

"Use that oil, there. Rub my feet with it."

Tommy looked at the bottle of oil, a bottle of essential oils his mother had purchased at some point. Tommy reached out with a trembling hand and took it, removing the lid, dabbing the oil into his palms, his hands covered in the viscous oil, smelling sickly sweet, and his stomach bent, but he swallowed down the threat of vomit, and took another breath.

Tommy anointed his father's feet. His hands were not his own, as he rubbed his father's left foot, his slick hands rubbing the flowery oil into his father's foot, covering his harsh skin and coarse hair in the grease.

"They were sent here by Satan, Tommy. They are sin made into flesh, and the world has become blind to it. If we accept it, if we turn a blind eye, we'll be complicit, and we'll be sent straight to Hell alongside them."

Tommy watched his hands as they massaged his father's feet, dabbing on more oil, rubbing the scent into his dad's skin, a bombardment of scripture, of verse, of dogma and hate, hitting him, over and over. He anointed his father, knowing it would be over soon, hearing Pastor David's words, of practicing patience, of seeing the time ahead of him, when he would be free. His father bellowed brimstone and fire, covering Tommy, an onslaught neverending.

Tommy anointed his father's feet, finishing one, working on the other, waiting for this to end, dabbing on more oil, vomit threatening again, and he swallowed it back, bile rising, his throat burning, his body covered in cold sweat.

He anointed his father.

"Good," said Dad. "Now. Kiss them."

The words brought Tommy back to the surface. He looked up, into his father's eyes, who didn't waver.

"I'm not kissing your feet."

"If you are to be forgiven, as the sinful woman was, you must cover them in kisses. It is only right."

A flame found purchase inside of Tommy. The heat burnt away at the cold.

"I'm not kissing your feet," said Tommy, iron in his voice.

"You will—"

"Pastor David is only trying to bring the town back together—"

"He is not! You shut—"

Tommy shouted him down. "I heard you, on the porch. I heard what you said. He wanted you back. He wanted us all back. Instead you hit him. You started this."

"I did no such—"

Tommy forced himself up, his thighs aching. "Yes, you did. You hate him. For what? Because he's gay?"

"He's a sin against God, Tommy—"

Tommy climbed to his feet, standing over his father. "He wants our town to be whole again. He wants the church to be whole again."

His father stared at him, his eyes peering into him. "Have you been talking to him?"

"So what if I have? He actually listens to what I say. He

actually respects my feelings. He doesn't just bark orders and expect obedience. He doesn't just scream at me about sin!"

His father stood then, taller than him, looking down, kicking the chair backward, clattering to the floor. The basin spilled, water covering the tile.

"How dare you! He'll infect you, Tommy! You'll be like him!" His father screamed now, filling the house.

The flame inside Tommy grew. Fury entered him.

"Like him? What would be so wrong about that?" Tommy narrowed his eyes. He stared into his dad. "Do you think we don't know what you do in the basement?"

A moment stood between them, infinite in length, filled with stark silence. The frogs and crickets, a constant soundtrack, disappeared. There was nothing, his father's face changing, a darkness entering it Tommy had never seen.

The moment lingered, a void, a nothing.

His father punched him in the stomach, as hard as he could, and Tommy couldn't breathe, filled with pain.

His dad didn't stop, and hit him again, bringing down his fist across Tommy's cheek, a hard crack against his face as Tommy bent over.

His father said nothing as he beat him, left, right, fists hitting Tommy in the face, in the stomach, in the arms and sides, over and over, Tommy only grunting in horrible pain, the dull thudding of knuckles cracking bones, of flesh absorbing punishment.

Tommy looked up for a moment, to beg, and his father punched him in the teeth, knocking one out. It rattled to the ground, and Tommy reached for it, until his father hit him again, beating him.

Tommy heard nothing but the rattling of his breath, blood streaming down his face, from his forehead, his cheeks, his eyebrows, his nose, his mouth. His ribs screamed in pain, unable to breathe.

His father stopped, standing over him, catching his breath, his knuckles dripping blood.

Tommy's ears rang, and he looked up, eyes lidded, and before he could find purchase in the world again his father grabbed his wrist and dragged him, across the wet floor of the kitchen, his shoulder screaming with pain, through the living room. He had no energy to resist, and his father pulled him into the entrance to the house, and threw open the door, and then pulled him over the threshold, scraping against his skin, onto the porch.

Dad

He pulled Tommy to the edge of the steps, and then pushed him down them, his body tumbling down the half dozen stairs, hitting the concrete at the bottom with a soft thud.

His father stood at the top, and Tommy stared up at him, in a daze.

"For if God did not spare angels when they sinned, but cast them into hell and committed them to chains of gloomy darkness to be kept until the judgment." His father stared. "Leave, and don't come back."

43

David didn't know how Tommy found his way to their doorstep, feebly knocking in the middle of the night.

He slept above them, in the guest bedroom, after a trip to the emergency room.

"A concussion. Stitches in his eyebrow, and in his forehead. Three cracked ribs. Bruised kidneys," said Jason, reading the doctor's notes.

"He's lucky it's only that," said David, sitting across from Jason. The sun had yet to rise. "When I answered the door—I didn't even recognize him." David blinked, a vision of Tommy's bloody and swollen face, looking up at him, half lidded eyes, begging for help.

"Do you think Eli found out?"

"No," said David. "I don't think so."

"What?" asked Jason. "Then why—"

"If Eli knew Tommy was gay, I don't think he'd be alive."

Jason stared at David for a moment in silence, and then stared at the floor, rubbing his eyes.

"What are we going to do with him?"

"He'll stay here, for now," said David. "Until we can find family to take him in."

"And what if we can't?"

"I don't know."

"We can't keep a teenage boy in the house—"

"Jason, please," said David, his voice like a knife. "I'm sorry. Please. He needs to rest. I don't want him to have to stay here."

Jason exhaled. "No, you're right." He paused. "Eli can't get away with this."

David stared. He rubbed his fingers together absently. He had washed his hands of Tommy's blood, soap and hot water, but he still felt it, tacky, the blood drying in dark patches. Tommy had said nothing on the way to the hospital. David had kept him awake. Asked him questions. But Tommy hadn't answered.

David's eyes went to the Bible on the coffee table. He felt a shadow loom over him. Of something large. He turned to look, and there was nothing.

"David—"

"We can't leave," said David. "Not yet."

"I know. I knew it when Tommy knocked on our door."

"I don't—"

David," said Jason, and David's eyes cast to him again. Jason got up, and sat next to him. "Are you okay?"

"I haven't been sleeping well. I keep hearing things. Seeing things," said David. He twisted his neck, and it popped, loudly. "There were circular imprints all over Tommy's body, Jason."

"David—"

"Eli's class ring. It was from Eli's class ring."

"David—" started Jason, and then David had sunk his face into Jason's shoulder, crying. Jason held him as he sobbed.

The tears came, and went. David shook them away, wiping his eyes, backing away from Jason. There was no time for tragedy.

"He won't get away with it."

*

"Agent Walt Fielding."

"Hello, this is Pastor David Ingram. I was given your number by the church, saying you're leading the investigation into Eli Parsons."

"That's correct. Wait—David Ingram. You're the pastor in Sacred."

"Yes," said David, holding the phone to his ear. He stood on the porch, the sun rising. Tommy still slept upstairs. He hadn't stirred since they'd put him to bed.

"You're on my list," said Fielding. "I'm surprised to hear from you."

"I was woken last night," said David. "By a knock at my door. It was Eli's son, Tommy. He'd been beaten half to death."

"Will he make it?"

"Yes," said David. "Concussion. Stitches. Busted ribs.

He's sleeping here, in my home."

"Eli did it."

"Yes," said David. "Without a doubt."

"I was planning a trip," said Fielding. "With my partner. We'd be down there next week, with any luck."

"With the Sheriff involved, I don't know who else to turn to, Agent," said David. "But Eli is dangerous. And getting more dangerous by the day."

Silence from the other end of the phone. "Agent?"

"Sorry, Pastor. I'm thinking. Is he an immediate threat?"

"I don't know." David looked over his front yard. "Maybe."

"Based on what the church told me, we were already preparing to make arrests. We'll be there Monday. Do you think Eli's son will be safe until then?"

"I think so," said David. "We have him. We'll protect him."

"Is there anything else I should know?"

"There are multiple members of the church who believe Eli and Sheriff Bronson are responsible for the death of the former pastor, John Grace. That they covered up his death, making it look like a car accident."

"Jesus Christ," said Fielding. "Sorry, Pastor."

"He forgives you, given the circumstances."

"Call me, if anything else happens," said Fielding. "I'll be in touch once we're in town."

"Thank you, Agent," said David, hanging up. Solomon babbled inside, playing with Jason.

David took a deep breath, and sat down on the porch steps. He took another deep breath, and closed his eyes, his hands together.

Dear Lord.

Tell me Lord. Tell me why. Why a child can suffer so much pain at the hands of someone who claims you? Why do you allow Eli to spread such venom in your name?

David looked down at the porch. The bloodstains had dried, trailing up the steps, concentrated in front of the door. Tommy's blood, his face a wreck, wearing a crimson mask, the remnants of Eli's ring worn on his body. Pieces of him falling to the deck.

The blood was everywhere. He sat in it, next to it, Tommy's beleaguered crawl up the front steps, an exhausted, delirious walk from Eli's home here, miles and miles, the same blood staining the ground from point to point. His suffering serving as a path between the two.

David looked at his hands again. He had washed them.

He still felt the blood.

He picked up his phone, and called Zeke.

"Pastor," answered Zeke, after a handful of rings.

"Hello, Zeke. Tommy—Eli's son. Eli beat him, last night. He's staying with us."

"Is the boy alright?"

"He will be."

"Good to hear," said Zeke. "You need something from me, Pastor?"

"No violence, Zeke," said David. "But I do need your help."

"Say the word."

David stared at the blood. "I need to speak to God."

44

David sat on the island and waited for God.

He had eaten the mushrooms, as instructed.

Zeke had taken him to the island.

"Isolated, and dark. Sit down, eat the mushrooms, and wait."

"Wait for what."

"Wait for God."

Zeke had left him. Told him he'd be back during daylight.

The dark was total, even as David's eyes adjusted. The sounds of insects, of frogs, of gators, surrounded him. The humidity of the summer night sunk in, his skin moist, sweat and bug spray mingling. Sweat dripped from his forehead, his clothes wet.

He waited, for the feeling. For something to change.

He had never done drugs, barely drank. He'd heard about bad trips, from his more adventurous friends living in the city as a student. Jason's art friends.

Zeke said it wasn't a concern.

David waited.

The minutes crept by, and David waited, sitting, his legs crossed in the wet dirt of the swamp.

The sounds of the insects, of the frogs and gators, of the various swamp creatures growing and growing, the din louder and louder, all David could hear, the wetness of his skin wetter and wetter, until he felt like he swam, even as he sat, floating in a pool, the dark growing darker, the slim light vanishing.

The dark grew and grew, surrounding him, the trees, the water, the creatures, the sounds, the sweat, the humidity—

And then David realized it was not those things that surrounded him. Something else did. There was something out there, a force in the dark. Something large, and strong, above him, over him. It was out there, in the scope of his vision but he couldn't see it, the presence of—

The presence of God.

The size of the presence froze him, and he held his breath, his lungs ballooning, feeling the air inside as much as he ever had. It lumbered around him, with mighty ponderous steps, filling the space outside of him.

But he could not see it, looming in the dark.

"Dear Lord," said David. "Is—is it you?" His voice cast into the darkness, into the Great Shape. A great fear arose in David, a natural feeling in the presence of the Creator of All Things. A fear, twinned with awe, feelings not twins, no, because all emotions sat in him at once, pulled from David by his presence.

The Shape moved again, containing the entire swamp, the creatures, the dark, the damp and wet, the mud and tupelos. David could not see it, but knew it moved—

No, not moved, but grew, no, not grew, but became more, the looming size of God bigger still, the swamp bigger inside of him. Because everything stood inside of God, the swamp, the water, the insects and creatures, sound itself, no light because God was light and darkness and everything.

And David realized he did not sit on the island in the middle of the swamp, but instead he sat in God, dwelling within the Lord. The Great Shape did not loom over him, but *around* him, because there was nothing else, and he'd been inside the entirety of his life, the Great Shape moving, dwelling, being, David a small piece of the entirety of everything.

God was there and said nothing. David felt him move, like the shifting of a massive ship at sea, David a humble passenger.

Like Jonah and the great fish.

David spoke again.

"Dear Lord," he started. He must consider his words. He took a breath, the God air filling his lungs. "I have never doubted you, Lord. I have never lost my faith. Even in the worst of times, I have believed and worshiped with my whole heart." He exhaled, breathing in more of the deeply damp air, swimming inside the whole of the Lord. "But I struggle. I struggle with Eli. Not that a sinful man exists, but in that he is a sinful man, compelled by the same faith as me. How can we both claim our faith in you, when our worship is so different? How can a man who sows only suffering and pain still sit in your church?"

Silence fell, a deep silence, no sound, not even the echo of David's heartbeat, and then a deep rumble shook the ground, shook the air, David's bones thrumming under his skin, the Great Shape ponderously moving, shaking, a movement David couldn't understand, far too great—

Then he saw himself.

He sat across from him, this him dressed as a pastor, in collar and tie and suit, in dress shoes and socks and slacks, his belt matching his shoes. He stared ahead, back at himself, and his other did the same.

David raised his arm, and his mirror self matched it. He stood, and the other followed suit, standing. It was him, his eyes in question mark, holding the same expression across.

He walked forward inside the dark body of God and holding caution close, reached out to touch his mirror.

David blinked, and he was gone.

Replaced.

Replaced by Eli, dressed in his Sunday best, staring at him. David stepped back in surprise, and Eli stepped back as well.

Eli had followed him here, and the surprise was replaced with rage, and David raised his fists, charging at Eli, and threw an overhand right, with all the might he had.

The mirror broke, Eli absorbing the blow, the force of the punch obliterating him. Eli's body exploded from the raw power of the blow, inch by inch, from his face through his feet, disappearing into viscera and gore, his skin, muscle, bone, and organs liquefying, splattering back into the nothingness.

But as Eli exploded from the force, David's fist coated

in blood, Eli was there again, from nothing, whole, a mirror, back, and David's rage was hot, molten metal slathered in his guts, and he threw another punch, and Eli exploded again, disappearing into a red rain of blood, flying backward, his body vanishing into liquid, only to be replaced again, another Eli appearing in the space between eyelids.

David swung again, and again, destroying them as they appeared in clouds of gore, but they did not stop appearing, even as the void filled with puddles of their viscous remains.

He swung until he panted, his tongue hanging out as he caught his breath, unable to move, his fists too heavy to swing, but it wasn't Eli anymore, his second mirror gone.

Christ stood in front of him now.

His Lord and Savior—

But no.

It was the Christ from the wall of the Holy Church of Sacred, the Christ of Eli, the Christ of suffering. Jesus the Tortured, Jesus, Son of Pain.

But not the same.

This one was nude.

And whole, the work of Ann Campbell undone.

David took a holy breath, the rich air of the innards of the God Shape, and he found in his hands his bat. The weapon.

He swung it now, at this imposter Christ, and the figure crumpled in front of him, but not into plaster and wood, nor blood and gore, but instead into an oozing slime, smelling of rot and sulfur. The bat launched the gray-white substance across the void, smattering into the gore of Eli, the blood turning pink, the organs covered in what remained of this Christ.

This Christ, he did not replace himself with new copies, no duplicates like Eli, but instead reformed in his eyes, and David screamed, a primal noise that tore at his throat, and he swung again, hitting the figure of this pain-Christ as hard as he could, the wooden bat thudding against the soft rot-cum of the figure, the thick substance flying in bursts across the darkness of in-God.

David swung and swung, the figure reforming, the awful substance covering everything, melding with the blood, David ankle deep in pink, and then as he swung he realized Christ was gone.

Replaced again, but not with Eli.

No, now it was Tommy. He stood there, mirror still, staring at David as David stared back.

"Tommy?" asked David, his throat burning, but Tommy held his stare, questioning, and then broke apart, his body in pieces, cut into disposable slices, the head, the arms, the torso and legs, falling down, into the pool of remnants, of ooze and blood.

Tommy fell, and David reached out, to grab him, to piece back together the broken child, but his hands were not hands, melded now into the bat, the handle and his hands the same, a solid piece, with no visible seam, and he had only the bat, the club, all he could wield.

Tommy fell into the shallow bog David stood in, the pieces vanishing under the surface, and there were no duplicates, no healing. Tommy was gone, and David waited, but his hands remained the bat, and he looked, looked inside the form, but there was only the void and the pinkish swamp he stood in, the remnants of his violence.

"Lord—" he started, but then the ground shook, another great movement from the God around him, and he fell, the shaking too momentous, plunging into the pink, and he couldn't breathe, the surface gone, upended, the world shaking, covered, God, where—

"Pastor David," said a voice.

David opened his eyes. He stared up at Zeke, his pale gray eyes staring down at Eli. The sun was up. His legs were wet.

He looked down, realized he laid on the edge of the island, his legs submerged in the swamp.

"You're lucky a gator didn't get you," said Zeke. "You alright?"

"I'm thirsty," said David. Zeke handed him a water bottle, and David drank, taking small sips, until his throat was soothed.

"You ready to sit up?"

David nodded, and Zeke helped him, sitting up on the banks of the island's swamp. He was caked in mud. His shoulders ached. Zeke stared into his eyes, reading him.

"Did you talk to him?"

David exhaled. "Yes," he said. "I did."

"What did he say?"

David stared down at his mud encrusted hands, filth underneath every fingernail.

David said nothing.

"Let's head back, Zeke."

45

Eli wrote his sermon as Christ watched.

He worked on the floor, the body of Christ in pieces next to him and nude above him, staring down, the head of his Lord next to him on the bookshelf.

The Bible laid open, and he copied from it, scrawling scripture down in his notebook, not in 3x5 cards, he'd learned his lesson, he wouldn't do that again. The notebook wouldn't smudge, the cover protecting from his clammy palms.

He copied scripture, word for word, damn Ingram, damn him—

Tommy's bludgeoned face appeared on the page, and Eli paused, gasping—

Focus, Apostle.

"I'm trying," said Eli. "I'm trying." He wiped the sweat from his eyes, but he missed an errant drop and it fell onto the page, staining his writing—

"Goddamnit!" yelled Eli, throwing his notebook across the basement.

Blasphemy, Eli. You disappoint me.

"No, please," he said, on his hands and knees, crawling toward the head, bowing toward. "I'm sorry, I'm sorry—"

Do you love me?

"Yes, of course, with all my heart, Lord," said Eli. "I do it for you. I do it all for you."

Not good enough. You can do better.

Eli bowed lower, placing his forehead on the cement, his sweat staining the stone.

"Please, Lord, please. I worship you. I love you. I'm sorry. I love you."

Look into my eyes.

Eli raised his head from the floor, his forehead stained with dust and grime. He stared into the pain-filled eyes of Christ.

Who do you belong to?

"I belong to you, Lord. I am yours, body and soul."

Say it again.

"I belong to you, Lord. I am yours, body and soul."

Again.

"I belong to you, Lord. I am yours—"

Eli's phone buzzed, vibrating on the shelf. He had turned it off, he thought—

He looked. Bronson. He answered.

"What is it, Bronson? I'm trying to write a sermon—"

"It's important, Eli." Bronson's voice paused with a trembling hesitation.

"What is it?"

"I got a tip, from a friend in the state police—"

"Get to the point, Bronson."

"I'm telling you, Eli. My friend, he heard through the grapevine—the feds are coming down here, Eli."

"What do you mean, the feds are coming down here?"

"You heard me. They're coming for us."

"What? Why?" asked Eli. "We took the church, fair and square. I told the rep the truth. We haven't broken any federal crimes—"

"The church is a national organization, Eli. And the feds get to decide what is in their jurisdiction. It doesn't matter. They aren't gonna come down and argue with us about whether they can arrest us. We need to get out of town."

"What?" asked Eli. He stared into the eyes of Christ. They wept.

"They're going to come down hard on us. We can't be here when they do. I've got family out west—"

"We cannot leave Sacred, Bronson. This is our town. This is our church."

"This is the feds, Eli. They do not fuck around. If we put up any resistance, Sacred will become another Waco. We can't stand up to them, and we can't just cover up what we've been doing, not anymore."

"We have been chosen by God, Bronson—"

"Eli, that's all well and good, but God is not going to keep us out of prison. When they get here, they're going to dig, and they're going to find out what we did to John. They already know we took the church by force—"

"I don't care, Bronson. We did right by God—"

"Eli, we have to put God aside—"

"Do you hear yourself? Put God aside, like everyone else in town has?"

"Eli—"

"You listen to me. We are not leaving Sacred. We are staying here. We are going to have service on Sunday, and we're going to make sure Ingram and his traitorous lot pay for their sins. Are you a coward, Bronson?"

There was silence on the other end of the phone.

"Answer me, Sheriff. Are you a coward?"

"No."

"Good to hear. We will stop them from worshiping. We will show the strength of our Holy Church of Sacred. And yes, God will protect and defend us. Do you understand?"

More silence.

"Say yes, I understand."

"Yes, I understand," said Bronson.

"Good," said Eli. "I'll call you when I'm done writing. Don't disturb me."

Eli hung up, and slid his phone back to where it was, putting it on do not disturb.

"I'm sorry," he said, bowing his head again.

No, you did well. Bronson is a weak man.

"We can't leave," said Eli. "We cannot lose the church."

Yes, my Apostle. Yes.

Eli took a great breath and walked over to his notebook. He picked it up, ripping out the sweat-stained page, and then kneeling next to his Bible.

He wrote his sermon under Christ's watchful eyes.

46

David came home before noon, walking upstairs past Tommy, who played with Solomon in the living room.

Jason sat reading in the bedroom.

"David—"

"Please, let me shower," he said, their eyes meeting for a moment. Jason took a breath and nodded, and David went into the bathroom, turning on the shower, letting the hot water run.

He stepped in wearing his mud stained clothes, letting the hot water rinse them, murky water running down the drain. David washed the worse of the mud off before he stripped and showered, rinsing away the dirt and grime.

The mud sloughed off him as he washed. He removed the grime, the muck, the caked on bug spray, the blood, the substance.

He cleaned himself with his hands. His hands were his hands.

But God remained all around him.

David got out, dried off.

Jason still sat, reading. Waiting, as David slid on clothes, his hair still wet.

David sat across from him, on the foot of the bed.

Jason slid a bookmark into place and put his book down, sitting in their lone chair in the bedroom. He looked at David.

"Where have you been?" he asked. His voice was quiet.

"I was with Zeke. I told you that."

"You said you were going to visit with him. To discuss Eli. You didn't say you were going to be gone all night. You didn't say you wouldn't be answering your phone for twelve hours—"

"Service out there is bad," said David. "We were out in the swamp, where it's even worse."

"Why were you covered in mud?" asked Jason. "What were you doing out there?"

"I—I needed to talk to God, Jason."

"What does that mean—"

"I don't know," said David. "I don't know." He buried his face in his hands.

Silence hung between them.

"I don't know."

47

David was up before the sun. He got out of bed soundlessly, showering, sweating even as he dressed, the heat never leaving the house.

He had been up late, working on his sermon, into the night, Jason, Solomon and Tommy long asleep.

Sleep had been brief, the alarm buzzing just as he closed his eyes. A pot of coffee would forestall his exhaustion. He could crash after the service.

Ann arrived just after dawn. David sat on the porch, drinking a mug of coffee as she pulled up.

"Pastor."

"Ann," he said. He gestured toward the other chair. "I was going to finish my coffee."

Ann sat, leaning her solid frame down into the seat.

"You expecting a good crowd today?"

"I don't know," said David. "I hope so."

They set up chairs after David had finished his coffee. They filled the house with a hundred chairs. As they set them up, Jason came downstairs, and finished tidying up, with Sol soon waking up too, and Ann played with him as they prepped for the arrival of the congregation.

The congregation arrived en masse.

John's loyal arrived, the house filling, but then more came. Some new faces, that David didn't know. Word had spread of the home service, and Sacred had arrived. Some new to the church, some who had left, young and old alike. At least a dozen new faces, some with children. The house filled more, with too many people.

"If you can stand, we're going to ask you to stand for the service, leaving chairs for those who can't handle it. And don't be shy if you need a chair," shouted Jason as they arrived, as people shuffled around inside, waiting in the front yard, in the back yard, in the kitchen. David and Laurie stood at the front door, as Ann and Jason and Zeke and Tommy shuffled the chairs inside, chairs folded back up and put outside, simply not enough room.

But it wasn't only new faces. It was old faces as well, some of those who'd been loyal to Eli. A half dozen families, faces he had seen previously. Those who had left the chapel with Eli, and had attended his lone service thus far.

They came, hats in hands.

"I'm sorry, Pastor. I truly am."

"Eli—I thought he had the best interests of the church in mind. I—I was wrong."

"We want in the true Holy Church of Sacred."

David smiled, and shook their hands, and accepted their apologies, and ushered them in, and told them to try and find room.

The box fans blew loud, the windows and doors open, but the heat still settled in the house, with men and women alike fanning themselves, rivulets of sweat running down faces, and shirts and dresses sticking to skin.

But still, they waited, gathering, crowding around inside.

"Can everyone hear me?" asked David, standing in the small corner of the living room. All assented. He nodded at Laurie, who stood up.

They prayed.

They sang.

The house was filled with the song of Christ, of God the Father, of the Holy Spirit. They belted out the lyrics, chests bursting with the songs of God, over the box fans.

Laurie paused, her forehead wet.

"Our scripture for today," she said, taking a deep breath. "Psalm 23:4. Even though I walk through the valley of the shadow of death, I fear no evil, for You are with me; Your rod and Your staff, they comfort me."

Laurie paused, and then took David's seat as he rose. He stood tucked in the corner, looking out over the elderly and handicapped, sitting in small rows, with everyone else standing.

"A familiar scripture. Perhaps the most known verse in the entire world. From Psalms, a book I revisit often. Is it because I share a name with King David? I don't know. It probably doesn't hurt." A light chuckle echoed, and David smiled.

"But it speaks to God as a shepherd. As our leader. As

our guide. We are but sheep in his presence. It is the metaphor I appreciate. The Bible is oftentimes poetic, but there is nothing in this verse that is literal. It is all metaphor. It is all symbol. Maybe it's because I'm a pastor, but I love scripture like this. It is rich with symbolism, and easy to understand, at that. 'Even though I walk through the valley of the shadow of death, I fear no evil, for You are with me.' We've all walked through this valley, in our lives. We've all faced situations that have felt like this." David paused. "We've all entered valleys in life. Deep troughs in the land, and we enter, seeing no other way forward. And we lose sight of the world. There is nothing but the valley, our vision dominated by the towering walls, and the slim path in front of us. The only choice is forward or back."

"'You are with me' says the scripture. God is with us. We are told, over and over, that God is omnipresent. That he is everywhere, at all times. We are told this as children. I remember it distinctly. And sometimes, I think we're told it as children as a reminder to behave ourselves, even when no one is watching, because it isn't true. Someone is watching. God is watching. That God is some great policeman in the sky, watching to make sure we don't break his laws. And you may be led to believe that on this verse alone. His rod and his staff, the scripture mentions. If you don't know, the rod and staff were tools of shepherds. The rod, a shorter tool, almost like a club, the staff, longer, with a crook at the end. Both used to move sheep, nudge them, the crook of the staff used to direct them when they've lost their way. The rod could also be used to defend the herd, a weapon against wolves or other wild animals."

"Tools. Maybe even weapons. To control, primarily.

But I want you to think about the second half of that verse. 'They comfort me.'" David looked at the humid faces of his congregation. They looked back. They listened.

"The rod and staff bring comfort. Because they are not weapons, not against the sheep. They are tools. They bring comfort because they guide us forward. When fear, or anger, or sadness could overwhelm us while in the valley—the Lord guides us forward. His presence provides us comfort. He is our guide, for when we are in the valley. When we need help, we take a moment, take a breath, and feel him there, guiding us—"

Everything moved quickly then.

A screeching of brakes outside, and David waited for the crash, but there was none, instead only hollow thoomps, one, two, three, four, five, in quick succession.

The crash happened then, not outside, but in, as windows broke inside the house, as heavy thuds landed on the floor, some breaking windows, others hitting members of the congregation.

The gas filled the house quickly, even with the box fans and the open windows, the gas noxious—

"Tear gas!" yelled Zeke.

"Everyone calmly—" started David, but then the room was filled with acrid, yellow smoke, and his eyes burned, first only slightly, and then they screamed in pain, the smoke too much, the house filled with it, and everyone ran for the exits, feet stomping on wooden floors, chairs pushed over, the elderly and infirm reaching for help, grunts and screams of fear as the congregation ran for the front and back doors.

Tears poured from his eyes, his nose running, his face wet and he squinted, reaching out in front of him. He saw

Mrs. Andrews, sprawled on the ground, her eyes shut against the gas, reaching, and he grabbed her hand.

"I'm here," he said, into her ear, and lifted her to her feet, his arms locked around her waist, pulling her out of the living room, the center of the house, away from the worst of the tear gas. There was still scrambling, back and forth, they had kicked the box fan over on the way out, and it blew senselessly into the air.

David helped her to the front door, and someone was there, and they took her hands, and David ran back, more people helping others on their way out of the house. He pulled his shirt over his mouth and nose.

David waded through the yellow smoke, his eyes screaming in pain, his nose clogged with snot, holding thin fabric over his face. His house was a maze, and he looked for others.

He blinked, and he was inside the Great Shape. The Formless God, now filled with tear gas, with choking poison. There was no way out from him, for he was everything. They were inside him now, inside the dark cloud of yellow smoke, God Containing All. No matter where he went, he was still inside. God watched them.

And then Zeke was there, deep in the smoke, and David was in his home again.

"Everyone's out. I checked every room," Zeke said, his face swollen and wet, tears pouring from him. His eyes were red, and they ran from the house, out on the patio, into the yard, where everyone had gathered. The hose was on, washing people's eyes and faces.

Mr. Danden sat on the ground, his head pouring blood. One of the grenades at struck him in the scalp. Ann held a towel to it, keeping pressure.

"I've already called 911," said Jason, holding Sol.

"How is Sol?" asked David, wiping at his eyes with his sleeve.

"I covered his face," said Jason. "I think he avoided the worst of it." David kissed Sol, once, twice, and then Jason, squeezing them both.

"How are you?"

"I'll live," said Jason. "Help them. Be their pastor."

David went from member to member, checking on them. The paramedics arrived within twenty minutes, multiple ambulances, helping those who needed it most, taking Mr. Danden away, lights flashing.

People left, as they were able. The tear gas dispersed.

Laurie sat on the porch steps, watching. Her hands trembled as she drank water.

David sat next to her.

"How are you feeling?"

"It hurts to breathe," she said. "And I can't see. But I'll live."

"Eli," said David. "Bronson."

"Did anyone see who did it?"

"No," said David. "But who else has tear gas?"

Laurie stared over the front yard, only a few left.

"You didn't get to finish your sermon," she said.

"No," said David. "I didn't." He blinked hard, his eyes still burning. "I was going to continue to the next verse." He took a harsh breath. "You prepare a table before me in the presence of my enemies."

"What are we going to do, David?"

David exhaled, forcing building anger out of him. "We're

going to do nothing, Laurie. Eli will reap what he sows. To-morrow."

He found Zeke. Zeke sat alone, intermittently spitting up globs of mucus, wiping his nose with a spare handkerchief.

"How you doing?"

Zeke stared up at him, his eyes blood red. He shook his head.

"I don't know, Pastor. I don't know."

David crouched next to him.

"Zeke—"

A vision of the God inside the gas clung to him.

"Yes, Pastor?"

"The mushrooms—" David started. "Do they—do they have aftereffects?"

"They shouldn't," said Zeke. "D'you see something?"

David stared into his crimson eyes.

"It was nothing."

48

Where were they?

Where was his congregation?

Eli looked out from near the pulpit, the head of Christ beside him, staring out over the pews.

Empty pews.

Eli preached, but his stomach ached, a cold hollow sitting inside. There were less here than last Sunday. Less by far, a couple dozen less. The Brooks, the Coopers, the Marshes—

They weren't here, along others, others he couldn't name, but those he had counted among his people, among his followers, his congregation. No one had filled in the empty pews left by Ingram and his people, and now the left side of the church was emptier still. Bronson still sat tall, now in the front row, but there was no one behind him, only sparse attendance.

The church was hot today, hot as it had ever been, the rising sun heating up the building, and Eli sweat, as did everyone else. They stared up at him, listening.

Were they listening?

"We are at war. Make no mistake," he said. He glanced over at the sorrow filled eyes of Christ, who stared back at him now, and Eli felt his presence, felt his commands. "Society is trying to change us. And for the longest time, I thought Sacred could withstand it. Maybe because we're a little tiny town, because of where we are, and how tight-knit we are, that we'd be able to resist the world."

Eli reached for the small towel, sweat running down his face, and he wiped at it, but the towel was already drenched—

Eli. Focus.

Eli put the towel back, staring at Christ, Eli's gaze meeting his eyes, and he swallowed.

"But we couldn't. And I would say Ingram brought it to our town, but it was here before him. The Church in Raleigh, deciding our morals for us. And even our late pastor, and his wife, trying to sway our church for—"

A bead of sweat rolled into Eli's eye, and he wiped at it—

John's bludgeoned face lurked behind his eyelids, black and red, blood and broken bones, John reaching for him with grasping fingers, feeble and weak, age and injury leaving him helpless, struggling as Eli and Bronson dragged him into the swamp, his body broken, shaking as he drowned, breathing in murky water.

Eli swallowed, opening his eyes, the church quiet, the meager congregation staring at him.

"—for—" he started, looking back at his notebook. "—for evil. Trying to sway our church for evil."

"They've turned us against each other. They've set us to battle, brother against brother. When we should be united. When we should become warriors in God's name, fighting for what he wants. Not pitting father against—"

Tommy's face, staring up at him, and Eli's fist, smashing down across it, a loud crack echoing. Tommy begging, begging for mercy, and Eli giving only suffering. Eli swung hard, punishing Tommy, punishing him, he knew, he knew—

Eli squeezed the notebook, contorting the tender spine.

His hand squeezed the Bible, hard, rubbing the leather texture, the pebbled feeling between thumb and forefinger.

"—father against son."

The congregation stared at him. Eli preached, his face covered in sweat. He glanced again to the head of Christ, his Lord, his Savior, his—

My Disciple. My Apostle. Focus.

Eli nodded, nodded.

"Jeremiah 51:20. "You are my war club, my weapon for battle—with you I shatter nations, with you I destroy kingdoms, with you I shatter horse and rider, with you I shatter chariot and driver, with you I shatter man and woman, with you I shatter old man and youth, with you I shatter young man and young woman, with you I shatter shepherd and flock, with you I shatter farmer and oxen, with you I shatter governors and officials." Eli yelled each word, squeezing the notebook in his hand, the paper contorting, his words bending under his fist. "We are the Lord's weapon! We are his instrument of war! A weapon for battle—"

The double doors of the congregation opened then, letting in a swath of sunlight, a figure in shadow. They marched in, avoiding eye contact with Eli, looking around the chapel, eyes scanning.

Eli squinted. It was Mark Brooks, one of the men he had counted on, who hadn't attended. He walked to a family, sitting in the pews. The Lincolns. Adam, Joan, and—Eli couldn't remember the child's name. Adam owned the Ford dealership in Marshall, Eli had bought his truck from him—

Mark whispered something to him, a back and forth, in hushed words.

"Mark, why are you interrupting—" said Eli.

Mark ignored him, only talking to Adam, and nodding emphatically.

"Mark—"

Adam stood up then, gesturing to Joan, and their child, a boy, and they rose too, moving past him, and leaving, Joan leading the boy by the hand.

"Adam, what is this—"

Adam stood, and stared at Eli.

"I was just told the church service Ingram is holding in his home was tear gassed. Right in the middle of the service. Multiple grenades were shot into the home."

Eli stared back, saying nothing.

"Nothing?" asked Adam. "Nothing to say?" Adam's eyes went to Bronson, still sitting, still staring forward, his eyes locked. He didn't flinch.

"I don't know what you think you're doing, Eli," said Adam. "But I won't be a part of it."

Adam left then, with Mark beside him.

"We are at war, Adam!" yelled Eli, barking, spittle flying. Adam didn't turn around, both him and Mark leaving the chapel. Others watched, and then another couple rose.

"Is that true, Pastor?" asked a man, Eli couldn't remember—

"We are at war," he said, his first instinct.

The man stared for a moment, and left, his wife with him. Another couple left then, following, and then another.

A dozen people followed Adam out. Less than two dozen remained, sitting, waiting, staring.

Eli swiped at the sweat that poured down his face with his shirt sleeve, but it did nothing, the shirt soaked through, and his eyes burned with the salt.

He turned and stared at Christ.

Finish your sermon, Disciple.

Eli stared at the head, and nodded, desperately, and finished his sermon.

49

Eli's shoulders bowed with the weight.

He bent, broken in half, worshiping his Lord. The head of Christ above him, staring up at his own father in pain, tortured, suffering forever.

Eli pressed his forehead into the cement floor, the house quiet above him. Angie had left, taken Sam, gone to her mother's, and he could focus, he could concentrate. He could pray.

Why God, why? He had done what was asked. He had fought the evil present in Sacred. He had taken back the church from the sinful men who had infiltrated the town, from the darkness that had insinuated itself into Laurie Grace, which had infected John.

John's fingers, grasping, squeezing his arm, tight, as he

breathed in swamp water, his body convulsing as he died, a Man of God—

Eli opened his eyes, away from the image, and he looked up into Christ's eyes. He pleaded.

"I don't understand," he said. "I did what was necessary. I did what was right. I have been faithful. I have never turned away from you. Even as—"

Eli closed his eyes and Tommy was there, blood filling his mouth, spilling onto the floor, staining the carpet. His hands up, begging—

"Please," he said, staring, his voice cracking. "Please—"

You beg me, Apostle. You beg, for what?

"I have followed your commands, Lord. I have done as you've asked. But still, still, they leave the church in droves. Every action I have taken has failed. What did I do wrong?"

They know, Eli.

"What?" he asked. Sour acid filled Eli, he had pushed the thought away, but now, it came surging back, and he swallowed back bile.

Tommy.

"No, he wouldn't. He wouldn't say a word, not after—"

You let him live. Why did you let him live, with the knowledge he has? Out of the house, out of your control? Away from the Lord, into the den of sin?

"No no no no no no no. He wouldn't he wouldn't, he doesn't know, he only said—"

Eli squeezed his fists, rising to his feet, pacing across the floor of the basement, barefoot, leaving wet footprints across the dust, his feet soaked in sweat and filth.

"They don't know they don't know—"

They do know. Or they will. Unless you do something

about it.

Eli froze, standing, and stared at Christ, their eyes meeting, Eli looking into eyes of pain. He approached the head, glaring.

"I don't—"

They are coming, Disciple. They are coming, Apostle. Bronson spoke the truth. They will take you, and him, and the church.

"I can't stay—"

You must stay. You are a weapon of the Lord, Apostle. You are my club. My axe. My hammer and anvil. You must show them the true power of the Lord.

"How?"

Bow.

Eli stopped, dropping to his knees, before Christ. He bowed, his body covered in sweat and dust, worshiping, submitting.

Send them to Hell, Apostle. All of them. Punish them for their sins.

Eli raised his head, staring up.

"But Tommy—"

Do you disobey me?

Eli lowered his head, closing his eyes.

"No, Lord. No. But, the church—"

Do not let them have it. No matter the cost.

"Yes, Lord. Yes."

Do you understand me?

"Yes, Lord. Yes, I understand."

Tommy was there again, in his eyes, begging, blood, Eli's fists the weapons of God, the grasping hands of John Grace, the firm grip on a Bible, the stock of a rifle in his hands—

Eli opened his eyes, and then bowed again, swinging down to the floor, his head smacking against the concrete, and he saw stars behind his eyes, but Tommy was gone, John was gone, and Eli did it again, smashing his forehead into the concrete, and blood welled from his forehead, the skin split, and he smashed it again, blood spilling down over his face, mixing with the sweat, warmth covering him, the blood staining the concrete.

He smashed it a final time, his head split open, the blood flicking across the concrete floor, the pain filling Eli's head, threatening him with darkness, but he opened his eyes, the world now red, and he stared into the eyes of Christ.

He suffered.

50

Laurie stared at her eyes in the mirror. Red skeins of veins shot through the whites, staining them nearly pink.

She had rinsed them for hours when she had gotten home, but the exposure to the gas would only fade with time. That's what the medic had told her, at least.

Laurie left the mirror, finding her glass of wine sitting on the kitchen counter, as she had left it. As she had gotten older, she had grown accustomed to a glass a night. To calm her down, help her sleep. It had gotten harder to come by.

But that was before John had died.

Now—well, now it wasn't a glass. More like two. Sometimes three. Sometimes, well—sometimes it was the whole bottle.

She kept the house cold, the AC blasting twenty-four

hours a day during the summer, and the wine warmed her, but more than skin deep. It warmed the cold part inside only John had touched, the part of her he reached with gentle words and a soft voice and a quiet strength that had given her more faith than God's Word ever had.

Or maybe it just numbed it.

She swallowed the last of her glass, and then filled it again, emptying the bottle. Her eyes burned less, as the wine worked its way into her.

She heard the sound then. The sound of multiple car engines outside, climbing up the slope of their long driveway, and a brief glance saw the slight reflection of headlights.

John had never noticed visitors. He would write his sermons at church in the winter, but in the summer he worked in his home office, studying, consulting, transcribing verse after verse, reading other sermons, comparing notes. She'd knock on his door, and leave him a sandwich, a drink, and he would glance at her, surprised it was time for a meal.

But Laurie always had. Observant was a word for it, alert, maybe—but her mother had always called her *squirrelly.* The slightest sound, the barest movement, and Laurie would notice.

Ready to dart away at anything her mother had said.

But Laurie didn't dart away at the sound of the engines. She stood in the kitchen, with her glass of wine. She was too old to run. Too tired.

There was a knock at the door. She waited a moment longer, and then tipped the glass to her lips, swallowing the entire thing, wiping at the thin red line that leaked from her.

Another knock.

Laurie placed the glass back on the counter, where she

just had it, and answered the door.

Bronson stood there, as large as the night. Eli was behind him. He held the head of Christ in his arms. His forehead was bandaged.

Bronson loomed, his mustache dark on his face, his eyes hollow pits. Eli's eyes glared at her, open wide. Bronson's two deputies stood on the front path, behind them both.

Laurie stood there, the door open, and then turned and walked away, back into the kitchen.

"If you're going to come in, leave the two idiots outside," she said. She heard the door shut behind her. "Y'all want anything to drink?"

There was no answer. Laurie was out of sight of the front door, and grabbed her phone from her pocket, and dialed David's number, silencing the audio, and then sliding it back into her pocket.

"Nothing?" she asked again, and then she turned around to see Bronson there, looming. "Well, fine. Suit yourself. I'm going to have some wine." She looked at the bottles on the shelf. Most were recent.

She grabbed the highest bottle. It was time.

Bronson stared at her, but she ignored him. She uncorked the bottle, and then poured herself a tall glass, almost half the bottle.

"Y'all want to talk in the living room?" she asked, speaking past Bronson. She passed him, with Eli sitting on the couch, the head of Christ in his lap, his hands holding the sides of the head.

No, not holding. Caressing.

Laurie sat down, opposite Eli. Bronson still stood, behind her. She sensed him there. She ignored him.

She wondered if David had answered her call.

"I didn't expect y'all, so late on a Sunday night," she said, forcing a smile.

Laurie smelled the wine, softly swirling it in her glass. She took a sip, and let the taste linger in her mouth. It was good. John should have tasted it. Maybe tonight.

"Laurie—" started Eli, watching her, his eyes wide, his pupils expanding.

"You really should have called, before you came over," she said. "I would have made you something. Shame you didn't bring Angie, or the boys. Although I know you and Tommy are a little bit on the outs. Teenagers. What can you do?"

"It didn't have to be this way, Laurie," said Eli, staring at her, his fingers sliding across the head in his lap.

"Be what way, Eli?"

"Don't play dumb, Laurie."

"I'm not playing anything. Sometimes, Eli, I just don't know what you mean."

Eli stared at her, pursed his lips. "You didn't have to push John the way you did. You didn't have to bring in Ingram. You didn't have to force my hand—"

"Force your hand?" she asked. "Oh darlin'. There's always a choice. Always a choice."

"God told me—"

"Did he?" asked Laurie. She looked at Eli. Sweat beaded on his forehead, despite the chill of the AC.

"He speaks—"

"This is a good wine, Eli," said Laurie. "Great, even. As far as I can tell, at least." She smiled. "John bought it for us, right after we got married. It was expensive. Too expensive.

But you know, John was a romantic. Thought we'd open it on our fiftieth anniversary. Told me we'd enjoy it then. And don't get me wrong—"

"Laurie, stop—"

"—and don't get me wrong, I loved John. Loved him so, so much. But when we got married, I wasn't thinking fifty years down the road. That felt like an impossible length of time. Couldn't wrap my head around it. But John—John was already thinking about it. He knew we would get there. He had faith." She took another sip. Savored it. "And I wish he was here to taste it. He always saw the best in people, me included." She stared at Eli. "And you, Eli. He always saw the best in you. No matter how much you argued about the direction of the church. He saw you had faith. That you cared. He thought that was why you argued. Why you fought. That you still wanted the best for the church. He thought—he thought you were a good man."

Eli stared at her, silent now, his eyes bulging. Bronson loomed behind her.

"Proved him wrong, though, didn't you?" she asked. "You showed him who you really are. And it took a little bit longer, but you showed Sacred, too."

"You bitch—"

"We made it forty three years, Eli. Not quite to fifty. Almost, though. Until you and your police dog killed my husband in the swamp."

"Shut the fuck up, bitch," said Bronson, his voice cold.

"No one's talking to you, mutt," said Laurie, not looking back. "The adults are speaking."

"It's your fault this happened," said Eli.

"Never your fault, huh? I forced your hand," said Laurie.

"God told you to. Did he tell you to beat your boy into a pulp, too? Hope you like prison, Eli."

"God will exonerate me," said Eli, his eyes blistering, his nostrils wide.

"I bet he will," said Laurie. She tipped back the wine glass, swallowing the last half of it in one fell swoop.

It warmed her, like John had.

"Still some of that wine left, Eli," she said. "I'm guessing you don't want any. We can save it for John." She stared at him. "What are you waiting for? If it's my forgiveness, you'll be waiting a while—"

Bronson's night stick hit her in the side of the head and a blast of pain ripped through her, numbed by the wine. Her eyes swam, and she fell to the floor.

Bronson threw the coffee table aside, and booted her in the stomach, and her air left her, she couldn't breathe—

He booted her again, this time in the head, and her nose broke with a CRACK, and blood ran down her face in a torrent. She wiped at the stream of red leaking from her, the sleeve of her blouse soaking through.

Eli watched, the head of Christ in his lap. He caressed it.

Laurie reached for the wine glass, breaking it on the floor and swiping at Bronson's arm. She cut him, and he cursed, and then booted her again, and again, the steel toe of his boots cutting into her, over and over.

She couldn't breathe, feeling cuts open up, bones breaking, in her arm, her ribs, and she tried to claw her way to her feet, but he stepped on her fingers, breaking them, and she screamed with what little breath she had.

Bronson loomed over her, and she turned, and stared into Eli's eyes. His lips moved, soundlessly.

Bronson raised his boot above her, and she closed her eyes. She saw John there.

Bronson's boot fell on her throat, and she couldn't breathe, she couldn't breathe, and then there was darkness.

*

David studied. He didn't notice the voicemail on his phone until a few minutes later.

He listened, his chest tightening. The muffled voices of Laurie, of Eli. Of Bronson.

They'd kill her.

It cut off after two minutes. He called Zeke first.

"I'm at the house," said Zeke. "I'll head your way, but can't make no promises about time. Just get over there."

"I can't leave Jason and the kids alone—"

"I'll call Ann. She'll cover your house. Go to Laurie."

Jason was reading. Tommy played with Sol.

"Eli and Bronson are at Laurie's. I'm heading over."

"David—"

"I have to do something."

"I can help," said Tommy, looking up.

"No," said David. "You stay here. Ann and Zeke will be here shortly. Be safe."

David grabbed his bat and left, jumping into the Prius and driving off.

They would be armed, he knew. Bronson's deputies might be there too. But he had to do something.

It was a short drive, and he pushed the car to its limit, speeding down the narrow two lane roads that connected the two houses.

Headlights passed him, but he saw nothing but the road ahead of him.

Only Laurie's car sat in the driveway when he arrived.

Please. Please.

He grabbed the bat and rushed inside.

He found Laurie. Her body broken.

David called Jason, his hands shaking.

No answer.

He rushed back to the car.

51

Ann watched out the front window, the curtains drawn. The window was gone, broken by the tear gas attack, her eyes still tender.

She saw the headlights. Three vehicles. Two sheriff's cruisers, and Eli's truck. Ann slid the barrel of her shotgun out the window.

"They're here," she said, quietly. "Jason, take Solomon upstairs. Lock yourself into your bedroom. Put furniture in front of the door. Do not open it for anyone but me or David."

"Ann—"

"No," she said, her voice low and hard, staring out the window. They were slow to exit their cruisers. Zeke would be here soon. Maybe they could stall—"

"I can help," said Tommy.

"No, Tommy. Upstairs—"

Eli approached the house, the Sheriff and his two deputies behind. Eli held the head of Christ, the very same Ann had removed.

"We want Tommy," said Eli. "Hand him over, and we'll leave, Ingram."

"I have a gun on you, Eli," said Ann, shouting out the window. "Any closer, and I shoot."

Bronson and the deputies took a step backward, but Eli stood still.

"Ann Campbell." He stared at the house. "Give me back my son. We don't want any trouble."

"I'm sure Laurie is safe and sound, then," she said. She heard Jason go upstairs behind her. A door lock. The sound of a dresser scraped along the floor.

Eli flinched, and narrowed his eyes, the front porch light casting sharp light at him.

"Where's Ingram?" asked Eli. "Let me speak to him."

"You're talking to me. Leave, or I start firing. You won't be the first man I've killed."

Bronson still walked backward, as did his two deputies, but Ann focused only on Eli, who remained in place.

"You can't shoot us all, Campbell. We will kill everyone in the house. We only want Tommy—"

The front door opened.

Ann realized. Tommy. He hadn't gone upstairs.

He was out the front door before she could move, and then moved down the front steps, and approached Eli, and Tommy was blocking her shot. Eli grabbed him with an arm, Christ in one hand, Eli using his son as a human shield, and something flew past Ann, through the window, through the curtains—

Ann turned, saw it—

A flashbang.

She moved, pushing up tired legs, sprinting away from it, and then it exploded, and waves of concussive light and sound blasted her, half deaf and blind, on the floor, and she crawled to a side table and knocked it over, the front door opening.

She hid behind it and fired, gunfire erupting.

*

"Dad, please—"

The two deputies rushed in and gunfire exploded from inside the house. Tommy struggled against his father's grasp, and pushed away from him, but Bronson was there, who clubbed him, and Tommy fell hard, smacking against the ground.

Bronson watched the door, riot gun to his shoulder, but there was no more gunfire.

"Morrison? Gilbert?" he bellowed, but there was no response. Nor any movement from Campbell.

"They don't matter," said Eli. "Help me."

Tommy pushed to his feet, facing his dad, Bronson still facing the door. His father stared, holding the head of Christ, his eyes dark.

"Dad—" started Tommy, but then he saw the eyes of his father, staring, nothing human in them, and he ran.

"Sheriff," said his father from behind him, and then the shotgun roared, ringing through the still night air, and a flare of screaming pain erupted from his right leg, and he fell, his leg failing him.

Tommy screamed, rolling over, seeing his leg, the calf and knee shredded, blood pouring from it. He couldn't move it, couldn't bend, the bones broken, and the pain almost overwhelmed him.

His eyes scanned for Bronson or his dad, but they weren't there, and Tommy rolled over, and crawled, pushing with his one working leg, the pain roaring through, leaving a trail of blood behind him, the meat and bone of his leg scraping across the dry soil.

He knew Zeke would be there, that David would be back. If he could buy some time—

And then a hand grabbed his good ankle, and Bronson was there, pulling him across the ground, and Tommy's hands sunk into the dirt, scrabbling for purchase.

"If we had more time, Thomas, you would have carried it here yourself," said his dad, and Tommy looked, and saw it, and a horror rose inside him, a deep, striking fear—

The cross was there, laid on the ground. It was attached to some cross bracing, to stand up.

No no no no no—

Bronson grabbed him by the throat and hair, and pulled him toward it. Tommy struggled, reaching for Bronson's eyes, clawing at them—

Bronson clubbed him again in the temple, and Tommy was dazed, his eyes foggy, and Bronson dragged him toward the cross, and laid him across it, his wrecked leg screaming in pain, rolling through him in torrents, the only thing keeping him conscious.

"I thought you had understood, Tommy. I thought

you had understood the sacrifice our Lord and Savior Jesus Christ had suffered through. But it's clear you didn't. You side with the sinners. I won't abide it. I can't abide it. Through sacrifice, you'll understand. Through suffering, you'll see Heaven."

Tommy blinked, trying to focus, trying to struggle, but a weight was on him, and it was Bronson, stepping on his arm and his throat, and he couldn't move, no matter how hard he pushed—

"Don't struggle, son," said Bronson, Tommy focusing as the barrel of the shotgun pressed to his head. He stopped struggling, tears rolling from his eyes.

"Dad," he said. "Please, don't do this. Please."

His father came into view. He no longer carried the head of Christ. Instead, he carried a one handed sledge, gripped tightly in his right. In his left, nails. Long, over six inches long, and pointed. He knelt next to Tommy. Tommy stared at him, his father's eyes black.

"You'll thank me, when we meet again," he said, and holding the nail over Tommy's wrist, brought the sledge down as hard as he could.

Tommy screamed as the nail drove his skin, through muscle, breaking tendon, the steel nail driving between ulna and radius, and through the muscle and skin on the other side, the point embedded in the wood. Tommy screamed, his voice hoarse, and his father hammered again, and again, until the nail was deep in the wood.

The pain filled Tommy, and he couldn't feel his hand, the fingers not answering his call, and Bronson switched sides, placing his weight on the other arm. He stared down at Tommy, his eyes narrowed, his mouth tightened into a sneer.

Tommy breathed ragged breaths, his body pain. He turned to face his father again. He had no strength to struggle. He barely had breath.

His father took a nail, and placed it carefully in the space between bones, and rearing back, drove the nail through Tommy, and he screamed again with what little breath he had, the blood leaking from the entry and exit wounds in both wrists now.

His body shook with the pain, and his father drove the nail deeper into the wood, Tommy's body reverberating with each blow, and both hands were numb, agony shooting down both arms, and Bronson removed the shotgun from his forehead with a slight departing pressure.

"We need to hurry," said Bronson. "Let's get it up."

Tommy couldn't move, only hurt, and they pushed the cross up, and his body rocked against it as it went vertical, and he hung, his shoulders wrenched immediately, desperately pressing against the wood with his one good leg, holding himself up, impossible to breathe—

They stood there, the two of them, and Tommy looked down from above them, blood pouring from his wrists and his leg. His shoulders strained, agony ripping through his arms, holding himself up with his good leg.

"His leg, Sheriff," said his father, and Tommy looked at him with harrowed eyes, but he was only an object now, and Bronson pulled his shotgun to his shoulder and aimed at Tommy's other leg, the blast rolling through the air, the buckshot obliterating Tommy's knee, his leg hanging, faint bone and sinew keeping him together, blood pouring from him.

He fell, the rest of his body weight pulling, and his shoulders dislocated with two sudden pops, and the terrible sudden pain sent spots into his eyes, but Tommy stayed awake, despite himself, and he breathed in, panting, but he couldn't breathe out, no strength to push, and he arced his neck and back to do it, but he couldn't—

Tommy looked down at his father, who stared at him, the sledge and nails now replaced with the head of Christ again, who stared up at him, twins in agony.

Tommy tried to speak, but the air wouldn't come, and the hollow, pained eyes of Christ were the last thing he saw.

<h1 style="text-align:center">52</h1>

They watched Tommy die in silence.

"Let's go inside and finish them off," said Eli, holding the head of Christ.

"Neither Bert or Dave have come out, Eli," said Bronson. "They're dead in there, pretty sure. Don't know if the dyke bit it, but I don't want to test my theory. The pastor will be back soon—"

"He's not a pastor," said Eli. "We can't let any of them live—"

"We got your damned son, we got Laurie. If Campbell was here, that means Laurie tipped them off somehow, which means Zeke ain't too far away—"

"What, are you scared of him?" asked Eli. "God will protect us—"

"God ain't gonna keep us out of prison, or from a bullet. We've done enough, we need to hit the road."

"I'm not running, Kyle. I thought you were in this to the end."

Bronson stared at him. "What are you talking about? You knew the deal. I've got no love for these sinners, but I'm not taking a bullet for it—"

Eli stared at him. "We're done when the mission is through, and the mission is not through until every one of these sinners has been destroyed, and Sacred is clean again."

Bronson stood tall, across from him, the hanging body of Tommy behind them. "Eli, we ain't got the time. We have to get out of town before the thunder comes down—"

A gunshot ripped through the air, a distant bark, and Bronson reached for his ear.

"Oh Goddamnit," he yelled, falling to the ground, and Eli followed him. "It's Zeke! Don't put your head up or you'll lose it."

"You hit?"

"He took my ear," said Bronson. "I"m getting out of here, Eli."

"You can't—"

"Stop me," said Bronson, and he alligator crawled to the second cruiser, which had cover from the treeline, and slid inside. Another shot rang out, the bullet winging the car, and Bronson drove off, another shot, and Eli sprinted, his head down, the head of Christ in his arms, and he jumped into his truck, and another shot rang out, the back window of his truck breaking, and he roared off, out of the driveway.

*

The cross was the first thing David saw.

"Tommy, no, oh God," he said, darting from the car, running to the boy's body, maybe he had survived, but he saw his legs, and he wasn't moving—

Jason.

David sprinted inside, the front room a mess, fragments of furniture and frames, everything broken.

Then he saw the bodies, and the blood.

Bronson's two deputies laid lifeless in the entrance to the hallway, both with awful wounds to the chest. They both held pistols in their hands.

"Back here, Pastor," said a voice, Zeke's voice, and David stepped over the bodies, through the blood, and saw Zeke, crouched, next to another body.

Next to Ann. David hurried to her, and saw her eyes were open, and thanked God, but then saw the blood pooling around her.

She sat up, against the wall, a thin table tipped over in front of her. It was peppered with bullet holes. Her shotgun laid next to her, forgotten.

Her hands were covered in blood, held together over the wound in her stomach.

"Ann," said David. "Let's get you to a hospital. I'll call the ambulance."

"I already did, Pastor," said Zeke. "But I don't know—"

"I can't feel my legs," she said, looking at her toes, and then at him. "And my hands, well—I'm telling 'em to move, but they're not listening."

David took one of her hands in his, and squeezed it, but there was no response. Ann only shook her head.

"Just hold on," said David.

"Think the bullet caught me in the back, on the way out," said Ann. "Just my luck. Got the two deputies though. Jason and Sol, they're upstairs. They're safe."

A tear rolled down David's cheek.

"Tommy?" asked Ann.

David met her eyes, and only shook his head.

"He ran out," said Ann. She took a deep, shuddering breath. "I'll get to meet God, right, David?"

"You will."

Ann half-smiled, blood in her teeth. "Good. Good." She closed her eyes.

"Stay with me, Ann."

Her eyelids fluttered open.

"I was a fool, David," she said, her words quiet. "Tell her, please."

"What?"

"Tell Sonja—" but she trailed off, blood dripping from her lips. Her eyes were still.

David squeezed her hand, with its fleeting warmth, and closed her eyes.

*

"Jason, it's me," said David, knocking on their bedroom door. "I'm here with Zeke. Bronson and Eli are gone."

The floor rang with the sound of furniture scuttling across the hardwood, and then the door opened, and Jason was there, holding Sol in his arms, and they embraced, and David squeezed them with all his might, and kissed Jason hard, and kissed him again, and kissed Sol on the forehead. Jason's eyes were wet with tears, and Sol looked confused and scared.

"Where—"

"What happened down there? Where's Ann, Tommy? Is Laurie—"

But David's eyes stopped him.

"They're all—" David held his breath, the emotion too much. "None of them made it, Jason. Bronson and Eli killed them all."

"What?" asked Jason. "Ann—she was just—"

"You heard the gunfire," said David.

Jason's eyes were wide, tears flowing.

"I can't—"

"Jason, look at me," said David. "I want you to pack up a few days worth of clothes for you and Solomon. Do it quickly. Get out of town. Find a hotel in Tallahassee. I'll meet you there. Go out the back door, and don't let Sol see anything downstairs."

"David, I don't know what you're thinking—"

David looked at Sol's face. Sol looked off, absent minded.

David closed his eyes, and opened them, staring into Jason's.

"Tommy is in our front yard, Jason. Eli, Bronson—they crucified him. Shot him in the legs so he couldn't support his own weight, after nailing him to the cross from the Holy Church of Sacred."

Jason said nothing, only staring, crying.

"I love you, and Solomon," he said. He shook his head. "I can't let him live."

Jason reached for him, but David was already gone.

*

Zeke was outside, by Tommy. He sat on his knees, his pack nearby. He cleaned his rifle.

"Pastor," he said.

David looked down at Zeke, and then up at Tommy's wrecked body.

"Let's get him down," said David. They tipped the cross over, laying Tommy's body down, and Zeke slid a crowbar under the head of a nail, and leaned down with all his weight, and levered one nail out, and then the other.

David reached under Tommy's body, and carried him away from the cross, laying him in a patch of grass.

He closed his eyes.

"Dear Lord," said David. "Please usher Tommy's soul into Heaven. And forgive us for our sins."

"Amen," said Zeke.

Silence settled in the night.

"Pastor," said Zeke. "What are we doing?"

David's eyes left Tommy, and went to Zeke.

"Did you see where they went?" asked David.

"Different directions," said Zeke. "Bronson took the cruiser west. My guess—his house. Probably to go on the run."

"Eli?"

"East."

"His house is west," said David.

"He's heading somewhere else," said Zeke. "If I was a betting man—"

"The church," said David.

Zeke nodded.

David took a breath. "You go after Bronson. I'll take Eli."

Zeke met his eyes. He nodded, and started to get up.

"Zeke—"

Zeke stopped.

"I need—I need God with me."

Zeke stared, and then nodded. Zeke went to his pack, and pulled out a baggy, shaking out a handful of mushrooms for David.

David ate them, one by one, chewing, swallowing. Zeke ate with him.

"Remember when you told me I'm a Man of God?" asked David.

"Yeah, I remember," said Zeke. "I saw the glow. Still do."

"And you said you would be my shepherd."

"I did."

David swallowed his doubts, looking into Zeke's eyes.

"Let's hope you were right."

"Thank you, Pastor. Good luck."

David nodded, and took Zeke's hand, squeezing it.

Zeke nodded, and then was gone, with his pack, jumping into the extra cruiser, and driving off with it, west.

David was alone now, and he sat with Tommy for a minute, rolling the two bloody nails back and forth in his hands. He held the steel, once warm from Tommy's blood, now cold again. Slightly bent from the hammering, and the extraction.

He rolled the nails, back and forth. The small sledge still sat in the ground, and David grabbed it, and then his bat.

He lined up the nails. First one, and then the other, using Eli's tool to hammer them through the thick wood of the head of the bat.

First one, then the other.

Covered in Tommy's blood, he handled the bat, the light

wood stained red.

He hammered, as Eli had hammered.

David worried the bat would split, the force and size of the nails too much for the wood to handle.

The bat stayed whole.

53

Zeke parked the cruiser down the road, headlights off, and approached on foot.

The mushrooms had kicked in, and he felt them working through him. Into his fingers and toes, into his heart.

Into his eyes.

As Zeke had turned into the neighborhood, the shadows had loomed larger, from the streetlights, from the porch lights. Longer, deeper.

Are the shadows still God?

As he parked the cruiser, and walked in the dark, the shadows surrounded him, and if he took a wrong step, or made a wrong turn, he would fall inside them. And if he fell inside, he would never come out.

What had Pastor David said?

His rod and his staff, they comfort me.

Zeke held the rifle tight to his body, clutching it as he navigated the light and dark.

But with those shadows, with holes of darkness, he also saw the light. And he saw Bronson, a beacon beaming down on him from Heaven above. Zeke knew his purpose.

Zeke found Bronson loading his truck, his ear bandaged. Shadows loomed around him.

Zeke stood ten yards from him, rifle at his shoulder.

"Running, huh?" asked Zeke. Bronson froze at his voice. "Turn around, Bronson. Slow. Hands up."

He turned from the bed of his truck, slowly raising his hands, facing Zeke.

"I'm not going to prison for doing the right thing," said Bronson, sneering. "You missed me, earlier."

"Not entirely," said Zeke. "But I've never been the best shot."

"What are you waiting for?"

Zeke stared at him, shadows roiling out from around the sheriff, longer, deeper, a dark highlight hiding behind his humanity.

"I'm giving you a chance, Sheriff," said Zeke. "To make right with God, before you die."

Bronson stared at him, peering, shadows curling. He smiled. He shook his head.

"Boy," said Bronson. He spoke slowly. "Do you think I've never been right? You tell me. As I beat Pastor John and broke his bones, and then drowned him in the swamp— where was God? Was he there? As I stomped ole Laurie Grace to a bloody fuckin' pulp—was he there? Either he was, or he wasn't." Bronson stared, darkness behind. "If he was—well, was he the thrill I felt as John's life left him? As his soul escaped his body? Was that God? The chills I felt as I crushed Laurie's throat underneath my boot? Was that him?"

Zeke only stared. The shadows surrounded Bronson now, full, and heavy. They threatened to swallow them both.

"And well, if he wasn't there—what does that say? It tells me he is happy for his men to do what is necessary. To do the dirty work. A King who averts his eyes, as punishment is handed out by his loyal men."

Bronson smiled wide.

"Is God here, Zeke?" he asked. "If he is—"

Bronson charged then, suddenly, and Zeke pulled the rifle tight and fired, but Bronson still charged, and Zeke chambered another round and fired again, but Bronson was right there, and pushed the rifle aside, pulling it from Zeke's grasp and throwing it away, and Bronson tackled him, driving him into the ground, and Zeke couldn't breathe.

Bronson wrapped his hands around Zeke's throat, squeezing with an iron grip. Zeke struggled, his hands wet with Bronson's blood, as he fought at Bronson's wrists, battering at them, but even wounded, he was too strong—

Bronson's face was shadow now, his eyes white orbs peering out from it. He moved closer, filling Zeke's vision, leaning all his weight onto his hands.

"If he is here, Zeke, he can watch you die," said Bronson, his mouth open, showing all his teeth, a terrible joyful grimace, and Zeke had no breath, and his right hand found his sheath on his belt, and pulled his knife, five inches, and slid it hilt deep under Bronson's arm pit, and Bronson screamed and let go, and Zeke slid out from underneath him, rolling to the side, taking in a deep breath, his heart pounding.

He scrambled to his feet, knife out, ready, his rifle on the ground ten feet away.

Bronson pushed himself up, the massive body rising back to its feet. Shadows still clung to him. Blood stained his shirt, a massive splotch of wet red in his stomach, where Zeke's round had found him. Gutshot. If Bronson felt any pain from it, he didn't show it, even as more blood poured from his armpit, where Zeke had stabbed him. He had hoped to hit Bronson's lung, but the sheriff was big, and he stared at Zeke with dark eyes, raising his hands as he approached, like a bear.

Zeke swung the knife out in small feints, and Bronson charged again, and Zeke cut, slicing through Bronson's forearm, a red river of blood running down his wrist and to the ground, and Zeke only watched him, time slowing as they danced. God shone a spotlight on them, a beacon in a lake of shadows, and Bronson charged again, and Zeke swung out, slicing again, the blade cutting through flesh, and Bronson grunted in pain, blood pouring from both arms. He flexed his hands, and Zeke had hit no nerves or tendons, and the sheriff smiled once again, and leaped, and Zeke switched his hold on the knife and buried it in the chest of Bronson, deep again, snagging on ribs, and it was yanked from Zeke's grasp, and he dodged Bronson, but lost his knife, rolling away.

He scrambled to his feet, and Bronson climbed up again, blood pouring from him. Bronson smiled, his mouth now wet with blood, his teeth red, and grabbed the knife from his chest, and pulled it out, drenched in scarlet. He was wreathed in shadows now, and Zeke saw only the darkness.

Bronson dashed at him, faster than seemed possible for a man his size, and his open hand grabbed around Zeke's wrist, and he held, his grip still strong.

God. Please.

Bronson reeled him in with terrible force, and buried the knife deep in Zeke's stomach, searing pain ripping through him, and Bronson stabbed again, and again, and again, shoving the knife deep into Zeke, once, twice, and Zeke lost count, and the wind was gone from him, and the fight had left him.

He only saw the shadows.

Bronson pulled him in close, his face filling his vision again, as he buried the knife deep a final time.

"Tell me, Zeke," he said. "Is God here?"

Zeke's vision cleared. The shadows moved.

He reached to his belt buckle, and pulled the small blade there, and with a quick snap, he slit Bronson's throat, opening up a deep gash across his neck, and Bronson let go, his mouth open, and he reached for the second mouth on his throat, to close the wound with hands unable, and blood poured from it.

He fell, no air, no blood, and he seized up, and he died.

The shadows fell back.

Zeke fell to his knees beside him. Blood poured from his stomach, dozens of stab wounds, pain filling him.

But he felt God.

54

God waited for David at the Holy Church of Sacred.

David drove through the night, the mushrooms slowly changing him, and he became aware of the presence of God as he drove through the quiet of Sacred. The shadow in the night was alive, and large, and it loomed around David, everything but the road, the crickets and frogs chirping in the night, now inside the Lord, and David drove inside him as well, and he pulled up to the church, the Lord was there, the Church inside him.

Eli's truck was there, parked haphazardly, the shadow of God lording over them, and David entered the church and God.

The chapel reeked of gasoline.

The fumes rose in cascading waves into the air, filling the

space, gas covering the pews, soaking into the carpet.

Eli doused the stage in fuel, upending a can. The head of Christ watched him. The cross from the back wall was gone, now in David's front yard, covered in Tommy's blood.

Eli finished dumping the gas, throwing the can aside. He looked to David.

"I knew you'd come," said Eli. "Christ told me you would follow."

There was no light inside the church but David saw, the darkness of the shape illuminating the chapel, the Lord outside, shifting, settling, his great weight pressing into the gravity of the Earth, onto the form of the chapel.

David carried the bat, squeezing the wood, his knuckles cracking as the wood yielded to his grip, soaked in Tommy's blood. Two nails stuck out from the barrel of the bat, the points near each other.

One side blunt, the other barbed.

Simmering anger threatened to overwhelm him, to force him forward in a sprint and to bury the nails in Eli's skull, to kill him with a single blow.

To end this quickly.

He thought of Tommy, and felt his blood between his fingers.

"You can't have it," said Eli. "You can't turn this place into something else. You can't corrupt it. I won't allow it, no matter what anyone else says."

"Still, you worship suffering," said David. He advanced, slow steps sinking into the wet carpet.

"I worship Christ in Heaven!" yelled Eli, staring out at David. "I've followed God's commands, and it has led me here!"

"To the death of both Graces. Of Ann. Of Tommy. Crucifixion and torture."

"Tommy will thank me in Heaven," said Eli. "It was the only way to redeem him. I couldn't let him follow your path. I couldn't let him—"

"—live," said David. He advanced, between the pews.

"You wouldn't understand, you sinner, you deviant!" Eli yelled, spittle flying. "You would drag Sacred into the darkness! You would turn the whole town to sin! You would—"

The building rumbled, God moving.

"Do you feel him, Eli?"

"What are you talking about?"

"God," said David. "All around us."

Eli looked at the head of Christ, sitting, staring up, its face filled with pain. It looked to the sky. It looked to the God that surrounded the church, around them, enveloping. It always had. At the Father that had tortured him.

"He's here," said David. "He's watching."

"I—"

David advanced, squeezing the handle of the bat.

"He's watching, Eli," said David.

"I'm not afraid of you," said Eli, stepping backward on the stage, toward the back wall, where the cross once stood.

"Am I a weapon, Eli?"

"What?"

"Am I a weapon?" asked David, climbing the steps.

"I don't—"

"Am I a weapon?" he asked, on the stage, moving faster now, Eli backing up. The building shook again, the floor, the roof, the walls.

"Please—"

David swung the bat hard, hitting Eli in the side, the two long nails embedding in Eli's flesh. Eli grunted, a horrible sound of pain, and fell, and David pulled the bat back, and swung again, into Eli's other side, the nails puncturing his flesh with a soft, wet sound, followed by a deep thud as the wood connected. He grunted again, and blood poured from him in the glowing shadows of the church, as the dark shape of God watched.

David pulled the bat back, and swung again, into the thigh, driving deep puncture marks, and Eli cried with pain, blood pouring from him, and David swung again, and again, in the sides, in the legs, in the arms. He punched twin holes in Eli, over and over again, squeezing the wooden bat soaked in Tommy's blood, the father and son together.

The walls and roof of the church shook, and broke apart, flying away. There was nothing but them, and God.

The blood splattered, flung, covering David, small drops at first, but as he opened up more arteries and veins he became covered in Eli's blood, his clothes absorbing it.

David booted Eli in the side, flipping him onto his back, and swung the bat into his stomach, over and over, opening up deep, bloody holes, new orifices, over and over and over again, and Eli covered up with his arms and hands, and David punctured them as well, the nails breaking bones and tendons.

Eli was a bloody mess, blood pouring from dozens of holes, red, leaking wounds, and he wept. He shook from the pain, his body trembling on the stage. The head of Christ sat silently.

David stared down.

"God is watching, Eli."

Eli trembled in agony, staring up at David, reaching with broken, crooked fingers, dripping with blood.

David swung the bat into Eli's face, the nails punching through cheek and tooth, through bone and skull, and Eli only grunted, and David swung again, and again, and again, pulling and swinging the bat down with full force, the nails punching into Eli's face, obliterating his nose, his eyes, his mouth, until there was nothing left but ruin, blood and gore rising in streams off the bat, flowing down onto David's hands and forearms like a river. Eli reached for a final time, and then his arms fell, and his heart stopped.

David stood there, the bat hanging, panting, his breath ragged, his chest heaving. He let the bat fall.

He walked to the pulpit, and put his bloody hands on the worn wood. He looked out over the empty church, soaked in gasoline.

David looked up, to the great shape of God, the full presence of him.

God trembled, shook, and David shook inside him.

Enjoy Words of Christ in Red?

Sign up here to be notified about Robbie's next novel!

robbiedorman.com/newsletter

And don't forget to leave a review. Reviews are a direct way to help your favorite creators. We appreciate it.

Acknowledgements

Thank you to my wife Kim, for her patience and support, and my team of beta readers: Andrew, Carrie, Matt, Megan, and Yousef. Thank you for reading.

About the Author

Robbie Dorman believes in horror. Words of Christ in Red is his seventeenth novel. When not writing, he's podcasting, playing video games, or walking his dog. He lives in Florida with his wife, Kim.

You can follow Robbie on all social media @robbiedorman

His website is robbiedorman.com

Subscribe to his newsletter at robbiedorman.com/newsletter